BENIN LIGHT

A Richard Mariner Adventure

Benin Light, the lighthouse marker for the bay that will lead to Granville Harbour, wild and inaccessible on the western coast of Africa, is a welcome sight for Richard and Robin Mariner. Until someone opens fire on them. The couple are shocked to see Sergeant Voroshilov, a Russian Militia man who left Robin lucky to be alive after their last encounter. And when armed guards arrive at their hotel to arrest Richard, trouble really begins...

Peter Tonkin titles available from
Severn House Large Print

High Wind in Java
The Ship Breakers
Cape Farewell
Resolution Burning
Wolf Rock
Titan 10

BENIN LIGHT

Peter Tonkin

Severn House Large Print
London & New York

This first large print edition published 2010
in Great Britain and the USA by
SEVERN HOUSE PUBLISHERS LTD of
9-15 High Street, Sutton, Surrey, SM1 1DF.
First world regular print edition published 2008 by
Severn House Publishers Ltd., London and New York.

British Library Cataloguing in Publication Data

Tonkin, Peter.
  Benin Light.
  1. Mariner, Richard (Fictitious character)--Fiction.
  2. Tankers--Africa--Fiction. 3. Sea stories. 4. Large
  type books.
  I. Title
  823.9'14-dc22

ISBN-13: 978-0-7278-7905-9

Severn House Publishers support The Forest Stewardship Council
[FSC], the leading international forest certification organisation. All
our titles that are printed on Greenpeace-approved FSC-certified paper
carry the FSC logo.

Mixed Sources

Product group from well-managed
forests and other controlled sources
www.fsc.org Cert no. SA-COC-1565
© 1996 Forest Stewardship Council

FSC

Printed and bound in Great Britain by the
MPG Books Group, Bodmin, Cornwall.

For Cham, Guy and Mark.
As always.

And in fondest memory of Uncle Mervyn
and Auntie Renee.

Acknowledgements

I last wrote about a major African river more than ten years ago when C.S. Forester's *The African Queen* was the inspiration for sections of *The Iceberg* and its sequel *Meltdown*. The inspirations for *Benin Light* were wider in time and focus. I have long planned to take Richard up a river, like Marlow in Joseph Conrad's *The Heart of Darkness*. Readers will easily see that this was that opportunity.

But Conrad's disturbing masterpiece was written the better part of a century ago, and was no more capable of supplying contemporaneous detail than the writings of H.M. Stanley, though consulting these and Alan Moorhead's *The White Nile* is a timeless pleasure. Sharp-eyed readers will also spot references to the works of writers as variable as Monserrat, Masters, Ruark and Hemingway; P.C. Wren, James S. Rand and Wilbur Smith – as well as Naipaul, Kinsolving and Achebe to name but a few. I needed still more modern inspiration if I was going to capture the spirit of a more modern continent – albeit one still fighting seemingly timelessly insoluble problems.

7

As it always does, *National Geographic* magazine came to my aid. In the February 2007 edition I found an article by Tom O'Neill, illustrated with the photographs of Ed Kashi, which revealed 'The Curse of the Black Gold' in the Niger delta. Port Harcourt became at once Granville Harbour, the Niger delta with its MEND insurgents became the Delta with its shadowy freedom fighters; and Bonny Light, the most sought-after of all crude oils, was transformed into the Benin Light of the title.

The next inspiration for the story came from contemporary headlines when a little girl was kidnapped in Port Harcourt and held for a while before being returned to her parents.

Names of important characters – as well as the conditions in the bay and delta – were supplied by Peter Marshall's *Around Africa*. An idyllic holiday in Egypt inspired the Granville Royal Lodge Hotel, which was simply upgraded from our hotel in Sharm El Sheikh.

But the greatest single inspiration came from the most modern source of all. Tim Butcher's wonderful *Blood River* (Chatto & Windus, London, 2007) not only supplied me with the wreck of the paddle steamer, but inspiration for the whole atmosphere of the novel with its lost cities and silence-haunted jungles. His narrative tells of following in Stanley's footsteps down the Congo to the coast as recently as 2004, traversing a dangerous wasteland of tribal warfare and post-colonial ruin. But it seems to me that what he conjures up could almost have

8

come from the pages of Rider Haggard's Alan Quartermain adventures or Edgar Rice Burroughs' *Tarzan* stories. Which takes us back to Conrad, and the great early literature of African adventure. Something that I hope I have captured in the pages of *Benin Light*.

Peter Tonkin, 2008.

One

Light

Suddenly the light was there. It glittered on the horizon, as bright as diamond on black velvet. The pattern of its flashes as familiar as the voice of a long-lost friend. There could be no mistake.

Richard Mariner felt his lips curl into a smile of quiet satisfaction. Even after all these years he knew exactly where to look, and when. It seemed like a kind of spiritual knowledge, something almost psychic. Of course, it helped that since his last visit this place had haunted his dreams. There was even a vague sense of homecoming, though he had never much liked the oil port or the frenetic city that leached on to it, sucking away its money and more. The dreams had usually been dark and disturbing. Only the light had stood against the nightmare gloom shrouding his restless memories, standing forever bright, steady and firm.

Richard crossed the dim vacancy of the night-lit command bridge and narrowed his eyes, staring fixedly at the bright beam that rose against the night, guardian to one of the most ancient and dangerous anchorages on the African coast. He briefly considered leaving the air-conditioned confines of the bridge to go out on the bridge wing for a closer look. But it was stultifying out there – upper 30s Celsius even at this time of night, with 100 per cent humidity. He was content to stay in here and use his supernaturally sharp memory.

In his mind's eye he could see the rocky out-crop of the island on which the lighthouse stood as clearly as if he was staring at its picture in the relevant volume of the Admiralty Pilot for Eastern Atlantic and West African waters. It resembled a giant rocky slug of coral just high enough to remain above the low heave of the waters here and bear the tall lighthouse on its back.

And, behind it, the broad mouth of the strange bay that it had guarded in one form or another since Portuguese explorers put a cairn of stones here while his own ancestors were still fighting the Wars of the Roses. Though it had been the Arab slavers and their English Tudor associates who had put up the first actual light. He seemed to recall a theory that the first settlement, little more than a slave pen, got its name from Fulke Greville, Elizabeth I's Naval Secretary. In time however it was adapted to its present form, Gran' Ville, by the French-speaking Belgians who ended up running the place after Henry Morton Stanley's explorations and annexations for Prince Leopold in the late 1800s.

Looking across the broad northern horizon,

Richard could see the restless red-gold glow of the never-sleeping city of Granville Harbour staining the lower sky away to port. And soon enough there would be the lesser constellations of lights and flares upon the rigs to the south-ward. But in the meantime, dead ahead, there was the bay of the river mouth and the nearly impenetrable forests of the delta behind it.

Like the lighthouse's island and the anchor-age, the wild riot of the delta was invisible in the predawn, except as a seemingly infinite darkness. A darkness that was much more than a vacancy. More, even, than an interstellar absence of brightness. A darkness that had a kind of form and enough of a presence to give off a brooding threat which he could feel, even out here. As though there was a kind of anti-brightness, like antimatter, that could pierce the air over the ocean as easily as the steady gleam of the Benin Light.

But now that Richard could see the light he knew exactly what to do. 'You need to start reducing your revolutions now, Captain Hand,' he said quietly. Or as quietly as he could, taking into account the steady rumble of the great vessel's motors, which pushed the massive hull through the water with enough power to make everything aboard shudder and rumble. 'You'll need to reverse your engines altogether soon. Your station will be exactly to the north of the light. That's where the pilot will come aboard, unless things have changed since my last visit here. And of course you'll need to be moving at slow ahead then or you'll lose way altogether and have to be tugged right across the harbour and into your berth.'

Richard was speaking as owner, and it was perhaps fortunate that his captain, New Englander Morgan Hand, was a patient and understanding woman. For he was thoughtlessly interfering with her near-sacred command responsibilities. But she was. And in any case, Richard's observations accorded exactly with the directions given by the supertanker's navigation computers. And these coincided with the advice she had taken from other captains experienced in the tricky procedure of coming into Granville Harbour, for she was recently returned from duties in the Kara Sea and this was her first visit. Certainly Richard's gently spoken advice meshed with the observations in the Admiralty Pilot.

Which would, no doubt, be echoed by the Granville Harbour harbour master as soon as they were able to raise him on the radio. And re-echoed by the pilot he dispatched to guide them in until the harbour tugs could snug her into her berth at the last possible moment. With the lowest possible extra expense.

Captain Hand translated the observations and the directions into orders, therefore, and gave them to the helmsman. The helmsman eased the engine-room telegraph back and the automatic answer rang up. Morgan knew the Russian chief engineer, Dimitri Poliakov, had departed from the usual routine and gone down there himself although the vessel usually ran with unmanned engine spaces during the night watches. Dimitri too had been in the Kara Sea until he was assigned to the new Russian-built tanker and he was as new to Granville Harbour as his captain and her new command.

Prometheus V's forecastle head, with its little jackstaff shrouded in limp house colours, eased dead north of the light and the long hull behind it began her slow and careful entrance into the broad but treacherous bay.

'They're a funny lot, the Granville Harbour pilots,' Richard continued, dreamily, hardly aware that he was giving voice to his thoughts and memories. 'They need to be a mix of deep-water men and river pilots. Like those sharks and crocodiles that swim in fresh water as well as in salt. There is surprisingly little in the way of surf or tide because the river's outflow controls everything for miles out to sea – or it does under normal circumstances. But there are other problems. Problems unique to the place.

'The bay is wide but surprisingly shallow because the delta pushes out so far into it. Shallow in both senses – from sea to shore, from surface to seabed. The river is huge and it never seems to rise or fall, like the Nile does for instance. It just channels millions of gallons of water a second out of the jungles and rain-forests of the river-basin upstream inland and pours it all relentlessly out into the Atlantic.

'The power of that outwash would be pushing us back out into deep water with its simple force, like the Congo or the Mau further south, except that the river itself seems to lose its way down here at the coast. It meanders into a massively complex delta – biggest after the Niger – then splits up into hundreds of little streams that get lost under the mangrove forests. Though when I say *little*, half a dozen of them are as wide as the Thames at Tower Bridge, one or two as wide as the Thames at Tilbury. All in all, they push every sort of rubbish out into the bay, with a couple of important results. The delta itself seems to be swelling, trying to fill up the bay of the anchorage altogether. And then the bottom's always rising and falling unexpectedly. Mudbanks and sandbars forever on the move. Like the dunes of the Sahara, of the Great Sand Sea, but more complex; much more dangerous. It's as though the seabed is alive, somehow, and fighting to keep all shipping well away.'

'Not much chance of that when it's sitting on top of the most valuable resource on the west coast of the continent, under one of the most densely populated oilfields on the face of the planet,' countered Morgan robustly, her Boston accent almost as clipped as his English tones. She looked across at her tall employer with a good deal of ready affection. He was in one of his dreamy, almost poetic moods. When he got like this, she secretly thought of him as Coleridge's Ancient Mariner, full of the wisdom of years of seafaring, able to see, recall and understand so much more than anyone else. The

16

Ancient Mariner as played by George Clooney, perhaps. Though even Mr Clooney did not possess eyes of that particular breathtaking blue. 'What was the spot price of Benin Light crude quoted on the exchanges this morning?' she asked, before her own thoughts were seduced too far from the matter in hand.

'Still well over a hundred,' he rumbled, his voice gravelly with fatigue.

Morgan nodded, without raising her own steady gaze from the navigation equipment, the radar and the collision alarm, which was already being closely observed by the slightly overawed second officer, who technically held the watch which would bring them into the harbour. Richard had kept the middle watch with the first officer, she knew, and remained here since she had joined the second for the morning watch at 4am. They were in strange, unsettling waters approaching a complicated, possibly dangerous anchorage – and *Prometheus V* could be a bit of a brute even at the best of times.

Richard had been on the bridge since midnight, called here by an impulse Morgan hadn't yet managed to fathom. An impulse that he hadn't really examined too closely himself as yet as far as she could see. 'They say it could go over $200 a barrel soon,' he continued. 'Especially Bonny and Benin Light crudes – these light grades that can be refined down and made near as dammit carbon-neutral. Even better than biofuel...'

Morgan nodded once more as she continued her train of thought. One of the bridge computers kept the watchkeepers up to date with all things to do with their cargoes – actual and potential. A glance at this would tell her all she needed to know about every grade and state of oil.

Morgan was only making conversation because she was a little worried about him and distracted by a lingering, unspoken and unrequited attraction towards him. She knew nothing of his Benin dreams and nightmares, nor how they had intensified as soon as the tanker had rounded Cape Palmas and started heading east under the sub-Saharan swell of Sierra Leone and Nigeria, robbing him of any real sleep for the last few nights at least. Instead, she suspected that Richard, like herself – like Chief Engineer Dimitri Poliakov – was being overcautious, made over-anxious by *Prometheus V* as much as by the vessel's nearing destination.

The supertanker was the first of a supposedly environmentally friendly series made in Russia, the result of a deal between Heritage Mariner and the consortium that owned the massive shipyards across the bay from Archangel. But the consortium had run into trouble with the capricious Kremlin. Or rather, business tycoon Felix Makarov, who ultimately ran it, had done so by managing to have a personal confrontation with the President himself – and he had been forced to flee the country with his old friends in the FSB close behind him. Things seemed to have cooled down now, but even so, there weren't likely to be many more in the *V* series.

Which was just as well. Morgan didn't like *Prometheus V* any more than Richard seemed to like the harbour they were bringing her into. And that in itself was incredibly unsettling, for the first four in the *Prometheus* series were simply the safest, best-natured ships afloat. Her last command had taken everything the Arctic could throw at her bringing oil out of the Kara Sea – but Max Asov, who owned the rights, had been the subject of a hostile takeover by the state. His exit from Russia had been almost as hostile as Felix Makarov's and the two expatriates were now close associates – with each other and with their mutual friend Richard Mariner.

Which seemed to be just as well for all concerned: the Kara Sea was closed to Heritage Mariner now, as Russia manoeuvred to bring all the mineral rights between the north coast and the North Pole into Kremlin control. But Benin Light seemed to be offering a lucrative alternative. Especially if it started fetching $200 a barrel. Which was why they were all down here in this godforsaken place.

Morgan picked up a handset and depressed the button marked comms. The radio officer answered at once. 'Sparks here.' It was typical of the ship that the Comms button for reasons of its own put the conversation on broadcast.

'Any joy from the harbour master yet?'

'Sorry, Captain. No radio signal at all. I've emailed. No reply.'

'Have you tried phoning?' asked Richard. 'Use your mobile. There should be an answerphone even if the office is closed. The harbour master's probably got a personal cell number too.'

'I don't have the number for the office, let alone for the man himself,' said Sparks a little frostily. Then he added, 'Captain,' as an afterthought.

'The Admiralty Pilot gives the Local Enquiries number. Hang on a minute.' Richard flipped over the pages of the entry on Granville Harbour. 'Well, the latest one they have is...' And he reeled off a long and complicated series of numbers.

A few minutes later, Sparks was exercising his French on an irate-sounding operator who explained that she should only be disturbed for emergencies at this hour. Emergencies or presidential business. But he persisted with a close approximation of Gallic charm, which proved effective in the end. A few minutes later, they were all straining their linguistic powers further as they battled to understand the slurred and crackling, all too casually recorded message on the harbour master's clearly ancient office phone. But this too yielded up a further set of numbers. Which Sparks duly dialled.

Six rings.

'J'écoute...'

The open line picked up the heavy breathing of someone fighting to get themselves awake. Bed springs groaned. A second voice gave a throaty, sensual groan as though the hand not holding the phone was engaged in an intimate caress.

'Is that the harbour master? This is vessel *Prometheus* inbound. We are approaching the Benin Light. Have you a pilot for us, sir?'

At least the answer came in English. 'What is time? Five of the clock? You wake me at *five of the clock*?' The second voice gave a less than sensuous groan. Whatever else was going on, the hour was too early for her, whoever she was.

'Have you a pilot for us, sir?'

'No. I have no pilot. You will wait at the light. All vessels wait at the light. I will send. We will see.' Irritation and sleepiness came and went in the harbour master's voice. His companion began to snore.

Morgan reached in and took the phone. 'This is Captain Morgan Hand of MV *Prometheus*. If we lose way, you will have to send tugs right across the harbour to get us to our berth as well as a pilot to guide us in. A waste of time and money.'

'Your time. Your money. You're wasting my time now, Captain. My sleep time. You will wait. It is deep water there. Almost no tide. No wind in this season. Sea dead calm always. You will be safe enough until I deal with you. I will send tugs and pilot. In the morning if you are fortunate. In the afternoon or later in the week if you are not.' He paused to let the threat sink in. The snoring gathered volume. His English improved as his head cleared and he warmed to his subject.

'There will be extra charges,' he persisted with practised fluency. 'You will need extra clearance papers. You will be given details when we contact you about berthing. Also the port taxes have risen recently. Customs charges. Immigration. Counter-terrorism. All passports must be checked for all crew members whether they are coming ashore or not and visas must be updated locally. Medical certificates must be in order and will be checked again locally. There are many procedures you will have to follow before you are allowed to berth, disembark any person or thing, take on supplies and chandlerage or load either bunkerage or cargo. These will all mean extra charges. Many, many extra charges.' And on that note the harbour master rang off.

The words *extra charges* seemed to echo on the air for a moment.

The Benin Light came on to the starboard beam of the bridge house four miles due south of them, exactly where it should be, and gleamed in through the length of the bridge wing. The utter blackness ahead seemed to have grown larger and even more threatening, as though it were one of the black panthers that famously hunted the forests here. A black panther almost as tall as the stars, in the deepest of giant shadows, crouching in silence and ready to spring.

'Reverse all,' said Captain Hand.

The last of the way came off her command and the knot-meter rolled down to zero while the ticking of the GPS slowly froze, as the Kelvin Hughes Coursefinder stopped trying to find a course.

Then she said, 'All stop.' And, almost unbelievably, the tanker settled into stillness in the dead calm of the deep water of the nearly tideless harbour mouth.

A strange, almost deathly silence settled over the vessel, which even the whispery fussing of the air conditioning could not disturb. A silence which, like the darkness, became associated in Richard's tired mind with the mangrove-furred flank of the vast benighted continent immediately ahead. Not a mere absence of noise – nothing restful or peaceful. The silence after thunder. The almost inaudible echo of a scream. The silence of that instant when something living becomes something dead.

The calm before the storm.

'Welcome to Granville Harbour,' said Richard drily into that gloomy, shadowy, strangely threatening silence. But his voice was no longer gravelly with fatigue. It had a lively edge of anger in it that warned his captain at least that he was not the kind of man to take the harbour master's threats lying down.

Two

Call

The phone rang and rang. Richard listened to the ringtone on the far end of the line and tried his hardest not to transfer any of his mounting irritation to the person failing to pick up and answer his call.

He had rung for the first time just as the sun burst up over the black panther of the delta two hours earlier at six o'clock. He had stood leaning against the radio-room door jamb at sunrise with the cellphone to his ear and the sleepy second officer just behind him bathed in the blood-red dawn. Dozing in the big black-leather comfort of the pilot's chair. A chair that looked as though it was going to be redundant for a good while yet. They were alone on the bridge. Captain Hand had dismissed the radio officer and the helmsman – both being equally useless at the moment. Then she had taken herself off to bed as well. One way or another it looked as though it would be a long day for her once the sun got up and the wheels of official-dom started turning. Turning all too slowly at first, clearly, until she or Richard could find some way of oiling them.

Richard had rung his London headquarters at once but there had been no one in the twenty-four-hour rooms except the Crewfinders people. It was their specialization to replace any crew member on any vessel anywhere in the world within twenty-four hours, so their offices were manned 24/7. But they were not the men and women he needed to bring pressure on a grasping harbour master. The people he needed to do that for him were his commercial and legal intelligence section, familiarly known as London Centre, but they would all be at home in bed asleep – and he could see no advantage in waking them up at the moment.

There were other contacts nearer at hand, however, who might just get things moving if they could be awoken and alerted. He waited until six before he tried for the first time.

As he listened to the distant buzzing of the connection, Richard stared almost mindlessly out of the clearview at the great vista dead ahead. The sun seemed to explode up out of the mangroves, reddened by a misty overcast that appeared to cling to the forest itself as all the winding waterways began to leak out fog with all the other effluent they poured relentlessly into the bay. The darkness of the delta between the light and the city became a kind of blood-letting for a moment, as though innumerable throats had been cut up there at once. And the great blades of light seemingly capable of such atrocities stabbed vertically up into the pale belly of the morning sky, shone horizontally straight into his eyes. And, as with the darkness last night, one of the strangest things about it was the silence. The light and the colours were so violently riotous that they should have produced a cataclysm of sound.

But no. Only the faintest ghostly whisper of the air conditioning. Only the most distant subterranean grumble of the generators running independently now that the motors were still. The last time he had been aboard a ship as dead quiet as this it was in Archangel. Aboard a derelict hull tethered to the end of the Komsomolskaya Pier. She had been as eerie and unsettling as *Prometheus V* was now. He had had her tugged to Archangel from Wilhelmshaven where she had been anchored 'in mothballs' for years, and was trying to sell her to the Russian business magnate Felix Makarov and his consortium. All that time ago when Felix had still led a consortium; when he still had a country to call home.

It had been one of Richard's most spectacular deals. But none of them aboard the rotting hulk at that time had realized she was full of corpses and getting ready to add his wife Robin to their grisly number. Robin had survived by a miracle. And the deal had gone ahead. Fortunes had been made – with more and more in prospect. Until Felix trod on the Kremlin's toes and the whole Sevmash Consortium was shut down.

After a decent interval, just enough to contain these darkening thoughts and drag the sun up

26

into the lower sky above the steaming delta, the girl on the hotel switchboard came on to tell Richard what he had known before he made the call. Mrs Mariner was not answering her phone. Perhaps he should try later.

And now, at eight, Richard was trying once again. The sleepy second officer was being replaced on the forenoon watch by a bouncy third officer replete with early breakfast and bursting with inquisitiveness as to their position and their plans. Against the repetition of the distant ringtone, further, more immediate distractions began to multiply. Third Officer Callum Mc-Kay had duties to perform, things to check and records to keep. And he had a habit of talking to himself, especially when writing, typing or reading.

'Third Officer McKay signing on to duty,' he dictated to his busy fingers.

A bridge phone rang.

Third Officer McKay answered it, held a one-word conversation, then explained to himself that engine-room watch was in place, as he entered the fact in the log.

'Now,' he continued to burble distractingly, 'speed, course and heading   that's going to be interesting. No, wait, Number Two's got that sorted. OK, then, state of sky and sea...'

Come on, Robin! Richard silently raged. *I knew it was a long shot trying to get you at six. But it's gone eight o'clock now, for Heaven's sake...*

'Hello?'

The reply was so strangely unexpected after the long wait and the distraction at the critical moment, and the voice so distorted by the line, that he half thought the operator was back to tell him off again and demand that he wait for a more reasonable hour.

'I'm trying to reach Captain Robin Mariner...' he began at his most reserved and formal.

'Richard? Richard, is that you?'

'Robin?'

'Richard. What time is it, for Heaven's sake?' Her tone was an exact echo of the harbour master's three hours earlier. Sleep and irritation warring for the upper hand. He half expected her to expostulate *'Eight of the clock?'* in a thick French accent.

But she knew him too well for that. 'What is it, darling?' she asked throatily instead. 'There must be something wrong. I was expecting you to wake me in person with a cup of English Breakfast tea.'

'It's a case of "Best laid plans", I'm afraid,' he answered wryly. He could see her in his mind's eye snuggling sleepily down in the big double bed at the Granville Royal Lodge Hotel. All golden ringlets and huge grey eyes made velvety by lingering sleep. He was suddenly filled with an overwhelming desire for her. Which gave a further edge to his already volcanic exasperation. 'Darling, I think I'm going to need your help...'

Quickly and concisely he explained why *Prometheus V* had not berthed as planned, why

28

he had not been able to come ashore – get dirtside as the tanker's crew expressed it – find his way to the Granville Royal Lodge and get up to her room with the promised cup of tea.

'So the long and the short of it is that this harbour master creature won't move until someone's bribed him?' she summed up when he had finished. Irritation had overcome sleepiness in her voice by now – and then been replaced with simple outrage.

'Him, his family and all his cronies by the sound of things.'

'Right. I'll get down to the harbour office and sort him out!' From the tone of her voice he did not doubt for a moment that she would sort the harbour master out. And then some.

'No. I want to do this myself. I can't see Exxon, Shell, BP or any of the others going through this whenever one of their tankers comes in to port. Someone somewhere must have a system in place. I want to set one up as well, or we'll never be able to get things done smoothly.'

Robin did not answer at once. He supposed – acutely – that she was coming to terms with the idea of Richard setting up a system of bribes and kickbacks to ease his business here. Not the Heritage Mariner way; not the Heritage Mariner way at all. 'Felix Makarov and Max Asov arrived with their entourages last night,' she announced, apparently apropos of nothing. 'They're in the Prince's Suite and the President's Suite respectively. Just across the corridor...' Robin let the sentence hang – but the implication was clear. It's their oil concession; it's their city. It should be their bribes. That would be more their style, after all.

But Richard was angry, more deeply unsettled perhaps than he cared to admit. Africa had always been a place full of deadly dangers for him. Deadly dangers on all sorts of levels. 'No, Robin,' he persisted. 'This is something I want to sort out myself. I know it's their oil and everything, but it's my shipping company. I'm the one who needs to sort it out.'

'All right, darling,' she acquiesced. 'What do we need to do?'

'I need to get off this ship, for one thing.'

'That shouldn't be too difficult, as it happens. Remember how the Raffles in Singapore and the old Mandarin Oriental in Hong Kong both had their own fleets of Rolls-Royces?'

'Yes...' Richard and Robin had been at the Raffles not too long ago. Robin was still angling for one of the new Rolls-Royce Phantoms the hotel used. To balance his own Bentley Continental, perhaps. Distracted by the thought, Richard abruptly had a flash of insight. The stories of Joseph Conrad had filled his head in the days immediately after the visit to Singapore while they had been adventuring in the Java Sea. It was Conrad's *Heart of Darkness* that was colouring so much of his thoughts at present, with its midnight-black story of murder and worse in the seductively uncivilized, ultimately deadly jungles of the Congo. He

30

looked up at the blazing multifaceted emerald wall of the delta beneath the early morning sun, so struck that he missed what she was saying.

'What?'

'Rolls-Royces aren't good enough for the Granville Royal Lodge,' repeated Robin. 'They have their own fleet of helicopters.'

'Good God!'

'Max and Felix came in from the airport in three of them last night. One each for them and their immediate circles and a third for luggage and assorted hangers-on. Max seemed quite impressed until Felix suggested that they use choppers here because the roads can be too dangerous.'

'But you think you can get a chopper out here to me?'

'Lover, I think I can *bring* a chopper out there to you. We may not be in the Prince's Suite or the President's Suite but we are in the Nelson Mandela Suite and you are every bit as thoroughly booked in as your Russian business colleagues, even though they've been in and out on a regular basis for months now. The hotel manager met them at the helipad and they're all on first-name terms. But the facilities are here for your convenience just as much as for theirs. Use them. Once you're here, at the very least you'll have access to the Heritage Mariner legal team. I mean I've had more bright young lawyers hanging around here with me than you can shake a stick at, all polishing up the contracts for the better part of a week

31

while you've been cruising and we've been waiting for Felix and Max to arrive. Polishing contracts and testing the poolside sunbeds at the very least. I can easily scare a couple up and bring them out with me if you want. Who would be best?'

'I need more than just legal advice here. I could do with some intelligence insight as well. Did Jim Bourne come out in the end? He did the initial briefing at London Centre – the intelligence stuff as well as the legal aspects. Jim'd be best if he's there.'

'No. He had one or two things to clear up in London Centre. He'll be here soon. I have Simeon Bourgeois and Charles Le Brun. They're both old west-coast hands. They've worked here. Port Harcourt, Mawanga. Simeon was in Kinshasa for a while; Kigali too, before he came into Heritage Mariner and we put him in legal and commercial intelligence.'

'But he doesn't like to talk about his Congo days. I know. Still, the west-coast experience will be just what I want. Fine. Bring Simeon. I'll be on my mobile number if you want to confirm flight time or whatever.'

Morgan Hand had arrived on the bridge during this conversation. She looked well rested and thoroughly alert after her three-hour power-nap. And, Richard noted with nostrils as well as eyes, a shower. *And*, from the faintest speck on the almost geometric swell of her starched white shirt front, breakfast.

'Captain on to the bridge at eight fifteen local

time,' Third Officer McKay dictated to his fingers as they kept the log.

'Jim Bourne, Simeon Bourgeois?' said Morgan, paying her watch officer no mind, but almost awed by what Richard had said. 'You wheeling out the big guns from London Centre?'

'You can bet on it. Robin will be here with Simeon to pick me up as soon as she can scare up one of the hotel's helicopters. Then I'll be on to head office as soon as they're in. Say nine o'clock London time in just under two hours from now. That'll give me time to chat through some things with our people on the ground and get set up. The hotel has first-rate video-conferencing facilities, according to its website.'

'And you have one of the fiercest legal and commercial intelligence sections of any business in Britain,' she said. 'London Centre. That is a lot of heat for one little harbour master.'

'It is. But I suspect that the harbour master's just the tip of the iceberg. Sounded like it from the list of other extra charges we were likely to face. The list of other authorities involved. So I want things straight and clear at once. And I want them to stay that way for as long as we do business here. Now, look, Morgan, I don't want you to do anything until you hear from me. If he calls again, stall. If the pilot comes aboard, let him sit in the pilot's seat. That's about all he'll be fit for in any case because I don't want you taking a line aboard or accepting any kind of an offer from the harbour tugs. You move when where and how I say. Even if that means reversing out of this harbour, turning around and steaming back home! And I'll tell you what to do in person after I've got all of this sorted out.'

'Right,' she said smartly. And, because Boston captains say *Aye, aye, sir* to no man, she added in her best clipped English accent, 'Righty-ho!'

It took Robin the better part of an hour to motivate the manager, call in a pilot and fire up a chopper. She called Richard from the right-hand passenger seat in the rear of an Aerospatiale SA316B Alouette III a little before nine fifteen local time. As she did so, Simeon Bourgeois was tightening his seat belt and the pilot was shouting at the air-traffic control officer in Granville Harbour Airport, getting clearance to hop down to the harbour and back as he throttled up the rotors. All in all, Richard really only understood that she would be there before nine thirty. Everything else was drowned out in a battering wall of noise that contrasted so strangely with the absolute absence of sound on the bridge around him.

Richard closed the cellphone and stood for a moment, right ear ringing, feeling the silence as an almost physical sensation. No log entries would be required until the chopper actually approached the ship so even Callum McKay had fallen quiet. Richard had not spent the interim since he had woken Robin in idleness.

34

With his mind whirling with plans and half-rehearsed conversations he planned to hold with Simeon Bourgeois, Jim Bourne and Robin, he had busied himself with preparations for going dirtside. He had checked his cellphone for messages for the fourth time that morning, then rung through to the automatic news and messaging service in his office at Heritage Mariner in London. He had checked his private, personal and business email accounts on his laptop. While he was on the web he checked the BBC News site, his preferred news service, but there was nothing relevant to himself or his business. Anything urgent would have come through to *Prometheus V* direct in any case – but he liked to make assurance double sure when he had the time and opportunity. Then, in the absence of anything needing his attention more urgently than the matter in hand, he had grabbed a bite to eat and packed his bags.

The Alouette clattered out of the lower sky and settled on the foredeck helipad exactly on time. Richard observed its approach from the bridge as Third Officer McKay babbled his log entry but was waiting on the white-marked green expanse with the strap to his laptop case over one shoulder and the strap to his grip over the other. In deference to the already stultifying heat, his jacket was folded over the grip itself and his tie was rolled in its pocket. He had hoped that the downwash of the chopper's rotors would act like a cooling fan – but no such luck. It simply funnelled hot and humid air over him as though a blast-furnace door had been thrown open in a steam-room. His shirt went from starched perfection to wet rag in the time it took him to scramble aboard. Settling in the left-hand passenger seat, he ran his hand back over the windswept riot of his hair only to find that this was literally dripping too.

'Hot,' observed Simeon Bourgeois, sympathetically. His slight figure rested in easy comfort, as though the very notion of sweat was foreign to his nature. The white cotton of his shirt lay as though recently ironed beneath the cream linen of his tropical suit, both emphasized by the mahogany glow of his skin. His brown-black eyes twinkled but he did not quite smile.

'As hell,' agreed Richard feelingly. He tightened his strap and shook Simeon's broad dry hand. Then he leaned forward, looking past his friend and associate as the Alouette lifted off again. Robin too looked cool and calm, as though she had just stepped out of a photo shoot for *Tatler*. 'Hi, darling. Thanks for coming out.'

He leaned back, pushed his kit to the far side of the little cabin with his feet and took a deep breath as he cleared his mind, sorting through the half-rehearsed conversations he had been preparing since the irritable harbour master rang off at five o'clock.

'Right,' he said. 'Let's get down to business.'

Three

Business

Like most large City businesses, Heritage
Mariner was a series of semi-autonomous sections. It had grown from Heritage Shipping, a
relatively simple maritime freight company,
into something much more than ever envisaged
by its founder, Robin's father Sir William Heritage. Soon the flourishing Heritage Shipping
had needed several sections. A financial section, a cargo-handling section, a maintenance
section. And, most importantly, a section dedi-
cated to finding cargoes and the hulls in which
to transport them. On top of these, there had to
be a personnel section designed to find and hire
men and women to crew them.

At first, of course, these sections existed all
together in Bill Heritage's brain as he ran a one-
man show. But then the business boomed. As
Richard joined, it moved into oil tankers and
boomed again. So Heritage Mariner continued
to expand as it met the demands of its success.
But it never lost that family feeling which on
the one hand engendered the fiercest employee
loyalty and on the other led to the house-style

habit of giving some of the sections names rather than dry business designations.

Nowadays Richard found himself CEO of a company which still had accountancy, mergers and acquisitions sections. There was always a need to balance the books, acquire new hulls and more recently to acquire entire businesses and shipping lines as well. There were increasingly few peer companies, even on the world stage, big enough to offer a realistic chance of merging; however the mergers section was always on the lookout, like sharks in 'eat or be eaten' mode.

But, more colourfully, there was also Crewfinders – at first an independent company founded by Richard himself. It was now the marine-personnel arm, recruiting, training and assigning crews all over the world from its office high above Leadenhall Street in the City of London. There was the Outback, the section that designed and oversaw the building of vessels from leisure craft to tankers. *Prometheus V* was the first ship in some time whose construction had been moved out of the Outback. Like most of the sections, the Outback got its name because of the man who led it – the Australian gold-medal yachtsman and award-winning boat designer Doc Weary. By the same token Heritage Mariner's business and executive recruitment arm was called the Bounty because it was led by ex-Royal Naval recruitment and administration officer Lieutenant Rupert Bligh.

Nobody was really sure whether it was Jim Bourne or Annie Bledsoe, his American opposite number in Heritage Mariner's smaller New York City office, who had decided to call the legal and commercial intelligence section London Centre. Certainly, the fact that there were a fair number of ex-naval and so-called secret-intelligence men mixed in with the business gurus and the legal eagles was an accepted element of its origin. The fact that the whole section had a slightly vague, almost cloak-and-dagger, remit added to things.

There were London Centre executives here whose legal duties went far beyond drawing up contracts and standing up in court. There were businessmen whose responsibilities took them well outside the office or the boardroom. There were the commercial-intelligence boys – who were mostly girls – who spent their days checking what was going on in all their rivals. The tanker, freighter, passenger, shipbuilding, business-running companies quoted on the stock exchanges worldwide and all of their properties listed at Lloyd's of London and far beyond.

And there were the doomsday men whose job was prediction. Everything from the implications of changes at senior government, presidential and prime-ministerial level in every active democracy to the demands by Russia to own the mineral rights between its north coast and the North Pole. From the intensifying effects of global warming on the oceans, the coasts and harbours beside them and the weather systems whirling over them to the chances of China completing its 'string of pearls' deep-water bases, facing down the Americans and gaining control of the three great straits of the China Sea, not to mention the Strait of Hormuz, gateway to the Gulf.

The doomsday men were almost all ex-intelligence; most of them, like Jim Bourne, ex-naval intelligence seconded to the SIS or, like Annie Bledsoe in New York, ex-NSA. But even their job went beyond mere predictive dreaming and blue-sky thinking. They didn't just move out of the box, they tended to kick down the sides. The name London Centre might owe more to the fictional creations of John Le Carré than to the real world, and certainly Jim at least was happy to emphasize how much he admired the writer, which seemed to foster the idea. But there were those who noted that the old-fashioned, nostalgic name had only appeared when the British secret-intelligence service MI6 had been moved lock, stock and barrel out of its old centre near Queen Anne's Gate and into the brash new building overlooking the Thames like the bridge of a cruise liner beached beside Vauxhall Bridge.

However it had originated, the name London Centre had stuck. And the fame of the section, inevitably a little stealthily, had spread worldwide. As had its recruitment policies, in line with its expansion into international markets on every other level.

Which was why Richard now found himself

sitting next to a French-speaking West African-born ex-undercover expert for the French 'Piscine', the DGSE and Service de Documentation Extérieure et de Contre-Espionnage.

'Tell me how things in Granville Harbour work, Simeon,' he said, pitching his voice over the thrumming of the Alouette's rotors. 'The whole business.'

Simeon Bourgeois remained silent for a moment as the helicopter eased up off the deck and into the lower air. Then he said, 'Better I show you, Captain.' And he leaned forward to tap the pilot on the shoulder. He shouted something in French that was lost to Richard under the noise of the rotors. The pilot gave a thoroughly Gallic shrug and the helicopter swooped away east of north. The dockside and the harbour buildings reared below them, seemingly close enough to endanger the undercarriage. They looked well built and fairly prosperous for the most part, but Richard's keen eye soon picked out signs of neglect and underinvestment. Faded paint on walls and signs; missing tiles on pitched roofs and lifting patches on flat ones. Sagging stucco and crumbling brickwork. Cracked and broken windows. Grass growing in dry brown tufts between dusty flagstones. Wide potholes in broad thoroughfares. No one had done any serious maintenance of these crucial facilities for a decade or more. Disorientated, he suddenly found himself confronted with a faded and peeling sign he recognized from his last visit here a decade since, advertising a company that

41

had ceased trading ten years even before that.

'Infrastructure's coming apart,' he called to Simeon.

'That's the least of it, Captain. Keep looking,' answered Simeon, shaking his head and frowning.

The Alouette swung north again to show the city blocks behind the port area. At first glance, the neat and angular urban layout could have come from any modern city. But a second glance revealed a range of more disturbing things. The roads were empty of modern motor traffic. One or two cars sat rusting at roadsides. Here and there a motor scooter picked its way gingerly between steep-sided, seemingly bottomless potholes. Bicycles seemed more frequent, but this was no Beijing with millions of cyclists pedalling athletically to work. A dozen or so ancient, ill-maintained machines were being carefully wheeled along crazily paved footpaths, all of them laden with goods. With a kind of a start Richard saw great piles of rubbish heaped in tiny garden plots and at crossroads. Rubbish that looked to have been discarded, picked over, scattered, picked over, casually re-piled. 'No civic amenities,' he shouted to Simeon.

'No gas,' shouted Simeon. 'No electricity most of the time. No phone lines – poles were made of wood and went for kindling. Only the port has anything like a reliable service – phone lines run underground down there. Some sewage but not much. No reliable running water

42

any more, not this far down. No drinking water. And these are the upmarket suburbs.'

'Upmarket?' broke in Robin, her laugh ringing with shock and disbelief. 'How can these be upmarket?'

'They are houses,' said Simeon. 'They are fairly secure; most of them have furniture. They have upper storeys, inside lavatories. Roofs.'

Richard and Robin looked at each other in wonder. Here was a modern city – more modern than London, Paris, New York. In its day a wonder of the city-planner's art with every modern convenience that infinities of oil revenue could buy. But it was being left, un-loved and unkept, to crumble into dereliction. Even the tall palms along the roadside stood dead and rotting, those that had not followed the telegraph poles into local fires – but from the look of things they were in better condition than the crumbling concrete street lights that stood beside them.

But Simeon was still speaking. 'And there are shops within fairly easy walk; important in the absence of a civic transport system. Not to mention the lack of a meaningful police force. And the shops are often quite well stocked, especially with local produce. There are still some farms running somewhere out there but it's mostly market-garden stuff.'

The Alouette swooped northwards and the city-clad hillside rose to meet it. Abruptly, there below them was a well-swept, litter-free boule-vard with green palms. A broad dual carriage-

43

way bustled with cars. Street lights gleamed even at this time of day. A taxi pulled into the traffic flow with a police cruiser on its tail. The cars eased past modest mansions, each on its own grounds, walled and fenced. There were cameras. Guards. 'Diplomatic district,' said Simeon tersely. 'Some of the senior presidential people live here too. But the top men and their families live in the presidential compounds themselves. The President keeps both his friends and his enemies close. Not that he has many enemies left. None that he knows about at all.'

The helicopter soared over a hilltop estate. Away to the west, a series of fairy-tale buildings glittered in the haze. 'That's the hotel area,' said Simeon. 'We'll be going there soon; and so we'll go down town now so you get a really clear picture.' He leaned forward and tapped the pilot on the shoulder once again. This time there was a lot more in the way of cajoling before that fatalistic shrug.

'He won't go far and he refuses to stay this low,' said Simeon as the helicopter swung round in a U-turn, gaining height as it went back south-eastwards even though the land beneath it was beginning to slope away again.

'Why?' asked Robin, her frown deepening.

'He says someone shot at him last time he was down at the delta.' Simeon gestured to the fuselage beside Richard's broad shoulder. There was a welt in the metal topped by a hole which none of them had noticed. The hole was just the right size for a bullet-hole and the welt showed the missile's trajectory clearly enough. And had the shot that made it been fired today instead, it would more than likely have put a nearly identical hole in the side of Richard's head.

Four

Shanty

Richard, Robin and Simeon Bourgeois sat in silence as the Alouette clattered back down towards that section of the city that lay along the side of the bay east of the docks. Richard shrugged off the uneasy feeling that the bullet-hole had brought. More to distract himself than anything else, he moved his head out of the line of fire and pressed his face to the window, hoping to see more. So it was that he was quick enough to spot the police roadblocks that separated the salubrious diplomatic district from its down-at-heel neighbours. To see the well-armed military patrols that cruised the rubbish-strewn streets in armoured half-track vehicles that took no account of potholes. To register the way the pall of unloved and unlovely hopelessness settled over the last of the ruined suburbs where even the armoured vehicles did not venture.

It was shocking how swiftly the regimented pattern of the city blocks broke down here. The fabric of the roads themselves seemed to have been torn from the living soil and carried away. Walls and fences remained as humps in overflowing overgrowths of garden flora – most of which was withered and drought-stricken. What multi-storey houses still stood in the strange sort of borderland were all roofless and open, windows eyeless and doors gaping, little more than crazy shells. Understanding was only a heartbeat behind observation. Everything of any worth at all had been stripped away. Slates and roof timbers. Rainproof sheeting. Copper pipes and electric cables. Anything plastic. Anything that would support weight, repel rain, provide heat. Anything that could be bartered.

Beyond the bleak stripped skeletons, a sort of shanty town clung to the bayside edge of the metropolis, crushed between the suburb and the overpowering wildness of the delta's mangroves. The jungle of the delta region seemed to grip the East Side shanties like the claws of some giant green creature come to tear them away altogether. It was simply amazing to think that this green riot of uncontrollable vegetation was any kind of kin to the rotting skeletons of the palm trees only a few kilometres distant where the ghost of urban civilization still haunted the dying streets.

Seemingly without pattern or the faintest semblance of organization, the corrugated-iron roofs of the one-storey shanties leaned together in one strange growth. Grey for the most part but splashed with garish colours here and there. Bright red rust on improperly treated metal. Peeling paint. Patterns and words where roofs had been fashioned from fallen hoardings. The walls between – tatty wood and plastic sheeting for the most part – were bright with peeling paint and unfading synthetic garishness. Flimsy enough to have been brought here and erected by one or two people. Showing a lack of time, energy and organization needed to use anything as complex or massive as brick or concrete. Which in turn explained why the shells of the houses had no roofs, floors or internal structure, but still had walls.

Between the confusion of little houses there were glimpses of narrow pathways that showed mud – hard and dusty or slick and slippery depending on their closeness to the waterside, the city or the jungle. But, unlike the roads in the ghostly suburbs, these paths were alive with humanity. A column of smoke rose from the heart of a rudimentary market, the oily black pall staining the lower air. 'Slaughterhouse,' said Simeon. 'All the meat, farmed or jungle, gets its hide seared before it's butchered and sold.'

'There are farmers who do that, especially to sheep carcasses, in England,' observed Robin quietly. 'They say it's to meet religious requirements. They call them smokies. It's forbidden. Illegal.'

'Nothing's forbidden down there,' Simeon answered. 'And there's no law so I guess nothing can be illegal.'

Richard considered saying something about the law of the jungle but then thought better of it.

The Alouette reached the slow polluted swirl of water again and turned, heading back up to the hotel compounds more than a world away at the top of the hill. Richard strained to look back once again as the pilot opened the throttles with every evidence of lively relief at having survived the overflight.

Then, with disorientating abruptness, something hit the side of the fuselage. There had been no sound of a shot, and, later, Richard would understand why – given the aircraft's height and the noise of its rotors and their slipstream. But the sound of impact was sharp. Like the impact of a steel-capped boot on a big tin can. The Alouette seemed to leap and swing. A second welt, parallel to the first, appeared in its side, but did not end in a bullet-hole. Mercifully, this shot had glanced off the helicopter's side. Even so, Richard's first instinct was to throw himself backwards. Only to rear forwards again almost instantly looking back down to see if he could put a face to his murderous enemy.

As they turned, powering away, therefore, Richard got a foreshortened view of the water's edge from the distant dock and harbour facilities to the shanty immediately beneath them. But he could see no individuals, simply crowds, as busy as foraging ants. But in the added vividness of shock, he seemed to see and understand things more clearly than before. It was strange to notice how the fences that bound the exclusive harbour with its Western-crewed ships and

49

oil workers seemed unable quite to contain the riches there.

Outside was a muddy, polluted foreshore where the detritus of ships was being picked over by swarms of people. Oil drums, crates, boxes, pipes, tubing, cans, plastic rope, discarded as rubbish by the vessels and swept round as jetsam by the sluggish tides and backwater swirls of the river's outwash, were precious prizes. Because they had practical or commercial value of some kind, he reasoned. But the foreshore was all too short, for the shanties crowded up to the walls and fences like desperate children starving at a rich man's gate.

There was no sense of any bayside or riverside organization down here in the shanties themselves. Houses reached right to the water's edge. Roofs overhung the water itself reckless of tide or flood. And half concealed beneath them sat the only things of any real worth in the whole sorry scene. Little boats clung to waterside hovels. Lines tied directly to window frames, door posts or roof poles. Small metal and fibreglass-hulled motor boats with rusty but functional outboards. Traditional native pirogues with paddles – little more than carved sticks designed to propel hollowed logs. Looking carefully, with straining, streaming eyes, Richard could see the little vessels stealing apparently silently in and out of the bright green overhang of mangrove, up and down invisible channels snaking with infinite complexity through the monstrous delta itself. Beyond the shanties, there was only the delta. And the delta, he remembered, was almost the size of Wales, where the illegal British smokies came from.

Here and there the empty oil drums floated amid the motor boats and pirogues tethered to the waterside shanties, lashed into dangerously unstable piers, staining the sluggish tide and current with deadly rainbows of oil. These were packed with fishermen armed with rods, poles and hand-lines, though any creature pulled out of that water would likely be as deadly as the pollution.

And then the jungle pounced out of the delta and on to the bay shore, gulping shanties, paths, water, fishermen, boats and all away.

'How's it got like this, Simeon?' asked Robin, deeply shocked and shaken.

'Greed,' answered the ex-French undercover man, West African and Congo expert. 'Who was it said "greed is good"? Not here it's not. Not like this. All the oil revenues, tourist dollars, all the international aid, every red cent that comes into this place goes to the President, his relatives and their hangers-on. When they've taken all they want, what's left starts filtering down. There isn't much and it doesn't go far. You can see it reflected in the city. That's why we took this little flight. There's a couple of thousand people high on the hog in the President's compounds. Maybe ten thousand fairly comfortably off in the protected diplomatic area. Tens of thousands scraping along increasingly desperately in the semi-derelict suburbs.

51

Millions starving to death in the shanties. And in the jungles of the delta – who knows?'

'But why don't they do something?' demanded Robin, outraged.

'You mean have a revolution or something?' asked Simeon, glancing across at the bullet-welted fuselage.

'Well...Yes, I suppose...' Robin's voice faltered as she saw the implication of her thoughtless remark.

'That's dangerous talk, Madame.' Simeon glanced over his shoulder at the pilot. 'Jim Bourne will update you on the latest details.' He lowered his voice so that the pair strained forward to hear him clearly. 'Basically the status quo remains in place for several reasons. One, the President has a lot of foreign support. We're working for Russians who have just got involved here – they don't want the apple cart upset. Neither do the Americans, the Chinese, you Brits...The list goes on. The President presents himself as the one man who can hold it all together in the face of Al-Qaeda-inspired African terrorism. And in a way, maybe he is. Look what happened in the Middle East after Saddam went down. Just think what might happen here with so many more people so much more desperate; with so much more to gain and so much less to lose...

'And the President's no fool. He makes sure that the army gets paid fairly regularly, and that all the top-cadre officers are absolutely loyal to him. He's invested some of his fortune in a top-flight security unit that runs the essential elements of the police force to make sure it will protect him and anyone else he names. Which includes everyone in the compounds, the hotels, the diplomatic area and so forth. Everybody on the oil platforms and in the dock facilities. I don't suppose you noticed, but all of the hotel helicopters like the one we're in have military markings. That's not just so they can be called up like the Territorial Army in times of national crisis. It's a very clear message to anyone down in the streets – take us on and you take on state security. Only the very brave or the very desperate would ever dream of doing so.'

As Simeon sat back, the Alouette settled lower. Richard glanced out of the window once again, wondering what had made the pilot feel suddenly safer, especially after being shot at for the second time. Beneath them was a long, straight boulevard which seemed designed to join the shanties on the outskirts to the derelict heart of the city. And there, a little to the north of the rule-straight east–west line of the roadway, was what looked like a fort in a Western movie. It could have been a Seventh Cavalry base armed against Comanche or Apache warriors commanded by John Wayne or Henry Fonda except that it was walled with iron instead of wood. Except that it had military-style watchtowers instead of almost medieval stockade outlooks. Except that instead of bunkhouses and stables it held what looked like a prison compound and corrugated-iron vehicle shelters.

'What's that?' he asked Simeon, struck by the strangeness of such a well-protected fort in the middle of a run-down city suburb.

'That's the central police station,' answered Simeon. 'That's where all the power outside the presidential compound is located.'

The three of them looked in silence at the strange fortress that seemed so far out of place, out of time.

Then Simeon continued, 'But don't get me wrong: this isn't an out-and-out police state. The President knows which side his bread is buttered. He even runs a parliament to keep the Western democracies happy. He's also happy to have an election every few years – especially when he's after something in particular. But he always wins. He presents himself as the Saviour of the Country – the Father of the Nation. But actually there's no real opposition. The millions of destitute and starving people in the shanties and the jungle may in theory have a vote. But they are split into more than a dozen factions who have been fighting each other since before the slavers arrived and started buying their captives nearly a thousand years ago. Oh, they've got guns – who in Africa hasn't? – but they tend to use them mostly on each other, fighting little turf wars over bits of territory too small to bury the dead. This is unusual.' He nodded at the bullet-welts on the fuselage. 'It'll bring down some painful retribution, I should guess. But the people will suffer in silence, I should think. If they dream of revolution, then that's all they ever seem to do – dream. They use their useless votes to vote for the President and they use their guns against each other and nothing ever gets any better. Anyone charismatic enough to pull them all together either politically or militarily comes to a sudden, sticky end. Or vanishes up-country and joins one of the wild militia groups up there.

'But the bush militias are as tribal as the rest. They spend all their time pillaging villages and wiping each other out. Or so I'm told. I don't know anyone who's ever been up-country and come out to tell the tale. Maybe Jim Bourne does. Down south in Congo, where I have been myself, there are reasons to try to get into the interior – minerals, diamonds, copper and cobalt in Katanga or wherever. People fly in and out of the heart of Congo all the time. But here it's different. As far as we know here there's only oil and it's all down at the coast, so why take the risk?

'And the result of all this, in Granville Harbour itself, is easy enough to imagine.'

'Pay structures as badly maintained as the infrastructure,' rumbled Richard. 'Anyone outside the magic circle you've named lucky to see any kind of a regular pay cheque at all. Most of them like the harbour master hanging on to their jobs because they have family responsibilities, mistresses, whatever and there's no real alternative. But forced to milk every opportunity possible for every penny they can lay their hands on. Living hand to mouth for the moment, but remembering how it was in the old days when the gas, the sewage, the water and the buses all ran – and hoping somehow to get back to that again.'

'Got it in one,' said Simeon. 'But once that kind of mentality takes hold it's hard to contain it. Everyone starts to go out after what they can get, whether they're one of the really needy ones or not. Mme Mariner has told me of this harbour master and what he said to you, of the list of authorities you will have to deal with. This is as good an example as any of the way it happens. It may well be that he himself is desperate, hasn't been paid, is trying to get what he can. But customs men are well paid – they're just holding out their hands for greed. Immigration and counter-terrorism are elements of the security service. They certainly aren't desperate. But everyone else is taking bribes – so why not them as well? And I noticed you looking down at the military patrols and police roadblocks on the streets. What do you think they are really after? Think about it – that's why the roads are so quiet. It's not surprising. It goes right up to the top. And not just here. How many billions of dollars were British Aerospace supposed to have paid to that guy in New York to ease the Mid-East contracts for them? *Billions?*

'And in the meantime, here we are trying to deal with some backwater small-fry who has just enough power to make himself a nuisance and try to cut a deal. And he's one of millions in this city – not to mention the whole damn country and the continent behind it. Gripped by a situation they can't begin to control but doing the best that they can with whatever power they've got. Lacking the spirit to fight back.'

'But somebody has the spirit, willingness and the wherewithal to fight back, even here,' observed Richard quietly as the Alouette settled over the great presidential compound with its palatial accommodation, swimming pools, paddocks and tennis courts, then began its descent into the hotel compound at the western end of the ridge above the city.

'Who would that be?' asked Simeon.

Richard gestured at the welts in the chopper's side and the bullet-hole with its bright beam of sunlight shining like a yellow laser on to his face.

'Whoever fired those shots, they've got guns and guts. What if they've got friends as well?'

Five

Lodge

There could hardly be a greater contrast between what they had been looking at and talking about ten minutes ago and what they were approaching now, thought Richard grimly as he pounded across the helipad towards the Granville Royal Lodge Hotel.

The fact that he had had to stoop beneath the Alouette's whirling blades seemed to emphasize the simple height of the dazzling frontage that stood less than a hundred metres distant and seemed to stretch right across the ridge-top. The snowy whiteness of the upper storeys reared as stark as an ice-cliff against the cobalt sky, its pristine beauty further emphasized by the design of the palatial area below. At first glance the Granville Royal Lodge Hotel's reception seemed to represent a huge royal hunting lodge built in the manner of the legendary tribal kings of the area. A huge circle of ebony columns the size of tree trunks three storeys high supported a thrusting overhang of dark palm thatch. The perfect curve of the frontage was broken only by a wide portico, which stood out from it between two broader columns that waited at the top of a short flight of red-mud steps. On each end of the steps sat exquisitely carved apparently gilded leopards stiffly erect, like hunting dogs on guard. Within the blessed shadows stretching away behind the frontage beneath the main umbrella of thatch, a forest of lesser columns supported a cloud-white ceiling which soared above half a dozen massive open-plan areas to the final, distant palisade at the back framed by further dazzling brightness beyond.

The first impression was that a substantial grove of huge trees had been torn from the jungle, erected here and left wedged in the heart of the white cliff hotel-front as a shady forest glade. A glade that offered welcome protection from the searing sun, but which nevertheless stood open to the winds which, even up on the ridge here, could still blow with furnace heat. As the Alouette's stinking exhaust proved all too well.

But when Richard reached the cunningly fashioned steps and realized that the hard red mud at his feet guarded by the six bright leopards was actually exquisite terracotta tiling, he further realized that he was the subject of a further series of breathtakingly expensive illusions. He paused beneath the twin tree trunks that supported the high, wide portico and glanced up. The palm-fronds of the overhanging thatch were the first trompe l'œil: each frond a match for the leopards – made of beautifully gilded metal. The outer circle of tree-trunk columns immediately in front of him did not in fact stand apart from each other – they were walled with glass so beautifully fine and clean as to be almost invisible. As he paused there, only distantly aware of Robin at one shoulder and Simeon at the other, a porter dressed in an old colonial askari uniform stepped smartly forward and opened a glass door the better part of four metres high.

'Welcome to the Granville Royal Lodge Hotel, bwana,' he said in a deep voice, sounding like something out of *Sanders of the River* or *King Solomon's Mines*. 'Please step through the security gate.'

Richard stepped through the arch of a security gate immediately within, into the air-conditioned reception atrium. He tensed himself automatically for the shrilling of the alarm. An encounter with a terrorist bomb some years ago had led to the reconstruction of his knee joints with a range of metal pins. He often set off security alarms. But not this one, however. It must be very discriminating; or not very efficient. The thought was fleeting because the impressions on the far side of the security gate were simply overwhelming and his sense of reality, if anything, diminished and receded.

At first, all Richard was really aware of was another set of contrasts. The invasive, humid warmth outside being replaced by the elegant, expensive chill in here. The random racket of wind and motors roaring even up on the portico outside the doors drowning in the purposeful hush that closed around him inside them like the pressured air of a jetliner. The avgas stench of exhaust fumes that had assaulted his nostrils on the helipad being swiftly washed away by the fragrant atmosphere that soothed them now.

And another telling contrast presented itself at once. So far the only local man Richard had dealt with was the harbour master. Now the hotel's manager stepped forward and identified himself with a smile and a tiny bow. The harbour master's irritable voice and accent had made Richard imagine a kind of rotund, ill-shaven Poirot in grubby underwear, with a darker skin and fewer little grey cells. A Poirot who had been alone except for his sleepy, grumpy bed companion.

What confronted Richard now was a vision from a gentleman's fashion ad in the *Tatler* or *County Life*, flanked by a platoon of equally exquisite underlings. They could all have been on their way to Royal Ascot or Cheltenham on a Gold Cup day. The manager's morning suit was perfect from head to toe. His silver tie was in a full-Windsor knot, his shoes shone like mirrors. His shirt front was pristine, his collar and cuffs a vision of white accented by the glossy ebony of the skin beneath them. There was the faintest fragrance of peppermint mouthwash and Chanel Pour Homme after-shave.

'I am André Wanago, the manager here. Welcome, Captain Mariner...' The very moment he started speaking, André gave a tiny gesture and more askaris relieved Richard of his laptop and travel grip. An immaculate waiter in starched white offered a silver tray on which stood a range of glasses full of waters and juices over shaved ice. Richard paused in his selection only to offer André a handshake which was immediately and firmly returned.

'My helicopter was shot at on the way here,' said Richard shortly, as the manager's speech of welcome reached its first hiatus.

André's brown eyes were almost level with his own. Their accommodating smile turned to a frown of sympathetic outrage as Richard's words sank in. 'But no harm done?' he enquired, glancing at Robin and Simeon.

'Only to your chopper...'

Richard released his hold and reached for a much-needed drink as the manager continued with his speech of welcome. 'Then you need concern yourself no further with this outrage. I will report it personally to the authorities as soon as you are settled.' The practised smile returned. The mellifluous tones flowed on and finally concluded. 'I am sure you will want to freshen up and cool down after your journey, sir. We will complete the formalities of registration when you are more comfortable.'

Richard sipped Perrier so cold it made his teeth ache and returned André's easy smile as his mind raced. He was not here to rest and relax. On the contrary, he was in the grip of an almost irresistible impulse to get on with things. The adventure in the chopper had been a distraction, but he needed to focus now. The harbour master would be in his office by now. The officious jobsworth might well have contacted *Prometheus V* already. Would certainly have called his vulture-friends and colleagues, on their cellphones if not on the risky landlines down in the harbour. They would all be sharpening their knives for a fat cut of the milch cow that the tanker represented to them.

It was not that Richard didn't trust Morgan, but he saw no reason to leave any of his captains alone and under pressure for longer than was absolutely necessary. The orders he had given her were clear enough, but enforcing them in the face of importunate officialdom would not be pleasant and hanging about here sipping Perrier and exchanging pleasantries wasn't helping matters in the slightest.

On the other hand, Richard calculated, offending André would hardly help things either, no matter how urgent the necessity. And, in the almost clinical confines of the massive atrium he did in fact feel in need of a shower as the perspiration chilled against his skin. He felt Robin beside him. Her hand on his upper arm squeezed in an old, intimate signal that urged calm and caution.

For André wasn't quite finished yet. 'In the meantime, however, there are several messages which have come to reception, marked for your personal attention. We have printed them out in anticipation of your arrival.' He clicked long, artistic fingers and they appeared in his hand as though he were a conjurer. 'You should understand of course, Captain, that our security is second to none and our discretion absolute.'

Richard saw at first glance why André added the seeming afterthought. The topmost message was in company code. That would be from Jim Bourne at London Centre, of course. And it must be pretty urgent for Jim to have even considered sending it like this. He flashed it at Robin and then at Simeon, who still stood at his other shoulder sipping what looked like mango juice. 'Several personal messages have been left at reception for you also. You are invited to an intimate gathering in the small corporate facility area by Mr Asov. Apparently at noon. But I cannot confirm that as both Mr Asov and Mr Makarov have left strict instructions that they are not to be disturbed before noon themselves. And they have their individual methods of ensuring staff compliance with their requests.' The elegantly sculpted lips tightened in a tiny smile signalling a shared confidence and understanding acceptance of the solecism of the encoded message. 'This is standard practice with them when they stay with us, of course.'

'Thank you,' said Richard shortly, understanding everything except the last, arch, reference. 'I shall take your advice in the matter of cooling off at once if I may.' He put his drink down decisively and there was a silver salver like a levitating table waiting to receive it. Simeon did the same.

Robin released the pressure on Richard's arm

but retained her grip as she guided him across the airy atrium of the lobby. To the right gaped a cavernous jungle hut of a reception, to which André was returning with his team. On the left, an apparent glade among the dark trunks was full of tables and chairs, bustling with other hotel residents taking tea and coffee and a range of other drinks. Their holiday costume seemed as bright as parrot feathers in the restful gloom, their cheery chatter scarcely more intelligible than the cries of the forest birds. Waiters in crisp and immaculate white passed between them, paused and hovered solicitously with silver trays. Askari-costumed porters, variously laden, came and went on various errands. Richard had a vague impression of busy bars and a bazaar of shops arranged in the cool forest clearings behind him with waiters, porters, guests coming and going amongst them.

'Simeon,' he said quietly, 'can you get the rest of the team together? I'll want to have a briefing in our suite in –' he glanced at the old Rolex Oyster Perpetual in its battered steel case that never left his wrist – 'twenty minutes.'

'Twenty minutes, Mandela Suite,' said Simeon and peeled off like a fighter plane leaving a formation. Richard had a vague impression of Simeon crossing to the rear of the atrium on his left. A glance that way revealed huge glass doors and beyond them a set of steps leading down into an open central area that dwarfed the atrium itself before the next wing of the hotel rose like an iceberg patterned with windows. 'What's out there?' he asked Robin as she led him between the final pair of columns and into the shady corridor of an accommodation wing.

'The biggest swimming pool in the universe,' she answered tersely. 'You'll see.'

Robin led Richard into a seemingly infinite corridor lined on each side with doors. Here the terracotta flooring was replaced by cool marble flags. The ceiling fell to a more human height – the contrast with the atrium explaining the apparent length of the corridor. Teams of men and women in neat traditional cleaners' uniform wheeled trolleys laden with cleaning equipment from door to door in the distance. Robin guided Richard to the nearest of several pairs of lift doors but it was the porter who pressed the button. He held the doors in courteous silence when they whispered open immediately, allowing them to enter before him, then stood guard as they hissed upwards.

'Suite nice?' asked Richard innocuously, aware of the porter and unwilling as yet to accept André's assurances of absolute discretion. Careful, therefore, not to raise any of the more politically questionable matters he was burning to discuss.

'It's the loveliest I've ever stayed in,' she answered brightly. 'Even nicer than our suite on *Tai Fun* last year. Though probably not energy efficient or carbon neutral.'

Tai Fun was the experimental sailing vessel cum cruise liner that had taken them round the

Java Sea last summer. The holiday had been designed to help Robin recover from her terrible experiences in Archangel. In the Russian city, Robin had been chased by a squad of militsia policemen before being trapped aboard the rotting hulk of an early *Prometheus* tanker which turned out to have been full of corpses. And, nearly fatally to all, but especially Robin, the corpse-filled derelict also contained a group of men who would stop at nothing to conceal that fact from the world. But the holiday aboard *Tai Fun* had caused its own unexpected element of stress as well, for the vessel had become the source of competition between Richard and Texan billionaire Nic Greenbaum. And then become involved in the international efforts to rescue the inhabitants of a tiny island trapped by a volcanic eruption. Unlike the rotting hulk moored helplessly in Archangel, the wind-powered *Tai Fun* had combined the most cutting-edge of green technology with the highest standards of elegance and comfort. If the Nelson Mandela Suite outranked *Tai Fun*'s palatial accommodation, it must be something unusual indeed.

After a few moments, Richard felt the lift begin to slow. The porter shifted his feet in anticipation of the door opening. Richard drew himself up and Robin slid her arm into his again, taking hold of his biceps with the gentlest of grips. The lift car stopped. The doors opened. The three of them stepped forward.

There was a surprisingly large square lobby

floored in pink porphyry marble slabs. On each of the walls ahead stood an imposing pair of double doors. Above each lintel was a plaque which announced the name of the suite within in a series of languages, exquisitely lettered. Outside each set of doors stood a seemingly fragile Hepplewhite chair. But the actual strength of the chairs – and the explanation for André's last, arch, remark – were alike demonstrated by the fact that a very large and powerful-looking man was seated in the one outside the Prince's Suite. He was wearing a beautifully tailored grey suit that seemed to have been cut for someone with a slightly larger chest, judging by the way the lapels sagged wide. His position was apparently relaxed, but his hands were on his lap all too obviously convenient to the gape of his jacket. A gape widened further by the weight of whatever he was wearing inside. A Grach, if Richard was any judge. Or a SIG Sauer if the bodyguard preferred Western guns to Russian ones.

The man was bald – shaven-headed – which made the earpiece in his left ear all the more obvious. But across his face above his eyes and below his nose sat two unbroken lines of shaggy hair. His eyes looked out from between these like the eyes of an angry hunter peering through the branches in a Siberian forest.

Robin gasped and her hand tightened on Richard's arm with painful force. Richard took a deep breath, almost as shocked as she was. But he stepped forward on the heels of the porter and confronted the bodyguard as he pulled himself erect with the deceptive laziness of a lion on the alert. The eyes between the branches of hair lost none of their fierceness. The hands stayed convenient to the gape in the jacket and the gun immediately beneath it. The thin mouth stirred the moustache in a fleeting smile of recognition.

This was one of the Russian militsia men who had pursued Robin through the streets of Archangel and then followed her on to the rotting hulk of the tanker. Both he and his partner Sergeant Paznak had been severely wounded in the exchanges of fire aboard the derelict. Like Richard and Robin, in one way or another they had been very lucky to survive. For both Robin and Richard himself, he had stepped straight out of a nightmare that could hardly have been more different to more recent nightmares of African jungles and faceless, night-dark horrors.

Richard recovered first and pulled Robin forward another, faltering step. He held his hand out and said, in English, 'Going up in the world, Sergeant Voroshilov?'

Voroshilov slowly returned the gesture, enclosing Richard's hand in his own big paw. 'Me and Paznak work for Mr Makarov now,' he said, also in English. 'Part of his 24/7 security team.'

Richard simply gaped. His hand fell and Voroshilov's returned to the ready position.

'But why on earth does Mr Makarov need

bodyguards?' asked Robin, finding her voice at last.

Voroshilov looked down at her. His fierce gaze softened fractionally. The thick bars of the eyebrow and moustache stirred again. 'You'll see,' he said quietly.

Six

Anastasia

Richard hesitated in the doorway to the Nelson Mandela Suite, simply awed. Robin walked inwards with the porter, apparently unconcerned by the fact that he was no longer following her. Voroshilov hovered at his shoulder, hand on pistol butt, seemingly caught between simple curiosity and the desire to give the place a swift security sweep. Then something occurred to Richard. 'Voroshilov,' he growled. 'Have you and Paznak swept this suite?'

'Mr Makarov insisted,' admitted the ex-militsia sergeant a little sheepishly. 'We sweep the whole hotel routinely whenever he or Mr Asov stay. He thought you would enjoy the same... ah...service.'

'Which of you does the food-tasting?' enquired Richard wryly. But Voroshilov had retired to his watch position, holding his hand to his earpiece. Richard turned back to the cavernous coolness of the suite.

The over-opulent style was best described as Hemingway hits Harrods – or perhaps Hollywood hits Harare, he thought, saving up his wry

71

observations to try on Robin later. Whatever, Richard strongly suspected, the man for whom it was named would never have approved. Even if the zebra-skin bench-seat on which the askari-uniformed porter was placing his brief-case was as false as the lion-skin rug beneath it, it was still too far over the top. The simple culture clash between the laptop and the rough-hewn mahogany work-desk on which it was placed in turn was literally mind-numbing. The ebony masks, ostrich-feather headdresses, war shields and crossed assegais on the walls were a relief only in that they were not trophy heads hacked off springbok, eland and gazelle. And they too clashed with the huge flat-screen TV currently switched to 'mirror' mode.

Massive leather-covered ox-blood Chester-fields squatted on either side of long glass-top-ped tables through which the skins of zebras and giraffe seemed to gleam as brightly as the huge arrangement of orchids and lilies at the centre of each. Along one wall, opposite the enormous TV, and also laden with flowers, stood a bar fit to entertain hard-drinking Hem-ingway himself – and most of the Hollywood stars, writers, artists and socialites he counted among his friends.

But there were blessedly few walls to be so tastelessly adorned, thought Richard, taking a deep breath of the clinically clean, air-condi-tioned, lily and leather-scented air. Like the lobby below, the suite's main reception room seemed largely to be sheathed in glass. Walls existed merely to support tasteless bric-à-brac and to frame doorways leading away to other, more private, equally tasteless rooms: bedrooms, bathrooms, dressing rooms.

Robin and the porter vanished through a double door almost as huge as the Great Gate of Sumer – and seemingly almost as ancient – beyond which Richard caught a glimpse of a bed-foot also draped in gaudy animal pelts. And an ivory-legged case-stand topped in some heavy grey hide – rhino, hippo or elephant by the look of it. And big enough to have taken most of the animal's skin to cover.

Richard closed the main door behind him and strode forward. This was no time to stand and gape. As he crossed towards the bedroom, he was given a widening view through the clear frontage. At first, this revealed the balcony that extended the floor outwards beyond the glass wall, seemingly hanging magically in the air, laden with more tables, sofas, sunloungers and sunshades disguised as modest palm trees. Then, beyond that – far, far beneath it – what truly seemed to be a jungle waterhole almost vast enough to be called a lake. Only the bikini-clad beauties that lay like sated lionesses sunning themselves around its sky-blue and silver edges revealed it to be the swimming pool Robin had mentioned earlier.

Richard put the flimsies of his messages down on the brutal mahogany desktop beside his laptop, the hotel's welcome pack, TV instruction booklet, touch-screen telephone and

73

all the rest. Caught a glance of his reflection in the huge TV screen and was struck anew by the fact that he urgently needed to shave, shower and change in spite of that fact that he had done all three only a couple of hours earlier. He paused for an instant, calculating whether he had time to give *Prometheus* a quick ring and update himself on anything new that Morgan had to report. But a glance at his Rolex showed that he had been dirtside for less than an hour, though it had seemed a good deal longer. And his main priority was to look like a man in control of things when the others arrived in fifteen minutes' time.

Morgan would have to wait.

Richard hurried onwards, therefore, all too aware that he had very little time to get himself ready – physically and mentally – before Simeon Bourgeois brought Charles Le Brun and the others up for their first conference. Their first council of war, perhaps. He glanced back wryly at the shields and assegais as he went in through the Great Gate into the bedroom. Perhaps they would come in handy after all, he thought, if things got really dirty here.

Had Richard known just how prophetic that casual thought would turn out to be, he would have taken Robin, turned around, headed back to *Prometheus* and sailed for safe home waters far away from the Benin Light at once.

But, as ever, Richard's ability to see into the future was obscured by the overwhelming busi-ness of the bustling present. And so he went bathroom to shower and change instead, bliss-fully unaware that the routine, workaday ablutions were simply further steps along the inevitable path to the deepest danger and death; as they meandered, all unsuspectingly, into the heart of darkness.

Fifteen minutes later, Richard was standing adjusting the golden perfection of his full-Windsor tie-knot in one of the full-length bed-room mirrors when his concentration was disturbed by an imperious rapping at the outer door. The porter was long gone, of course, and Robin had vanished into her own bathroom. He glanced at the Rolex beneath the double cuff of his gleaming white shirt. Even here, in this heat, he insisted on full-length sleeves; weakening only in that the shirts were of the finest, lightest silk. 'I'll get it,' he called to Robin, reaching for the crisp fawn cotton of his perfectly tailored suit jacket. Cotton with a little stiffening rather than more fashionable linen because he preferred his creases to stay where they were put – and to stay vertical, for the most part. 'Though they're a minute or two early,' he added, speaking to himself. He shrugged his jacket on, squared his shoulders, shot his cuffs and buttoned the single-breasted garment across the firm flatness of his stomach where the point of his perfectly tied tie just touched the golden buckle of his slim leather belt. He paused, trying to make sense of Robin's reply – lost

75

beneath the thunder of the shower that she in her turn was enjoying.

The mirror reflected his tall, lean body, stylishly if conservatively draped in the closest his London tailors would come to the khaki-drill tropical uniform used by the military in the days before ubiquitous camos conquered the soldiering world. Fortunately, perhaps, it was not all that close to the military original – for that was what was worn by the porters here. Naval tropical whites would have been too much ashore, of course; as far over the top as the war masks and headdresses on the walls. And for the first time he could remember he was wearing shoes that he could not shine – pale suede desert boots that reached up past his trouser cuffs and high above his ankles. The outfit was more than slightly outdated affectation, of course. Like much about Richard, it was carefully calculated. It emphasized his air of decisive authority – put him as firmly in charge here as he was on the command decks of his supertanker fleet.

The thick crêpe soles of the boots took him silently back out to the main door. There was a security screen but he didn't bother even glancing at it, secure in the presence of Voroshilov and his automatic outside. So that when he opened the door, expecting to see Simeon, Charles and the rest, what actually confronted him was quite a surprise.

She stood five foot seven or so, a hair shorter than Robin, and she was lissom, muscular and powerful-looking. But it was the piercings that he noticed first. She had four rings in the upper section of each ear and a further four – all heavy gold – in the lobes. Her forehead boasted four more studs, two each distorting the dramatic curves of her thick black brows with more gold, diamond-studded. A diamond emphasized the aristocratic line of each nostril while a third sat squarely above the dimple in her all too determined chin. But it was the ruby at the corner of her black lips that was really disturbing.

For she looked exactly like a vampire. Her face was white, except for the thick black eyeliner and lipgloss. Her rough-cut, boyish hair was black, though its roots were fine ash-blonde. The fingers that she ran through it were long and pale and clawed with sharp black nails. The hands clad in fine black leather fingerless gloves. She wore a long black leather coat that covered her from her square shoulders to the ankles of her black CAT Colorado boots. Except that it gaped open at the front to reveal the fact that all she wore beneath it was a cropped white T-shirt as tight to her chest as a layer of paint. A navel ring framed by a less than tasteful tattoo. And a huge studded belt whose lower edge sat perhaps a centimetre above the hem of her black leather micro-mini skirt.

'Heeeeeeeeeey,' she said in a purr that mixed Russian, French and American as her sharp black eyes appraised him frankly but approvingly. 'You must be Richard. They told me you had arrived and I couldn't wait to meet you. I'm Anastasia.'

Richard looked up at Voroshilov, his eyebrows raised. The Cossack shrugged as though helpless in the face of this overwhelming apparition. And as he did so, the door that he was guarding swung open behind him and a second, older, woman swept out. The bemused Richard was carried back to his days as a young commander on the first great tankers and the piles of *Playboy* all too often discovered under cadets' bunks on his notoriously thorough captain's inspections.

The second woman sported all too many long blonde ringlets, far too much deep-tanned cleavage and all too little high-cut, semi-transparent skintight bathing costume in a distracting leopard-skin pattern.

But when she spoke, it was in the icy accents of an offended Swiss matron. 'Anastasia!' she spat shrilly, drawing out the long 'a' to *Anastahahahahahsia*. 'What are you thinking of? It is time for your studies! You must return to your books! At once! Your papa will be outraged. Once again!'

The woman in the bathing costume spoke in Swiss-accented French. Anastasia swung round and answered in fluent German. 'Of course, Frau Hoffman. I have no wish to outrage my poor papa. It is biology today. I will study the ill-effects of ultraviolet radiation upon human skin.' She glanced back at Richard and winked as though they were old friends already. 'Especially upon *ageing* human skin!'

It was at this point that the lift doors whispered open to reveal Richard's war council. And it was, perhaps, the fixed nature of their gazes that reminded Frau Hoffman of just how much of her skin was currently on display. 'Messieurs!' she said icily, and swung round to retreat into the darkness of Max Asov's suite. The instant of rear view before Anastasia followed her allowed all present to satisfy themselves that there was not, in fact, a little white bunny tail sewn on the seat of her suit. But then, as it plunged upwards and downwards like a thong, lost at once between two full moons of red-bronzed flesh, there wasn't really room for a bunny tail in any case.

'*Enfin*, Richard,' said Simeon brusquely, crossing in front of Voroshilov as the door to Max's suite clicked decidedly shut. 'I see you have made the acquaintance of M. Asov's execrable daughter Anastasia and her delectable companion Frau Hoffman.'

Charles Le Brun swept past him, ebony hand held out, cinnamon eyes roguishly a-twinkle. 'Though if you find Frau Hoffman easy on the eye, you wait until you see the other playmates that M. Asov and M. Makarov have brought along with them!'

The men that Robin had brought out from London Centre on Richard's instructions could hardly have made a more strongly, contrastingly businesslike team, if Frau Hoffman was anything to go by. Together with the local

79

experts, Simeon Bourgeois and Charles Le Brun, there were Alex Magnus and Hal Cornelius, the international-contract experts who would oversee the global implications of anything to be signed. They were accompanied by John Day and Bill Bushell, the oil-contract men who could focus on the more local issues.

To be fair, none of them looked as though they had spent the last few days poring over lengthy business documents in shaded rooms well out of the sun or far away from the pools, the bars or the restaurants. But they were a businesslike team who settled to work at once, discussing *Prometheus*'s predicament and what they, Morgan Hand and London Centre led by Jim Bourne, could do about it.

The discussion became so focused and so intent so quickly after Richard made contact with *Prometheus* and Charles brought Morgan's worried face up on the big TV via the hotel's videoconferencing facility that Richard hardly noticed Robin slipping out to join them. Until she began to speak – for she was a vital, knowledgeable and insightful member of the war council at once. But the fact that the tanker had received no further contact from the harbour master, who was currently blocking their attempts to contact him, was a problem.

And Jim Bourne's coded telex was a further sticking point. Richard sat at the desk and typed the message into his laptop, pushing the series of keys that would translate it into plain English. As he worked, so he read out what came up on to the screen in front of him as the others sat round frowning with worry and thought. "'I advise you most strongly – in the strongest possible terms – to wait until I arrive in Granville Harbour. I advise you to do nothing until I can talk to RM face to face." Why we should do this he does not say. Nor does he give any further details. The only extra piece of information comes in the form of a postscript which comes out as: "The Doctor is back in play." But Doctor who?' demanded Richard, swinging round, looking away from the laptop screen and scanning the frowning faces, trying not to think of childhood television programmes, Cybermen and Daleks.

The others merely shrugged and exchanged looks of uncomprehending ignorance. Morgan on the video screen shook her head. In the room in front of her, Robin unconsciously echoed the action. A little silence began to lengthen out.

'There's only one Doctor I can think of,' began Charles Le Brun hesitantly.

When the imperious rapping at the door was repeated once again, interrupting Charles mid-thought, Richard rose to answer it quite automatically, still lost in thought himself. A glance at his watch showed that it was coming up to midday and he supposed it would be Max Asov or Felix Makarov – or more likely one of their acolytes – come to remind him of the invitation to their reception. As he touched the handle of the door he had a fleeting thought that it might even be Anastasia returned from her biology studies to renew their brief acquaintance.

But no.

Richard opened the door to be faced by a short, square officer in army uniform so neat that he might just have stepped off the parade ground at Sandhurst or West Point. Behind him stood six men in camouflage kit, all armed to the teeth, with modern-looking automatic rifles sloped across their chests. And behind them stood Voroshilov, with his hands very pointedly well clear of his underarm pistol.

'I am looking for Captain Richard Mariner,' said the officer suavely. His accent would have fitted into the Royal Military Academy at Sandhurst as flawlessly as his uniform and the black toothbrush moustache almost invisible on his upper lip. And the men behind him might be as well placed there in their khaki berets, universal camouniform and their all too obviously updated British SA80s.

'I am Captain Mariner,' said Richard, his face gathering into a frown as his icy eyes swept over the soldiers and their armaments. The fact that the guns had no trigger-guards emphasized how well trained and reliable the threatening little command must be. 'What seems to be the problem?'

He heard the stirring behind him as the others began to stand up and gather at his back. But his eyes never left the level brown gaze of the officer standing squarely in front of him.

'If you are Captain Richard Mariner, then I must inform you that you are under arrest.' The officer raised his hand and ticked off Richard's transgressions on his fingers as he spoke, looking absurdly like an irritable schoolmaster berating an unruly youth. 'You have entered the country illegally; you have avoided security, customs and immigration. You have signed no papers and you have paid no taxes. You have not even completed the required registration at this hotel. I repeat, you are under arrest, sir. You must come with me at once.'

And, to emphasize the seriousness of his words, the little phalanx of soldiers behind him snapped the safeties off their SA80s.

Seven

Zinderneuf

Robin was at Richard's side at once, her face aflame with outrage. Simeon and Charles were mere centimetres behind her. 'Now just a minute here,' she began.

The officer seemed to give no signal, but the six SA80s were all suddenly aimed at them. The only thing that – very pointedly – stopped the gesture being absolutely life-threatening was the fact that the officer remained calmly and patiently standing in the line of fire. 'I'm afraid I must insist, Captain,' he said gently.

Robin held her tongue.

And Richard shrugged. It was all too clear that in the game as they played it here a room full of lawyers was by no means equal to a lobby full of soldiers. 'Can I get some stuff?'

'Your passport and papers. That is all. I will accompany you.'

As Richard and the officer passed Simeon, he said, 'We'd have needed a local brief anyway.'

'I know just the man.' Simeon nodded once.

'Where should my lawyers come to find me?' Richard asked the officer.

come. Major Kebila and I are old acquaintances.'

The major gave a little bow as though Simeon had greeted him at a presidential reception. But he made no reply and remained silent as Richard collected together his papers. But Robin wasn't finished. 'I'll come with you,' she announced as Richard returned with Kebila punctiliously at his shoulder.

'I'd rather you didn't, darling,' he answered softly, placing his empty hand gently on her shoulder and meeting her worried gaze with a confident half-smile. 'You stay here and pull all the strings you can. This is only what we might call *a little local difficulty*, after all.'

'Perhaps Simeon, then—'

'I'll come with you, if the major will permit,' interrupted Charles Le Brun smoothly.

'But the major will *not* permit,' said Kebila, allowing a little steel into his pompously formal tone at last. 'Captain Mariner is not a minor under the age of discretion requiring adult supervision in detention. He is a grown man of legal age who has transgressed several laws. He will be taken to the station and he will be charged. When you and your local representatives have made due representation to the relevant authorities, you will find him waiting, comfortable but bored and repentant no doubt, in a holding cell.'

'If I can't accompany you, Richard, I must at least give you a little advice,' said Le Brun

Richard's hands. 'You know how much your passport is worth, to you as an identification document – but also to their people as an aid to illegal immigration; terrorism, even. But you may not be aware just how precious the various medical certificates are worth. Documentary proof of inoculation against malaria and yellow fever are each worth a fortune here. As are certificates of immunization against the various types of hepatitis, rabies and the indigenous fevers...'

Richard nodded once to show that he heard and understood, but his hand remained on Robin's shoulder and he gave it a reassuring squeeze. 'I would also like you to tell Max and Felix not to worry,' he added pointedly. 'And give them my apologies, will you? I don't think I'll be able to attend their reception after all.'

Richard rode down with Major Kebila and two soldiers in the lift, then waited until the other four arrived. Then the eight of them crossed the huge atrium swiftly and silently, uninterrupted by André Wanago or any of his assistants. One of the military half-tracks he had seen prowling the city was waiting outside and he was struck by how much larger and more intimidating it looked from ground level than it had seemed from the helicopter.

The back doors swung wide and he climbed in immediately behind the major. He took his seat beside the punctilious officer on the bench that reached down one side and the soldiers sat along the other. The steel box of the vehicle and the sheer number of automatic and semi-automatic weapons within it seemed to make handcuffs, at least, unnecessary. But the half-track was of military design and spec. There were no comforts. The benches were narrow and hard. They had no backrests other than the burning metal of the armoured side. There was no suspension system to ease the lurching of the tank-like drive. There was most especially no air conditioning. After a while, the heat built up to such an extent that Major Kebila gestured at the rearmost men to open the doors a little.

By chance, Richard found himself sitting opposite a large window covered with thick but pristine bulletproof glass. He concentrated on the view as the half-track lurched away from the hotel and the hotel district, and down into the city itself. And when the rear doors were swung back, his view was broadened considerably.

Richard realized at once that even the few hundred feet of vertical distance resulting from the helicopter's altitude had made things seem better than they were in fact. Or rather, less awful. For by the time the rear doors opened, the half-track was in the residential area that had seemed so relatively well maintained from the air. And yet the stench alone gave the lie to that as wafts of hot air stinking of uncollected rubbish and overflowing effluent swept in and out of the hot steel cell. They brought with them clouds of gritty dust that told of concrete and road surface breaking down badly.

Richard narrowed his eyes against the dust and the glare even as he tried to pinch his nostrils closed against the stench. From between the curtains of his eyelashes he could see the seemingly strong white stucco was webbed with cracks and crumbling. He could see the rust on the apparently strong security gates. He could see the wires dangling from the burglar alarms. He could see the disturbing contrast between the military precision of the uniforms around him and the disturbingly careless sloppiness of the police patrols and roadblocks that waved them through. The desperation all too evident in the suburbs and the shanties was spreading like a canker even to the more affluent middle-class areas.

And it was almost always the intellectual middle classes, his history lessons taught him, who were really responsible for revolutions. The lawyers, the businessmen, the doctors... Even in those revolutions like the French and the Russian that ended up consuming them in the end. Them and their sons, their daughters and their dreams.

But, then, between the easternmost roadblock that marked the edge of the diplomatic area and the well-guarded gates into the military compound containing the central police station, the half-track passed through one of the seemingly derelict districts that had made the chopper pilot so nervous. And it seemed that the pilot was by no means the only careful one. As the vehicle ground past the most dilapidated road-block yet, Kebila gave one of his tiny gestures of command. The rear doors slammed shut. The little command sat up straight. The atmosphere within the little cell changed, subtly but re-markably. The unit went to battle-readiness. The soldier opposite Richard put his hand on the raised screen of the metal cover designed to close over the bulletproof window, leaving only the narrowest letter box of vision, in case of heavy weapon attack. But Kebila lifted one finger and the metal flap stayed up. Richard began to suspect that the major himself was observing the passing buildings with a keen, possibly tactical, eye.

And Richard realized, with something of a shiver, that the derelict, rotting and roofless suburbs, with their breeze-block walls, their gardens overflowing with rubbish and inter-connecting piles of undergrowth, their wide but empty boulevards and public squares, would make a potent killing ground if whoever shot at the chopper could find a large enough army of like-minded, similarly armed friends.

The only way to get a squad of determined freedom fighters out of here would be to bomb the buildings flat. And what sort of president would be willing to risk the international pub-licity that razing sections of his own capital city to the ground in smoking ruins would bring? Certainly not the man who basked in the spot-light of international approval as the father of his nation, the one force for stability in an otherwise fractured country.

The half-track lurched sideways suddenly. The movement was so unexpected, abrupt and disturbing that for a moment Richard thought that they had been hit by a mortar. But no. They were simply swinging north into the wide roadway leading out of the disturbingly hostile suburbs and up towards the distant gates of the police station's military compound. The movement had a couple of unexpected effects, however. It threw Richard half out of his seat. He looked forward automatically and saw that the long, straight road down which they had been travelling led directly to the shanty town and the jungle of the delta immediately beyond.

And it was only then that he remembered the way the Alouette had settled during the overflight an hour or so earlier. How he had looked down and thought of Western cavalry forts deep in Indian country, isolated and under constant threat. Major Kebila might look more like Adolf Hitler than John Wayne or Henry Fonda – or Colonel Custer, come to that. But Richard could see in the intentness of the soldier's gaze that same disturbing awareness that he might find himself the target of attack at any moment.

And that meant that the major at least thought that whoever had shot at the chopper was by no means alone. A supposition given added weight by one extra element revealed by that swinging lurch northward. The shanty town they had overflown this morning was now alive with

90

soldiers as well as citizens. That could only mean trouble, as far as he could see.

Richard's grim assessment of the situation was more than confirmed a few minutes later when the half-track ground between the watch-towers and under the apparent portcullis of the heavily armoured gate. 'Welcome to Fort Zinderneuf,' said Kebila almost to himself. And Richard looked down at the frowning officer, fighting to read his true expression. To calculate what capital he could make out of the major's unguarded words. For where Richard had been imagining Kebila as Custer outnumbered and isolated far out in Indian territory, the major apparently saw himself more like Beau Geste trapped in a Foreign Legion outpost marooned in the Great Sand Sea surrounded by deadly Tuareg and Bedouin warriors.

But, given the location and the situation and all, thought Richard as the rear doors slammed open to reveal a parade ground backed by an all too modern municipal building labelled POLICE and GENDARMERIE, Rorke's Drift might be more appropriate after all.

Or, Heaven help them all, Isandlwana.

Now that his head was filling with great military disasters of the African continent, Richard had just started thinking about what little he knew of the fate of General Gordon at Khartoum when Kebila and his command led him through the double airlock of the security section. The squad cleared a passage for Richard through a line of men waiting under armed

91

guard and guided him through the open door frame of the security arch that passed through an extremely robust-looking blast-proof wall into another smaller blast-proof room with heavy doors closed against further entry. Here Richard surrendered his papers to Kebila and put watch, keys and phone in a tray while a second security man double-checked him with a pair of wands like those used at airports. Then and only then did Kebila hand him back his personal effects as the silent unit opened the inner doors and conducted him through into the blessedly cool shadows of the gendarmerie's main reception area.

Better pull yourself together and start to focus here, Richard thought grimly, abruptly aware of the tricks his tired mind was beginning to play on him as Charles 'Chinese' Gordon joined Beau Geste and George Armstrong Custer in the depths of his subconscious, together with their lonely forts, their lost and slaughtered commands.

Richard glanced around, and was struck immediately by how busy it was in here, when it was so difficult and time-consuming to access through the security. When it seemed so quiet on the outside. When it stood so isolated within the eerily vacant suburbs that it served. The reception hall was spacious but it was quietly and grimly bustling. On one side there was a desk where a sergeant sat behind bulletproof glass taking the papers of everyone being admitted today. High above, the ceiling was festooned with lazily spinning fans that looked large enough to propel a supertanker. But it was the more modern air-conditioning units on the walls that cooled the heavy air. Deeper in the shadows, those already on their way to the cells were shuffling in a sizeable crowd, silent and depressed – like spectators at a match who have just seen their team defeated; annihilated. Beyond them, through an arch, there were corridors just partially visible to Richard because of his towering height, lined with doors made of iron bars. Locked cells like animal cages already packed with angry, muttering men and women.

Only Kebila's uniform, it seemed, took Richard to the head of a long line waiting under the guns of yet more armed guards to be booked in on whatever charges they all faced. The weary-looking desk sergeant straightened up when he saw the major. Put his papers in proper order, shoved some steel into his spine. 'Papers!' he spat at Richard, transforming from a slob into a martinet with dazzling speed.

Richard held out his passport and his various other documents and it was only after Kebila had taken them and handed them to the sergeant with the most cursory of glances that he remembered Charles Le Brun's warnings. 'My lawyers have a list of all the documents there, Sergeant,' he said in his best French. 'We will be making a full account of all of them when they are returned.'

'Don't worry,' said Kebila in his flawless

English. 'I have also...ah...*accounted* for them all.' And his glance rested on the sergeant for a moment like the point of a fencing foil. Or the red dot of an automatic's laser sight.

'Personal effects?' demanded the sergeant, grimly. That at least would be a novelty for him, thought Richard glancing around. The poor souls that had passed through here so far today looked as though their only personal effects were the rags they were wearing.

'I will look after those,' decided Kebila. 'We will perform only the most basic induction now, Sergeant. You are far too busy to be wasting time. The identity and personal details of the prisoner are available from his passport. These will be sufficient for your paperwork. I will take Captain Mariner through into the interview room behind Holding Cell One.' He paused. Let the steely gaze rest on the sergeant again. 'I believe the captain's legal team will be arriving soon, even if they have to land a helicopter on the parade ground in order to get here.'

It was a very thoughtful Richard who followed the sturdy officer through into the packed corridor and then into the unsettlingly empty holding cell. The cell was large and designed to accommodate half a dozen men, judging by the number of bunks against the wall. Its barred door looked across the corridor to its twin opposite – where the better part of twenty men and women were being held. And the next beside that seemed as crowded. And the next. Richard paused, looking back at the dark and desperate caged faces all along the corridor, frowning with concern, as Kebila went through into a room beyond. He recognized none of the strangers, of course. Registered none with his conscious mind. Would never have recognized any of them ever again, had things turned out even a little differently. None, except for one woman, who stood tall; seemingly less cowed and more simply outraged than the rest. Richard's thoughtless gaze passed over her and then returned. Her clothes were slightly more urban than those of the others. A skirt and jacket that looked to have been tailored. It was not quite a twinset, but it was almost chic – enough to set her apart. He looked up, interest quickening. And their eyes met. A kind of electricity ran between them, as though they were old friends recognizing each other after years of separation. Meeting in the most unlikely of places.

And this was the next step along the deadly path he didn't yet know he was following, and he could not begin to imagine where it was going to lead in the end. Or who would be waiting when he got there. Like the madman at the head of the river in Conrad's *Heart of Darkness*. He turned to ask Kebila who the woman was, but the officer was still in the inner room, beyond earshot of anything other than his loudest bellow. He turned back again. But the young woman was gone, swallowed up by the sullen mass of humanity confined in the cell around her.

Richard did have another clear impression, however. There was something unsettling going on here. Was it just ill chance that had thrust him into the middle of it today? Were he and *Prometheus* more than innocent but unlucky bystanders? Were the oilfields, Asov and Makarov involved? And that was not an idle or an overly speculative question. He remembered Simeon's briefing as well as he remembered how this place had looked from the Alouette. It was clearly oil money that kept Major Kebila's buttons so bright, his half-track so full of petrol. That kept Fort Zinderneuf full of living police and soldiers, perhaps, instead of the regiment of dead men that filled it at the beginning of P. C. Wren's great adventure story. But on the other hand it was the brutal sequestration of that income that led to the shanties, the shots fired at the Alouette and the crowds of people being held here for questioning – or worse.

He had as many questions for the major as the major probably had for him. He finally followed Kebila through into the interview room, therefore, still lost in his brown study of speculation. The frowning officer was sitting on one side of a table, his elbow on the wooden top, one finger stroking that Hitler moustache, apparently as deep in thought as his prisoner was. But before either of them could even open their mouths, Richard's cellphone began to ring. He took it from his pocket automatically. Then glanced down at the major, frowning a silent question. Kebila gave a minuscule nod.

Richard opened the screen and pressed Receive. There was no face or ID – so this was not a number in the phone's capacious memory. Inconsequentially he noted that the clock on the screen read 12:00 local time.

'Richard?' shouted a familiar voice, resonantly baritone and overpoweringly virile, rolling the R of his name like a villain from a James Bond movie, carrying to Richard's ear long before the phone got there. Carrying to Major Kebila as well.

It was Felix Makarov. Of course it was. 'Yes, Felix?' he answered, knowing to hold the earpiece clear of his head from previous, deafening, experience.

'Alex and I have just talked to Robin and the men of your legal team. What can I tell you, old friend? We are coming to get you at once, Richard. And we will be bringing the big guns. The *big guns*. You understand?'

Eight

Celine

'I have no idea what *big guns* he's talking about,' said Richard folding himself carefully into the chair opposite the still-thoughtful officer. 'But they'll need to be very big indeed to blast their way into your Fort Zinderneuf.' He gave a wry smile to show he wasn't entirely serious.

Kebila paid no attention to Richard's attempt to lighten the atmosphere. 'It is a serious thing, Captain, to enter a sovereign state without having met the legal entry requirements,' the major answered pompously. 'Customs. Immigration. Health. Security. Do you think of yourself as being above the law?'

Richard's smile vanished. 'Not at all,' he answered soberly.

'Perhaps you believe my country does not take itself and its laws all that seriously?' persisted Kebila, his quiet tones allowing some anger and frustration to show.

'On the contrary...' Richard looked around the room. The angle of his chair – calculated to keep his knees well away from the underside of the table – allowed his gaze to sweep through the holding cell and across the corridor outside. The glance made the point that here was a system of law apparently taking itself very seriously – and working with extreme efficiency – very well indeed.

Kebila was not in any way mollified. 'Then perhaps you feel that this is some kind of banana republic where everything is run through bribery and corruption rather than by due process?' he snarled, his anger fully on show at last.

Richard hesitated on that. This was what the harbour master's demands and Simeon Bourgeois's briefing had indeed made him believe. 'And is it?' he countered at last.

'No!' snapped the major angrily. 'This is a country where the laws apply to foreign businessmen and their comings and goings as surely as they apply to our own gun-happy citizens!' He tore himself out of his seat and crossed the interview room, swinging the door shut so forcefully that it slammed like a gunshot. The bustle outside stilled at the sound, then slowly reasserted itself.

Richard's eyes narrowed. All this activity over one shot at one chopper? he wondered. Was he in fact responsible for this? The flight over the shanties had been his idea. He had known that the Alouette had already been targeted once. He had reported the second shot – as had Simeon, André Wanago and, no doubt, the outraged chopper pilot. A sudden disorientating feeling of guilt threatened to overwhelm him.

But then he got a grip. This reaction was out of all proportion to one gunshot. Either there had been another, much more serious outbreak of violence, or the authorities were using the incident as an excuse to do some checking on the situation in the shanty town. The latter was the more likely, for Charles Le Brun at least would have heard of anything serious happening in Granville Harbour and he would have mentioned it during the all-too-short briefing before Kebila and his men arrived. So the likelihood was that Kebila's superiors were simply rousting out the shanty town. A counter-terror tactic that verged on terrorism itself. The only thought that persisted to disturb that satisfactory little exercise of logic was the niggling question arising from Jim Bourne's coded message. Who was the Doctor? How was he back in play?

The President and the forces that backed his rule were clearly not trying to win friends in Granville Harbour – though they were trying very hard to influence people. Richard's head tilted interrogatively to one side. 'Where is this leading, Major?' he asked quietly. Though just for one minute even he was uncertain whether he was asking about his own position – or that of the hundreds of imprisoned men and women outside.

But before the angry and frustrated soldier could answer there was the muffled *CRUMP!*

of a detonation fierce enough to rattle the door in its frame and an instant of silence followed by a wave of automatic fire and a simple bedlam of shouts and screams. Without a second thought, Kebila and Richard were both in action. Kebila tore open the door he had just closed and sprinted out into the holding cell. Richard followed him through into the corridor and stopped there, looking back over the heads of the crowd in the reception hall. The security doors opened as Kebila reached them, and the security airlock beyond was briefly revealed. It was a bloody shambles. But, Richard guessed grimly, it had proved its worth. For although someone had detonated a bomb or a grenade the blast-proof walls had contained the explosion and protected the mass of prisoners and their guards.

But just for a moment it looked as if the guards would need more protection yet. The prisoners were shouting, screaming, dangerously close to open riot. Those in the reception hall surged this way and that while the men in the cells rattled the iron-barred doors and screamed to be released. The atmosphere had gone from weary resignation to mob madness in an instant, the sound from that acquiescent murmur to an ear-shredding roar like a volcanic eruption. Richard's heart pounded. The short hairs down the back of his neck prickled and rose, and he found he was swallowing – his throat was suddenly dry. And, incredibly, as he stood there, calculating his next move, a clear female voice cut through the din. 'I can help,' it said in French. 'Tell Kebila I can help.'

Richard swung round. The young woman in the tailored suit was standing against the bars looking out at him, her face folded into an earnest frown. 'I am a doctor,' she persisted. 'Dr Celine. Tell Kebila. He knows me and he knows I am innocent of any association with these outrages!' She took a breath to say more but was suddenly choking and coughing.

Richard realized that what was catching in his own throat was gun smoke. He looked away from the doctor's earnest face back across the reception hall to the blast doors, thinking perhaps the choking smell had wafted in from there, but they were closed. Then, bizarrely, shockingly, he saw the mob in front of the sergeant's desk falling row by row to the floor. In less time than it took his reeling brain to compute what he could see, the whole reception hall was floored with prostrate bodies. And the roaring in the cells behind him faded uncertainly so that he could hear the thudding of automatic-rifle fire echoing deafeningly around the all-too-enclosed space.

It was only when it started raining splinters of fan-blade on to writhing and protesting men that Richard realized Kebila had ordered his men to shoot above the crowd's heads. A kind of quiet returned with the last deafening rattle of gunfire. But the atmosphere had changed. Richard's mind leaped back to his thoughts of revolution. This is what it must have felt like to be standing in 1790s Paris with the mob howling *Ça Ira!* as the tumbrils rolled towards the guillotine. This is what it must have felt like to stand on the steps of the Winter Palace in October 1917. But all that popular hate and passion was caged, controlled – for the moment at least. And, Richard noted with growing respect, controlled by the calm authority of one punctilious officer with a brilliantly drilled squad of soldiers and a disturbingly apposite Adolf Hitler moustache.

But Dr Celine was right, thought Richard. Kebila was going to need help with the wounded if he was going to do anything other than put them out of their misery at once. He glanced back at the woman, feeling instinctively that her detention here was little short of an outrage, nodded once and began to push his way towards the major.

The blast doors opened then and more soldiers poured into the place. Behind the first, well-armed, battle-ready wave came officers whose badges of rank showed them to be Kebila's superiors – even if they did not gleam quite as brightly as the major's. First among these was a plump, soft-looking little man whose doughy body was in stark contrast to the hard-muscled major. But he wore the pips and epaulettes of a full colonel as well as a most fearsomely pointed military moustache, and Kebila favoured him with a quiveringly precise salute. The colonel returned it with a languorous sort of a wave. He looked around the room, his pudgy features marked with disapproval and disdain. Disdain that only deepened when, at last, another plump stranger joined them – this one in what looked like a senior police officer's uniform a couple of sizes too small. But it was hard for Richard to be certain, for the uniform was by no means as well preserved even as the colonel's. And although the crumpled cloth looked like blue serge, the badges of rank did not match the Belgian gendarmerie's in the same way as Kebila's matched the army's. The three exchanged a word or two, then began to pick their way through the massacre on the reception-hall floor, walking back towards Richard as he hurried out towards them. The colonel slapped the thighs of his uniform trousers with a fastidiously rolled pair of leather gloves, a gesture clearly showing impatience and frustration at the very least. More soldiers poured in through the blast doors, followed by more police.

Richard reached the little group. 'Major Kebila,' he said, in his best French, 'at least one of the people in the holding cells tells me she is a doctor. Dr Celine. She says she can help with the wounded.'

Kebila hesitated, caught off guard by Richard's importunate approach in the presence of his superiors.

'Who is this?' demanded the colonel.

Kebila gave a short explanation.

'If this man is being questioned, then he should be in a cell,' decided the colonel immediately. 'In a cell or on the floor.' The colonel finally condescended to look at Richard. 'Living or dead. It makes no difference.'

And not for the first time – but perhaps for the most memorably intense – Richard felt the shadow of Death itself sweep over him.

With Kebila punctiliously at his shoulder, his every gesture signalling almost uncontrollable outrage, Richard retired thoughtfully to the interrogation room and folded himself back into the chair. 'Please wait here, Captain,' grated Kebila, showing just as much irritation as the senior officers – but with a very different target. He slammed out of the door into an echoing silence, which at once filled with the sound of marching feet, shouted orders and the sinister clicking and snapping of automatic weapons being readied to fire.

Richard cleared his mind of all speculation. He had been in dangerous situations before – though few as immediately threatening as this one. He knew his own metabolism and how it worked under pressure well enough to know he would be filling with adrenaline without scaring himself with distracting possibilities. Whatever was going to happen next would require quick thinking and instant reaction. He concentrated on breathing slowly and calmly, like a scuba diver confronted with a shark.

Kebila returned with four of his squad. The powder-smell from their recently fired weapons filled the room at once. The officer was holding Richard's passport and papers. Which might be good, he thought, or might be bad. 'Come with me, please, Captain,' commanded Major Kebila shortly.

'Of course, Major. May I ask where you are taking me?' Richard stood up slowly, his eyebrows raised interrogatively. His heart pounding uneasily.

'As you would expect,' answered Kebila shortly, 'I have been ordered to take you at once to the big guns.'

The prisoners in the littered waiting area had picked themselves up off the floor and were being herded over towards the sergeant's desk by a mixture of soldiers and gendarmes, all armed to the teeth and very dangerous-looking. Kebila led Richard through the newly cleared passageway towards the closed blast doors. He snapped an order to the guard beside them and the man slammed to attention as Kebila opened them. The stench of explosives, metal, burning and death washed in at once as a wall of wind battered in through the ruins of the security arch and the fallen wreckage of the outer doors. Richard glanced around at the room, which seemed to have been recently repainted in thick red, black and brown. He stepped over a miraculously preserved security wand – and the dismembered hand that still held it. For a moment it seemed to him that, apart from himself and the soldiers surrounding him, the only other living person in the place was the woman in the tailored suit moving quietly and purposefully through the carnage. Dr Celine. He met her eye. She gave a nod, a tiny, sorrowful smile of thanks. She knelt beside something that suddenly resolved itself into a wounded survivor who looked unsettlingly like meat on a butcher's slab. 'Perhaps a grenade,' she said to someone Richard could not see, 'but the scatter of body parts make it look like a suicide bomber to me...'

Hurried forward by his escort, Richard stepped over other piles of offal, blessedly less human-looking, and followed Kebila out through the blast-splintered wreckage of the outer doors on to the parade ground.

Here the source of that stinking wall of wind sat sedately, with its rotors still spinning. And under them, approaching at a run, was the stark bald head of Felix Makarov. As soon as he was clear, the towering Russian straightened, matching Richard's commanding height, inch for solid inch. He tucked the scarlet of his tie down across the front of his shirt and fastened his double-breasted blazer to keep it there. Then he strode forward, hand held out. Richard went forward and found himself pulled into a bear-hug embrace. The avgas and slaughterhouse stench vanished for an instant beneath a cloud of Eau Sauvage cologne.

Over Makarov's shoulder, Richard saw a tall, angular stranger easing himself out of the Alouette like a spider coming out of a corner. Behind him came another, shorter figure in a full-dress uniform whose badges of rank were

107

as familiar to Richard as Kebila's and the colonel's. Richard recognized the first man's thin, lined face with its permanent disapproving frown from his briefing notes as easily as he recognized the gold braid on the second man's shoulders. Felix had brought the Minister of Justice with him and an army general to back him up. A pair of very big guns indeed.

Over the buffeting of the downdraught and the incomprehensible bellow of Makarov's hearty greeting, he heard a familiar sound which could only be that of poor old Kebila slamming to attention and saluting once again.

Five minutes later, introductions made, orders given and thanks expressed, three of them were back in the helicopter. Fort Zinderneuf was falling away beneath them as the Alouette soared into the flight path and back towards the hotel. Richard looked down and saw the foreshortened statue of Kebila turn on its heel and go marching towards the battered, bustling gendarmerie like a clockwork soldier in the wake of the general who had stayed to take charge – and to grab any headlines or glory that was going, Richard suspected.

He glanced across at the passport and documents lying safely accounted for in his lap. 'I must thank you all again, most sincerely,' he repeated, still looking down, unusually embarrassed at having been rescued from such a strange position by such powerful and important men. Then he looked up at the cold dark eyes of his associate, sitting like two black

pebbles in the otherwise hearty smile that creas-
ed the Russian's cheeks.

Richard glanced uneasily across from the
tiger-smile on his partner's face to the disapproving frown on the minister's. A lot of
favours seemed to have been called in here, all
in all, he thought, though the senior officer and
the government minister had fallen into a
situation from which they could, with luck, get
a lot of credit – all of it based on poor old
Kebila's quick thinking and decisive action.
Was it staggering ingratitude, though, to wonder whether Felix's reaction smacked of over-
kill? Certainly, the Russian had conjured up an
unsettlingly massive sledgehammer to crack a
little nut. A full general officer and a minister of
state – when all that was really needed had been
a local lawyer, if Simeon Bourgeois had been
right. There was a disorientating lack of proportion. It was like sending a regiment into the
shanty town and arresting every man they could
find there, just because a couple of shots had
been fired at a passing helicopter. How on earth
would these people react if something really
serious occurred? How *were* they going to react
to whoever or whatever had blown up the
security sections of the gendarmerie?

But it was all over and done with as far as
Richard was concerned. Except that he suspected most acutely that he and Heritage Mariner
would end up paying the piper. 'What on earth
was it all about, Felix?' he asked, glancing back
at the toy-soldier fort all alone out in the

seemingly deserted south-eastern city suburbs.

Felix Makarov tapped the side of his nose with his finger and leaned forward conspiratorially. 'Did you by chance meet a Colonel Nkolo a little while ago? Major Kebila's commanding officer?' The Russian's words just reached Richard across the battering of the chopper's motor. They certainly did not reach the preoccupied minister. Unlike the cloud of Parma Violet-scented breath that they came in.

'I certainly met a colonel, though I didn't get his name,' answered Richard frowning slightly as he tried to see where this was leading. 'Short, tubby chap with a turned-up moustache.'

'That's the man. Hercule Nkolo. Among his many duties and responsibilities he is the officer in charge of port security.' The tiger-smile on Felix's face widened, allowing white teeth to glitter just as coldly as his black eyes. 'And that is very convenient, you see, because it is the colonel's brother Herold Nkolo who is Granville Harbour's harbour master.'

Richard nodded, understanding shining into his mind, showing a simple pattern where there had only been confusion. It was typical of Felix that he should have this kind of knowledge. It occurred to Richard that his well-prepared associate would probably know about the mysterious and memorable Dr Celine too – who she was and where she came from. For an instant Richard considered asking Felix about her. He felt an obscure bond with the woman. An almost measureless respect for someone brave enough to come to the bars of her prison cell demanding that her jailers let her out to help tend people who might well have been wounded by associates of the men in the cell alongside her. At the very least he wanted to follow up on their slight acquaintance and see if there was anything that he or Heritage Mariner could do to help her in turn. And Felix seemed a logical place to start.

But something held Richard back. And that, too, turned out to be another little step along the almost inevitable path they all seemed to be following here, up into the heart of the darkness.

Nine

Reception

The reception in the hotel's small corporate entertainment suite was still going on when they got back, even though they paused twice on their way. First, they stopped off at the presidential compound so that the Minister of Justice could return to his ministry with a minimum of inconvenience. There was a serious situation requiring his immediate attention after all. An escalation of civic unrest from a couple of casual shots at a chopper to the suicide-bombing of the central police station represented a considerable deterioration of security. The President would need to be briefed in person. The government would need to take action; would need to direct the security forces at the very least.

Then Felix lingered with Richard at the reception desk as Richard took the opportunity to hand over his passport and papers so that he could register fully and formally at last. All his experiences that morning had shown him how important it was to be punctilious with your paperwork in Granville Harbour, even in times of calm when civic unrest was merely a distant spectre. So he took the earliest opportunity to get his own in perfect order, in spite of his burning desire to find Robin and show her that he was all right – living proof of his phone call from the Alouette on the way in from the President's compound. And to give her the news – if she didn't already know it – that a repentant harbour master was now in contact with *Prometheus*.

Richard had contacted Morgan as soon as he had broken contact with Robin. By which time the supertanker was in imminent expectation of a pilot and a team of tugs which would berth her at the port authority's expense. Whatever else was happening at Fort Zinderneuf, Colonel Hercule Nkolo had clearly had an opportunity to talk to his brother, Harbour-master Herold.

But André Wanago was waiting at the security gate as they arrived, full of apologies for his failure to stop Major Kebila – or at least to warn of his approach. Richard accepted the apologies gracefully but with a shade of mental reservation. The fragrant, winning André was clearly part of the system. As much so as the brothers Hercule and Herold Nkolo. Perhaps, given the most recent events, in league with the Nkolo brothers; certainly in league with Major Kebila and his superiors. Which Granvillian wishing to survive here – let alone flourish – could afford to be otherwise?

So, with restlessness and double-dealing all too obviously in the air, the opportunity to get his paperwork in order was too good for Richard to miss. And, truth to tell, he wanted to think things through a little before he saw the Heritage Mariner team again. That, and his awareness of the fact that he absolutely had to visit the cloakroom to check on whether any of his adventure was lingering about his person or clothing. Anything in the way of smears or specks of red on his supposedly immaculate fawn cotton clothes or desert boots; the odd reek of cordite or excrement in place of his favoured Roger and Gallet aftershave.

He could not get out of his mind the sight of Dr Celine ruining her carefully maintained and religiously preserved two-piece suit by kneeling in the pools of blood and body fluids beside the butcher's-slab wounded at Fort Zinderneuf. Frankly, Richard felt diminished by the comparison with her as he checked his immaculate cotton and suede. He had done all that the brave woman had asked of him, but he still felt that he could – should – have done more.

But once his business was done and his mind put at rest regarding his appearance, he pushed the doctor firmly to the back of his mind. Then he allowed the ebullient Felix to lead him through to Max's party as though nothing much had happened during the last couple of hours at all.

The small corporate entertainment suite looked to Richard to be about the same size as the ballroom at Grosvenor House in London. It was a blessed relief from the brutal Africana of some of the other public rooms, and of the Nelson Mandela Suite, however. Its white walls and parquet sprung dance floor, its tasteful mixture of old-fashioned fans and discreetly contemporary air conditioning, could have been taken from any modern building. Only the huge David Shepherd-style paintings on the walls gave a clear African theme, with their lions, elephants and rhinos roaming the edges of jungles and the vastnesses of veldt.

And that theme was extended beyond the almost invisibly pristine glass doors designed to open out on to a huge veranda that gazed down, like the outlook of some Serengeti hunting lodge, over the artistically jungle-shaded huge-ness of the pool. Where Frau Hoffman would have found herself one of the lesser beauties by a long chalk – and her costume a model of repressed retro respectability beside the minuscule confections sported by the men and women lounging there.

But Richard had precious little time to admire the decor or the view. His arrival transformed the atmosphere. His immediate impression on entering the room was of muted anxiety over-lain with a sort of forced jollity. But the instant Robin saw him and called his name, the party really seemed to get under way. Within mo-ments he was surrounded. Robin had tight hold of his left arm – as though hugging his biceps as hard as she could was the same as hugging him. Simeon and Charles were just behind her, pumping his right hand with every sign of deep

115

relief. Behind them, oddly, came Anastasia, all smiles. Against the flesh-filled backdrop of the poolside, even her outrageous costume seemed quietly conservative, though bizarrely out of place in both the tropic heat and the bright daylight.

And finally, Max Asov, their nominal host. A shorter, darker, more wiry version of Felix Makarov. But every bit as forceful. Every bit as dangerous. He had trouble shaking Richard's hand because he held a champagne flute in each fist. And he wore a woman on each arm, neither of whom looked much older than Anastasia; both of whom seemed to have been snatched from the kindergarten at the Playboy Mansion. Each of whom, it seemed, had been called inside a moment ago from the most outrageous company at the scarcely covered poolside, if their clothing – or lack of it – was anything to go by.

It was understandable, perhaps, that after the shock of his arrest and the worrying hours of his detention, the relief of his release and return should swing the reception away from its original purpose. Richard suddenly discovered an overwhelming hunger that was only slowly sated by the seemingly inexhaustible array of canapés on offer. He had heard of survivor guilt, he thought wryly as he tucked into quails' eggs stuffed with caviar and crostini topped with pâté de foie gras. But survivor starvation was a new one to him.

So there was no real business done after all.

Instead, the two teams of businessmen, their business associates and their social – family – circles got to know each other in a cheerily informal atmosphere. And as the afternoon progressed, the alcohol level rose and the barriers of decency went down, so the doors to the pool veranda were opened and the party spilled out into the bronzing near-nudity at the water's edge.

It was fortunate that the press arrived fairly soon after Richard and Felix, for the jollity was fuelled by champagne and vodka as well as by the potent sense of having escaped from a dangerous and damaging situation and it was spiralling pool-wards far too early in the proceedings. But the local press did arrive – and in some numbers.

Richard and Felix agreed to be interviewed at once in a convenient annexe away from the increasingly raucous reception – and they made a sober and sensible impression. Robin came with them, like a mother hesitant to let a recently hurt child out of her sight. But for once, and for the time being, she was content to remain in the background, standing beside Simeon Bourgeois, who attached himself to them, and watch Richard while he worked. Indeed, Richard was able to learn a few more details about the situation he had been snatched away from by Felix, and how things were progressing in the suburbs and the shanties – and in Fort Zinderneuf.

While Felix sat cheerfully in the centre of the

limelight, offering expansive answers and flirtatious observations to the questions of the local TV's breathlessly delectable roving reporter, Richard went to one side and talked to an intense young man from *Le Monde du Granville*. They discussed international business matters, oil and shipping. They discussed the upcoming Admiral's Cup and what chances the *Katapult* series of multihulls stood of dominating their class once again. They talked in much vaguer terms of Richard's planned contract with Max Asov and Felix Makarov. 'You'd better ask Felix himself,' said Richard. 'He's more up to speed than I am.'

'Mr Makarov is today's news,' said the young reporter with a wry smile. 'But I'm after tomorrow's.'

He showed Richard the front page of today's edition, with an arresting picture of the Russian tycoon dominating. The picture showed Felix, his current beautiful young companion and Max's daughter Anastasia. The not very accurate caption made them sound like one very rich and powerful family indeed. The byline above the story gave Richard an idea of the reporter's name, however – Patrice Salako.

But then, as though trying to make amends for the editorial inaccuracy of the caption, the young reporter suddenly went for the really hot news. 'Your arrest was for...What, Monsieur?'

'A misunderstanding over paperwork,' answered Richard easily, glancing across at Robin and meeting Simeon's gaze as he fleetingly looked away from the TV interview. Then Richard went after a nugget of information in return. 'Is it usual for army officers to do police work like that here?'

'Indeed, Monsieur. There is some...what shall I say...*overlap* between the responsibilities of our uniformed services. It is not unusual. Our services are based on the Belgian model, as I am sure you know, and even there the military association between the army and the gendarmerie lasted into the present millennium. But you were taken to the central police station, were you not?'

'I was,' Richard confirmed. 'It is known as Fort Zinderneuf, I believe.'

'A literary joke among some of the better educated. But the place itself is no joke, Captain. And it was there that you witnessed the atrocity, I am told?'

Richard hesitated infinitesimally. He felt he had witnessed several atrocities at Fort Zinderneuf – not least the detention of the brave young doctor Celine. He glanced across at Simeon again but if he hoped for guidance there he hoped in vain. Simeon seemed entranced by the bright lights and the brighter eyes focusing on Felix Makarov. But Richard had no real doubt what the eager reporter was talking about. 'Yes,' he purred. 'Some kind of explosive device. I did not see exactly what happened. I heard it may have been a suicide bomber.' He paused, thought better of admitting that he had heard the speculation from Dr Celine herself, then continued smoothly. 'Have you got any details, Mr Salako?'

'Please call me Patrice, Monsieur Mariner. I have been told there was a bomb of some sort. Perhaps, yes: a suicide bomber. You saw nothing to give us more detail yourself?'

'I saw the aftermath, Patrice. The explosion was powerful. If you asked me to guess, I'd say it was certainly a suicide bomber. There was much loss of life. The police station was very full...'

'Ah yes. There was a sweep of the township. Such things are not uncommon, but the number of security personnel involved was unusually large, I understand. Shots had been fired at a helicopter. Such a reaction was to be expected. But this...'

'There has never been anything like this bombing before?'

'Not in Granville Harbour, Monsieur. And in the heart of the police station itself...And that such a thing should have occurred when you were in the station yourself. It is incredible. But we have been told the situation there is well under control now. Colonel Nkolo was on the scene with Kaptaine-commandant Moputo. And of course both the Minister of Justice and General Bomba were there within minutes. An extremely impressive reaction from the government. I understand the majority of those being questioned have been released now, and just the hard core of suspects are being questioned by the general himself.' A shadow passed across the eager, intelligent young face. Richard got the impression that being questioned by the general was a sharply unpleasant experience.

'Is he a good man, this General Bomba?' asked Richard.

'Oh, yes!' answered the reporter enthusiastically. 'He is the President's brother-in-law!'

Richard digested that nugget of information, then he changed tack. Or rather, he addressed a worryingly vivid mental picture that the reporter's words and look had conjured into his mind – that of Dr Celine, no longer wearing her bloody, soiled and ruined clothing; no longer wearing very much clothing at all, in fact, being questioned by General Bomba himself.

'Do you know of anyone called Dr Celine?' he asked. 'I met someone called Dr Celine in the prison.'

'Of course!' enthused the reporter. 'The Angel of Granville Harbour! Dr Celine is famous! Worldwide!'

'Really? I don't think I...'

But the interview with a mere newspaperman was interrupted at that point by Felix and his irresistible TV reporter. The Russian literally dragged Richard to the hot seat, but on the way he was able to slip an arm round Robin and so they arrived in the full glare of media publicity as a couple. Simeon lingered with Felix in the outer shadows.

The TV reporter's name was Charlotte Uhuru. 'It's her stage name,' whispered Felix as she was setting up the interview. 'Uhuru means "freedom" in Swahili or something. You would not be able to get your tongue around her real name.'

'I don't suppose there's much Miss Uhuru can't get her tongue round,' observed Robin darkly. But then she switched on her most charming and dazzling smile for the doe-eyed reporter as she breathlessly informed her live audience of the treats in store from yet more international A-list guests.

'Treat her with respect,' warned Felix, masking his whispered words with his most open, boyish smile. 'She may be every bit as dim as she looks, and every bit as overproduced, underdressed and easily available. But the President himself is a fan to put it mildly – and politely. And what she wants she gets – until he gets bored with what *he's* getting, at least. So, watch yourselves...'

Fortunately, as it turned out later, Simeon heard none of this hurried and sotto voce conversation. He was much more interested in watching Miss Uhuru getting ready for the next section of her broadcast.

Both Richard and Robin were old hands of this kind of thing. They had graced magazines and newspapers, radio and twenty-four-hour TV channels all over the world. Though Robin preferred to keep a low profile now that she could be an acute if innocent embarrassment to her twins at university simply by appearing on the box, and Richard was more used to gracing the business news than the social sections on both TV and radio.

Between them, they could with confidence, ease and charm have answered questions on a simply dazzling array of subjects, even without recourse to their advisers, spontaneously on a live chat show. Even with Felix's sinister warning ringing in their ears.

Miss Uhuru seemed more interested in making sure her wide eyes, blinding smile and fathomless cleavage were right up front at all times. Then she was interested in showing off her Western-style couturier outfit. Then she was interested in her guests – Richard first because he was a man. Then she was interested in garnering their first impressions of her beautiful country. Like a cheap celebrity magazine columnist, she was more interested in shallow first impressions and vapid personality gossip than in learning anything more substantial. Carefully selective first impressions of her country and city were the order of the day, of course – with no room for Fort Zinderneuf, suicide bombers or the Angel of Granville Harbour.

Next she sought their views on the international reputation of the country's beloved president. Only positives and superlatives allowed again – no question of nepotism, bribery, corruption, financial collapse or simmering revolt. Finally, more breathlessly still, she demanded their thoughts on the glittering surroundings and how impressive were the lists of film stars, rock stars, sports stars, magnates and royalty who had stayed here recently. And of the mouth-watering range of celebrity chefs who had been flown out here to cater for them. Not a mention allowed of the real people living outside the magic boundaries of the international Neverland of the hotel and presidential compounds. No whisper permitted of services in meltdown, citizens in medieval desperation, professional classes reliant on blackmail, bribery and handouts; of derelict cities, polluted rivers and Stone Age shanties.

Richard's tact was put under strain at once. He soon became restless and after five minutes only Robin's deft and well-practised interventions kept him from seeming downright rude. And this was just as well. For Simeon, picking up on his employer's mood, became increasingly restless – his worry almost dangerously distracting to both interviewer and interviewees. And Felix's cellphone started ringing before the interview was over. As Felix, frowning, turned away and became engrossed in a clearly important conversation, the information he was giving and receiving proved a blessed distraction to the eavesdropping Simeon. And as it did so, an irresistible combination of Charlotte Uhuru's breathless enthusiasm and Robin's easy courtesy covered even the impatient Richard with a suave patina of gruff charm. Appearances were kept up until the credits rolled. By which time, Felix was able to flip his phone closed with a flourish and inform them enthusiastically, that the whole lot of them had been invited to a reception at the President's palace.

'This is very impressive, Richard. You are a master of communications, a media wizard. It took Max and me months of...ah...*negotiation*, if you understand my meaning, to get our first invitation. And yet you have one within twelve hours!'

'We're here to do business, Felix, not to go dancing off to receptions. Not to waste time and money *negotiating*, as you put it!'

'But this is how business is done in Granville Harbour. And receptions are where business is done.'

'It's the business between us that needs to be settled first, Felix...But yes, I see your point. It is too good an opportunity to miss. And whatever business we might be able to do at the palace might well have an impact on what our respective legal teams are trying to thrash out. Still and all,' he added, half to Felix and half to Robin as they all swept back into the increasingly raucous reception accompanied by Charlotte Uhuru, her camera team and the earnest young newsman Patrice Salako, 'I'd be happier with all this if Jim Bourne was here.'

Ten

Dress

News of the presidential invitation had a sobering effect. The reception, teetering on the edge of drunken excess, quietened the instant that Felix's news was understood. Even the rowdiest there became like chastened school-boys beneath the gazes of Felix and Max, Richard and Robin. Jackets were retrieved from chairs by the balcony windows. Dress was adjusted from poolside to boardroom in a twinkling. A small pink and brown invasion of sunbathers was ushered out into the blinding heat. The doors were closed and cool calm returned.

Richard's team, fuelled by high spirits more than by alcohol, clustered around him as he and Robin fought to come up with a plan of action that might maximize the potential of this un-expected opportunity. If only they could calcu-late what that potential might be.

Max and Felix gathered their own men a little more slowly, no doubt trying to do the same thing. On the one hand, Bashnev-Sevmash Oil and Power were a little ahead of Heritage

Mariner, given more knowledge of the likely benefits awaiting them at the presidential palace. On the other hand, Max and Felix were faced with more of a challenge in maintaining the focus of men whose high spirits were largely in excess of 40% proof and whose attention was still distracted by the hot and dangerous curves outside.

In the Heritage Mariner camp, Simeon Bourgeois proved an ace in the hole and a fount of knowledge right from the start. Although he had never been invited to a presidential reception, he had clearly seen it as a vital part of his job here to keep on top of social as well as political and business matters. He knew Patrice Salako. He read the society column which the young reporter produced weekly. And he was one of Charlotte Uhuru's little army of local fans. Long before it occurred to the wily Russians to seek advice or information beyond their own closed ranks, Simeon had persuaded Richard to exercise some genuine charm. And Charlotte Uhuru in one respect – perhaps in one respect only – proved a useful replacement for Jim Bourne. 'If anyone knows the inside dirt on what the President is planning,' insisted Simeon in a whisper every bit as fierce as Felix's, 'Charlotte will!'

And so she did. 'Oh, yes!' she admitted over a tall cool golden glass of Dom Perignon, her bitter-chocolate eyes almost fiercely on Richard's intensest ice-blue gaze. 'I am always invited to the President's receptions! I am sure you have seen the broadcasts he occasionally allows me to make. Of course they are syndicated Africa-wide...'

'Of course,' enthused Simeon more loudly; perhaps a tad too loudly. 'I watch all of your programmes...'

Charlotte graced the intense young businessman with a passing glance that seemed to rank him just above the waiters in her personal pecking order. But she further graced him with a smile and a sigh that strained the buttons of her jacket and threatened to tear the swelling lapels apart. Though, Robin noted, the Grand Canyon of her cleavage was aimed precisely at Richard.

'And I am sure the President sends you a guest list with the invitation,' added Robin, thinking faster than any of the distracted men. 'How else could you prepare your interviews properly and professionally?'

'Of course...' Charlotte's smile wavered slightly and her gaze wandered almost myopically over the tall blonde beauty before returning to the men like a laser beam.

'And warning of any particular dress requirements,' Robin persisted, all too poignantly aware of her invisibility.

'Oh, yes! He likes me to dress. *Most of the time...*' Her eyelashes fluttered coyly like a pair of Japanese ceremonial fans. She glanced meaningfully out at the almost naked beauties displayed around the pool's edge. Dared them to imagine the rest.

* * *

Half an hour later Robin had dragged the men away from the reception and up to the Nelson Mandela Suite, where she could address a distraction of her own. A distraction that was suddenly at the centre of her attention as surely as Charlotte Uhuru's soft coffee mountains had been at the centre of theirs. The only such thing, in fact, that could tear her less testosterone-fuelled focus away from the business matters that still needed so much urgent attention.

The question of dress.

The unanswerable combination of Simeon and Charlotte had established that the President would be wearing traditional native robes this evening. But his entourage and guests were expected to be more Western in their attire. The minor European royalty and more major Hollywood stars that were topping the guest list were all famous for the quality of their tailoring. A certain latitude might be allowed to the African and South American sporting personalities and the new-wave Chinese rock stars, but everyone else was expected to be in, as Richard wryly put it, 'Posh frocks and monkey-suits.'

'What I have with me hardly counts as a ball gown,' said Robin, frowning, as soon as they were alone. 'But it will pass muster, I'm sure.' Her steely grey glance dared him to disagree with her – especially after his shameful exhibition with the TV reporter. But, fashion-conscious and elegant though he might be, he was in no position to comment on such niceties of wardrobe. So he wisely held his peace. 'What have you brought with you?' she demanded after a moment, still angry with him, still looking for a fault or shortcoming to punish him with.

'To the hotel? Nothing even remotely suitable. What I'm wearing is the most formal thing I have here.' He looked down at the perfectly tailored cotton of the fawn tropical suit. All too obviously daywear; not evening wear at all. 'I've a big kitbag aboard *Prometheus*, though,' he persisted in the face of her icy stare. 'There should be a dinner jacket at least in that. Or mess kit. Or whites.'

'You've no idea, really, have you?' she said, her voice betraying how near the end of her tether she was as she strode across to the video-conferencing facilities.

Before Richard could think of an adequate reply, she had summoned the startled face of Third Officer Callum McKay on to the screen. 'Where's Captain Hand?' she demanded shortly.

'Ah. Preparing to come dirtside and report to Captain Mariner – ah that's Captain Mariner your husband, Captain Mariner...We're safely docked and awaiting further orders. Captain Hand's just waiting for the chopper. There's a bit of a hold-up...'

'Tell the chief steward I want Captain Mariner's kit to come ashore with the captain. All of it.'

'Captain Mariner's kit. Coming dirtside with the captain as ordered. *All* of it...'

As the picture faded, so McKay turned away, still talking, to enter the order into the log. And, hopefully, to hurry up the chief steward before the chopper finally arrived. But within five minutes the phone was shrilling and, with the instrument held to her ear, Robin pointed the remote and switched on the TV to video-conferencing mode once more. This time it was Captain Hand herself who appeared in HD quality and multiphonic sound. 'There's a problem with the choppers,' she said shortly. 'It looks as though I may be trapped aboard for a while. The same goes for Richard's kit, I'm afraid.' Callum McKay hovered at her shoulder and, considering that they had just docked in a secure anchorage and a safe haven, the pair of them looked anything but relaxed and happy.

'What's the matter?' asked Richard, his antennae twitching, sensitive to trouble as always.

'It's nothing I can put into words,' said Morgan. 'But there's something...'

'Oh, for Heaven's sake!' snapped Robin, slamming the handset back into its cradle. 'Is it Friday 13th today or something?'

'Let me,' said Richard and retrieved the phone. 'Hello, André? Where is the hotel's helicopter? Refuelling? Good. I need it at once. No, I'll come straight down. No. I'll be down at once.' He hung up, a little more gently than Robin had. 'A little local difficulty,' he said. 'I'm going down to reception. If I'm not back within ten minutes then I'll be back with Morgan and my kit in an hour or so.'

Robin opened her mouth to say something but he was gone.

The lift hissed open and Richard strode out into the lobby. André Wanago was there behind the reception desk, a worried frown upon his face. 'Captain Mariner—' he began.

But Richard was not going to take no for an answer. The look on Morgan Hand's long face was more than enough to arouse the never deeply dormant knight errant in him. It wasn't often that tanker captains looked like they needed urgent help but this was one of them and Richard was the man to deliver it. 'Wherever it's going I need it to take a little detour,' he insisted. 'To my ship and back. Ten minutes, fifteen, tops.'

'But General Bomba himself has ordered—'

'I won't tell him if you don't,' interrupted Richard ruthlessly. 'And I'll be chatting to him, as likely as not, at the President's reception tonight. Chewing the fat about the experiences we've already shared today, with Major Kebila, Colonel Nkolo and a range of other officers and ministers at Fort Zinderneuf!'

It wasn't subtle. Richard could see at least three levels of threat in that one little speech and the paranoid André could probably see a couple more. But it seemed to do the trick.

'Very well, Captain,' the manager acquiesced, and reached for the phone. 'Give me the heli-

132

pad, please...'

Five minutes later, Richard was seated in the seat beside the two bullet-welts that he had occupied earlier that day. The Alouette was skipping straight down towards the bay – and, as there was no need for sightseeing on this trip, the short jaunt straight from the hilltop to the harbour took surprisingly little time. The speed of the trip was further emphasized by the fact that *Prometheus* was now in the prime anchorage, right outside the harbour master's office, where the closest possible eye could be kept on her – and on all aboard her.

Perhaps that was part of Morgan's all too evident concern, thought Richard.

The helicopter hardly settled into the white-painted circle on *Prometheus*' deck before Morgan Hand was running beneath her rotors, her long slim body folded forward over a modest overnight case, while Callum McKay laboured out behind her laden with Richard's big kitbag.

No sooner was everything in place than the chopper was off again, racing low over the ageing dock facilities and out across the semi-derelict suburbs. 'All secure?' bellowed Richard, glancing back at the vanishing *Prometheus*.

'Safe and sound,' she answered, 'with First Officer Oblomov in command. Perhaps I was silly to get so worried...' She nudged his kitbag with a questioning toe and glanced up at him, her eyes veiled. 'Should I thank you or the kit for this rescue?'

'Don't ask! But the paperwork's all in place?'

133

'Shipshape and Bristol fashion. Boston fashion, rather. What's so important about this old kitbag, anyway?'

'You'd never believe it if I told you. Just be thankful that you and the kit were in the same place at the same time.'

'You really know how to make a girl feel appreciated, boss!'

'Like Lancelot. I know. What was it that you were so worried about?'

She grinned. 'More like Percival,' she countered, stirring the kitbag again, 'before he got his armour on.' Then she frowned and answered his question more seriously. 'I don't know, but there was an atmosphere. It was almost threatening. Nothing I could put my finger on, but...' She shrugged. 'Quite frankly I'm glad Oblomov's in charge for the moment. He's a very competent man of action. Ex-Russian merchant marine. You know he single-handedly fought off two boatloads of pirates off Somalia?'

'You think he's going to have to do the same in Granville Harbour?'

'No! Of course not. Except...Still and all, he's doubling the harbour watch. And he insisted I leave him the keys to the gun locker.'

No sooner had she said this than the Alouette tilted off course and swung westward towards the airport. The pilot looked over his shoulder. 'We go via the airport. One more passenger,' he called. 'One last passenger.'

Still frowning over Morgan's formless but deeply disturbing worries, Richard pulled the kitbag over and settled it under his legs as the Alouette dropped on to the landing circle of the apron outside a white-painted, modern-looking terminal building.

A group of three men ran out, but the first two paused only to sling cases aboard then stood back to let the third climb nimbly in. The new-comer was broad-shouldered and slim-hipped. One glance revealed a deep chest and long, powerful-looking legs. He had jug-handle ears, thick black Brylcreemed hair faultlessly in place astride a rule-straight parting and an open, weathered, square-chinned face. With eyes as blue as a far horizon and pencil-line of moustache reaching across his upper lip above his wide white square-toothed grin, there was something of the Great White Hunter about him. An impression emphasized by his open-necked short-sleeved khaki-drill shirt, cotton slacks and desert boots. He should have been carrying an Express repeating rifle or an elephant gun, not a laptop, thought Morgan. And he should have spoken with a Rhett Butler drawl, not a clipped Cambridge accent. Cambridge, England; not Cambridge, Massachusetts.

'Richard,' he said as he settled back. 'What a pleasant surprise. Good of you to meet me, old man.'

'I was passing in any case,' said Richard easily. 'Taking a little jaunt out to *Prometheus* and back.' He paused, as though about to launch into one of his focused and heated discussions. But then he closed his mouth. Sat back. Thought better of it.

When he started to speak again, he was back in social mode, his thoughts and fears on the back burner for the moment. 'But I don't think you two know each other. Jim, meet Morgan Hand, captain of *Prometheus*. Morgan, this is Jim Bourne, head of London Centre.'

Eleven

Doctor

It was not so much a case of 'pecking order' when they got to the hotel, thought Richard wryly, as of 'packing order'. Or, rather, of *un*-packing order.

Trailed by a solicitous entourage of porters who fell away like planes in an aerobatic display team as they passed the rooms reserved for Morgan and then for Jim, he hurried them up to the Nelson Mandela Suite. Here, secure in the knowledge of Paznak and Voroshilov's security sweep, safe from all ears except Robin's, and perhaps the Russians', he held the little conference he had been hesitant to risk aboard the Alouette.

So, while Morgan and Jim had to rely on hotel staff to empty their cases and closet their necessaries, Robin went through his own kit while he talked. The downside was that she kept tutting, increasingly irritatedly, at the thoughtless abandon with which he had stuffed suit-bags along with everything else into his kitbag immediately prior to his hasty departure for *Prometheus*. When Robin herself, of course, had already been sunning herself like another sated lioness around the pool.

Be that as it may, she came and went from one room to the other as Richard left a series of messages for the rest of the team, and a couple more general calls at reception and the pool bar. Then he settled into the immediate requirements of his conference. Typically, he had been multitasking; using the busy little hiatus to finish his detailed consideration of how he needed the meeting to run, and what he wanted to learn from it in what order. Robin, multitasking herself, made only one call – an emergency call to the hotel's dry-cleaning, laundry and clothing-repair service.

Multitasking or not, Robin would normally have been a well-focused and active member of the discussion group, but her first glance at the maze of creases left in the first business suit that she found distracted her. And it seemed that every time she unzipped a grey plastic suit-saver it revealed a new sartorial horror. So she followed the conversation from a little distance as she shook her head with wifely concern over the shortcomings of her uncharacteristically careless husband.

Robin observed how Jim's information seemed to chime with Morgan's feelings and both struck home to Richard's increasing concerns as he guided the conversation with practised ease. The atmosphere of threat that the worried captain had sensed in the port was new – and seemed to have arrived only this after-

138

noon. Though apparently the more Richard thought about his conversation with the harbour master that morning the more he regretted the clinical distance lent by a helicopter overflight.

Especially as the overflight seemed to have sparked off something out of all proportion when the second shot ricochetcd off its fuselage, observed Robin brusquely.

'That was before the bombing, wasn't it?' demanded Jim. 'The one you were caught up in?'

'I only really got a feel for the city when Major Kebila was transporting me to Fort Zinderneuf,' he said. 'And things must have been going to pot even then. The bomber must have been heading there at the same time I was.'

'Or waiting there already,' added Morgan.

'Yes, I suppose so.' Richard glanced over at Robin. Their eyes met and she saw the familiar shift in his expression that signified an attempt to pull the wool over her eyes; to put her mind at rest. 'But it's just coincidence,' he continued brusquely. 'There's no question of me being any kind of target. Of any of us being a target, surely. What do you think, Jim?'

'Well,' the intelligencc man answered, 'there's no doubt that President Banda's beginning to lose his grip. Or that there are people in the country – the city, even – who blame us Westerners for supporting his excesses for all these years. In the old days it'd be the Russians fomenting any unrest. Now the Russians are on the other side of the coin, of course. But wherever there is unrest, there's always someone who sees an opportunity if they can make it a little worse. But the latest intel is that President Banda's problems are more likely to be in the shanties, in the delta and upriver. I hadn't heard a whisper of any trouble in Granville Harbour itself. Nor that there were any targets beyond the security forces. Indeed, that elements of the security forces may not be quite so *secure* any longer themselves, if you catch my drift. The Doctor—'

'Ah, yes,' Richard interrupted. 'The Doctor. We simply couldn't work out that reference. I thought maybe I made a mistake in the translation when I decoded your message. Neither Simeon nor Charles could quite get it either. The only doctor I came across was called Celine. But that's another story...'

'Maybe so. Maybe not,' answered Jim with a lopsided grin. As he opened his mouth to explain more there came a knock at the door.

Richard held up his hand and crossed the room. For once he looked carefully through the security spyhole. 'Speak of angels,' he muttered and opened the door at once. He returned with Simeon and Charles, who wasted no time at all on greetings before they settled to join in the discussion.

But before they could discover what Jim was talking about, there came yet another knock. This time Robin answered it and all discussion stopped as she admitted the hotel's chief tailor and one of his dry-cleaning staff. Like undertakers, they accompanied Robin to the master suite and returned a moment later with a battered and shrivelled outfit of white tie and tails that might, by the look of them, have accompanied Fred Astaire through a train-wreck. 'I don't know how long we're planning on staying here,' Robin informed them as she showed them out, 'but if it's less than a month then you'll have your work cut out trying to rescue all of this.' She gestured back to the half-unpacked kitbag on the master bed.

Richard had the grace to blush. For once in his life his gaze just failed to meet the stares of the men and women at his little meeting.

'Madame,' promised the tailor bowing with lugubrious formality, 'we shall return the evening wear to you within the hour at the most. And it shall be –' he sought the mot juste – 'resurrected...'

'Right!' said Robin, joining the group at last and cutting impatiently to the chase, all her irritations apparently forgotten for the moment. 'The Doctor. Tell us about the Doctor, Jim.'

'Right.' Jim's earnest gaze swept around them all. 'In the coded message I was referring to Dr Julius Chaka. Up until the first elections of this millennium he led the Opposition Freedom Party, as I'm sure both Simeon and Charles remember.'

'But then his advisers, his main supporters and his family were all wiped out, purged or arrested in the 2002 crackdown,' said Simeon.

141

'He vanished. It was always assumed that he met the same fate as the others.'

'The same fate as poor old Lumumba in the Congo,' added Charles darkly.

'Apparently not,' answered Jim with absolute certainty. 'Apparently the CIA got him out. Though why they did so is anybody's guess. Maybe someone owed him a favour. Maybe it was some kind of investment. A kind of extra-ordinary rendition in reverse. Snatching someone from danger and putting them in safety. The exact opposite of the usual process. He ended up in Rwanda, so I've heard. He's been in hiding in Kigali ever since. Well, not just hiding. From what I now understand he's been hard at work in deadly secret. Raising an army, training it, getting it ready to sneak down the river from the eastern borderlands, infiltrate the delta and, eventually, the shanties. It's the old story, isn't it? We have a one-city state here. When Granville Harbour falls, the whole lot goes. Well...It was a done deal for William the Bastard when he had himself crowned in Westminster, Christmas 1066. After that he was William the Conqueror and London was his. He just had to clear up a little local difficulty or two and the rest was history.'

'So that's what you meant,' nodded Richard. 'The Doctor's back.'

'And, given what happened to everyone he cared about in 2002, he's not likely to be a happy man,' said Robin darkly. 'Was it tribal? Like Rwanda, now you've brought it up? Was

142

Dr Chaka's party the equivalent of the Tutsis while President Banda unleashed his Hutus on them?'

'No. There was no massacre. And if there were atrocities they were done in secret. A surgical strike by one branch of the tribe against another branch of the same tribe. An un-expected benefit of slavery, apparently. There is only one tribe here. They call themselves the Matadi. This area has been so relentlessly milked for the original form of "black gold" for so long that all the minor tribes were wiped out long since; slaughtered or slaved. You want to start a tribal war in Granville Harbour, you'd have to depopulate the Caribbean. No. Julius Chaka is Matadi, the same tribe as almost everyone in the country. Same tribe, same religion. Only his politics are different and that's apparently enough.'

'More importantly than all that,' said Richard thoughtfully, 'is whether he's a sufficiently powerful man to control any forces he un-leashes. He may have plans and ambitions. He may have power and backing. But can he ride the whirlwind, as the saying goes?'

Jim, Simeon and Charles exchanged looks. 'You're right,' said Jim after a moment. 'The usual process of this kind of thing involves a good deal of anarchy. But again, there's no reason to expect any in Granville Harbour itself. In the short term, at least. And there's no reason to expect any of it to be aimed at any of us. As long as President Banda keeps a grip. I mean, look at what happened in Kenya in 2008. Borderline civil war after the election. Did untold damage to the tourist trade. But were any tourists actually killed? None that I heard of.'

The next knock interrupted them and Simeon did door duty to admit Felix. 'We'll be slumming it over to the President's palace, apparently,' he informed them cheerfully, his Russian voice booming and echoing. 'General Bomba's requisitioned all the choppers so we'll have to make do with the President's fleet of limousines. Mine had better not be a Zil...'

Twelve

Crash

Richard's evening wear seemed to define his relationship with Robin during the next couple of hours. Which was apt enough in his calculation – as the evening wear seemed to have caused most of the trouble in the first place.

The tail suit was still steaming when the tailor brought it back. Richard hung it up while he showered and shaved – banished to his own bathroom because now that they were alone, Robin seemed still to be steaming too. But he hung it too close to the air conditioning so that when he eventually pulled up the black, braided trousers and shrugged on the perfectly tailored tailcoat, the silk lining was like ice against his hot skin. But not quite as icy as the blonde-haired, grey-eyed vision that proceeded into the master suite from the secret recesses of her own bathroom just as André called up to warn them that their limousines had arrived.

And the arrangements for the limousines added substantially to the frost in the Mariners' domestic atmosphere. They were the last down because Robin's deep garnet silk dress had

145

required some last-minute adjustment, as had her jewellery, hair and make-up. And she had wanted to dab just a little more Chanel behind her ears. So, when they arrived, they were presented with something of a fait accompli.

The first of the three stretch limos already contained a full complement of bodyguards and lesser Russian advisers. The third contained, Max, Felix, Fedor Gulin, their closest associate, Simeon, Charles and Jim Bourne. There was a seat reserved to Richard. Robin's seat was in the middle vehicle, already packed with Max and Felix's current companions, Anastasia and Frau Hoffman – Anastasia's black gothic dress far and away the least revealing attire there. And seated opposite them, trying not to get caught looking down cleavages or up miniskirts, were Voroshilov and Paznak – the two bodyguards who only a year or so ago had been chasing Robin through the icily benighted city of Archangel.

Robin swung round on her heel and glared back at Richard. But he was already stooping to climb aboard, his practised hands reaching behind to separate the tails of his coat so that he did not sit on them and crease them. And she found herself confronted by an askari gallantly waiting to hand her into her own conveyance like Buttons beside Cinderella's magic coach. 'You *shall* go to the bloody ball!' said Robin fiercely but obscurely and climbed in beside Anastasia. The door slammed solidly enough to tell the ex-militsia men that the limousine was heavily armoured, then the little cavalcade eased into motion. It took Robin five tries to release the inertia mechanism of her seat belt because she kept jerking it so angrily.

There was no direct route from the hotel compound to the presidential compound, so Richard found himself repeating the first part of his earlier ride with Major Kebila, though in very much more comfortable circumstances. Following the other two limousines, Richard's eased across the grounds, past more swimming pools, exclusive little villas and the narrow end of at least one golf course – all of which seemed to have escaped his notice this morning – before it rolled out through the tall security gate. Now Richard found himself observing the more familiar bustle of the prosperous diplomatic suburbs of Granville Harbour. Darkness, which had arrived at six on the dot, hid the more dilapidated sections from the distantly interested gaze of the Russians. Their comments made it clear that neither Felix, Max nor Fedor Gulin had ventured outside the security gate before. Or had bothered looking out of the chopper on the flight in from the airport, come to that. Only the courteous professionalism of the Heritage Mariner men stopped some heated discussion about the Russians' more outrageous assumptions and misunderstandings as to the reality of the Granville Harbour status quo. Consequently, discussion in the third limo was stilted and short-lived.

Not so in Robin's. Max's companion was called Bambi or something like it. Felix's was called Irena. They talked up a storm in a mixture of excited Russian and American-accented English as to which film stars would be there. Listening to the bits she could understand with any clarity, Robin was moved to poignant sympathy for Brad Pitt, George Clooney and their like. The girls' conversation seemed so predatory. The merest scraping of the most casual acquaintance could be worn like a designer label. And an actual liaison of any kind – from a quick grope in a broom closet upward – could be sported like the most exclusive outfit. She was abruptly put in mind of the scene in Nathaniel West's novel *The Day of the Locust* where an unprotected film star gets literally torn to pieces by his rabidly souvenir-seeking fans.

Where Richard would have – and, unknown to Robin, already had – escaped into silent surveillance of their surroundings through the window, Robin turned inwards and began a conversation of her own. 'Are you looking forward to the reception, Anastasia?' she asked in her liveliest tone.

Anastasia silently regarded her as though she was insane. The dim brightness of the street-lighting glittered off the jewellery adorning the myriad piercings in her face. And, oddly, off the kind of golden locket that any doting father might give his daughter on the occasion of her first real grown-up ball.

'Aren't you interested in meeting the film stars and famous people who'll be there?' persisted Robin. Then she suddenly realized she was using a tone that she hadn't used since the twins – much of an age with the sullen girl – were ten years old.

'*Please!*' responded Anastasia, drawing the word out into a long, familiar teenage whine. 'B-list losers, the lot of them! What kind of a person with half a brain would want to meet that lot?'

'Anastasia!' said Frau Hoffman. 'Don't be so rude!'

'Whateveeeerrrrr...'

'Who would you like to meet, then?' persisted Robin with a larger smile and a less patronizing tone.

'People who make some kind of a difference! If Mandela was there I'd want to talk to him. Or Desmond Tutu. But this guy, this Liye Banda, he's a repressive loser who just calls himself a president – and a field marshal, come to that – when he's actually like a vampire sucking away everything that's good in this place. I mean, do you and Richard actually know who you're doing business with?'

'Indeed we do. Primarily we're doing business with Mr Makarov and your father, as the Bashnev-Sevmash Oil consortium. And I would not let your father hear you talking like that!' warned Robin, shocked.

'Like he'd actually *listen*. He's an eye man,

149

not an ear man. Not a brain man when it comes to women. More a bum and boob man...As you can tell...' Anastasia's withering glance took in Bambi and Irena – and only just stopped short of Frau Hoffmann.

Robin swung round, suddenly fascinated by what the girl was saying. Here was a woman well worth talking to, she thought. Here was the Russian equivalent of her own vividly intelligent and sorely missed daughter Mary. Robin's unconscious movement revealed another little link between the two of them, for it released from beneath the garnet silk and the black satin of the ball gowns a fragrant cloud that could only be Chanel No. 5. The perfume Robin always wore.

As she opened her mouth to speak, her nostrils full of the fragrance that they shared, she felt the car begin to slow. But it didn't occur to her to look up. Not to begin with, at any rate. Not until, as Anastasia put it later, the shit really hit the fan.

The Russians had put a man beside each of the drivers just in case. The man in the first limo was called Ivan Vrithov. He called the driver 'Katanga', though this was not the driver's name. Katanga called Ivan 'Boss', though he did not think of him as such.

'Why are you slowing, Katanga?' asked Ivan.

'There is a car by the road here. It is burning, Boss.'

'All the more reason to speed up, stupid!'

Ivan leaned forward to get a better view. It was like Katanga said. A little local runabout was burning by the side of the road. It had run over a junction by the look of things where the lights were no longer working, swerved to avoid a guy with a laden bike – and ended up hitting both him and the concrete post of a dark lamp-standard. A clear enough little story, revealed in a fire-lit tableau. They needed to get past as quickly as they could. But Katanga did not speed up. He continued to slow. The door of the burning car opened. Someone staggered out into the street right in front of the car, weaving starkly through the bright beams of the headlights. Katanga braked hard and came to a stop across the mouth of the side road just behind the burning car.

'What the fuck...' Ivan began. But what started out as a belligerent question for Katanga suddenly became something much more general. A shriek of surprise and horror.

The armoured half-track must have started well back along the shadowed side road, then revved up as fiercely as Katanga was braking at the end. It was going at nearly 50 kph when it roared out into the firelight and hit the limo side-on. The big car reared and might have flipped right over, but the big bull-bars on the half-track caught on the roof and held it down. Instead, it was hurled sideways, going from nought to fifty faster than a Ferrari. Its tyres all burst at once, then its wheel rims gave brief but vivid showers of sparks as they scored the last few metres of road before the whole mess hit a surprisingly solid house-front with a sound like a mortar exploding.

Immediately on the first impact, the half-track's driver braked. Although the side windows starred and shattered in one or two places as the wheel rims sparked and the chassis juddered across the road, the armour-plated screens to front and rear remained solid, even when the car came to rest against the wall. And wedged there, so that had anyone felt ready, willing or able to get out, they couldn't, because both the windscreens were equally impenetrable from either side and all the doors were clamped tight closed either by bull-bars or brickwork.

Paznak and Voroshilov did not see what was happening because their backs were to the driver and their eyes were focused firmly on the pale hot satin gusset of Frau Hoffman's underwear. They heard the first impact, the immediate explosions of the tyres and the shrieking howl of wheel rims on roadway as though in a dream. And it all happened so fast they had hardly had time to look away from Frau Hoffman before their car slammed to a halt. The lady herself arrived bosom-first in Voroshilov's lap, closely followed by Irina and Bambi, for none of them had wanted to risk creasing their outfits with scat belts. Only the more practical Robin and Anastasia, sisters under the skin, had played it safe.

Paznak bellowed a fortunately obscure Slavic obscenity and hit the nearest handle, shoving the heavy door wide and rolling out into the stultifying night. Had Voroshilov – who was the quicker thinking of the two – been less pre-occupied with exactly who was piled on top of him and precisely what lay quivering between his reaching fist and his pistol grip, he would have called a warning. But Paznak's mistake took only a microsecond to make. And an eternity, perhaps, to rectify.

Therefore, when Ivan Vrithov's colleague, the second Russian security man beside the second driver, hit the universal lock switch, Paznak's door was already open and the passenger section of car remained unsecured, while the driver and the bodyguard were safe from any-thing short of an anti-tank round. So that when Bambi followed her own first animal instinct – flight – she was able to push past Robin and Anastasia, and shove the other rear door wide.

Only now did Voroshilov, shrugging off Irena and destroying Frau Hoffman's soft décolletage with the uncompromising solidity of his SIG Sauer, shout the basic orders drummed into any competent security guard in preparation for situations such as these. 'Stay in the car! Lock the doors! Don't panic!' But by then it was far too late.

Frau Hoffman spilled out of the limo as swift-ly and spectacularly as her considerable chest spilled out of what little was left of her dress.

Then she was off into the shadows just behind Bambi as Paznak, suddenly remembering what he should actually be doing, pulled out his Glock and covered them, shepherding them up into a safe-looking side street which ran away opposite the one the half-track had come from.

When Irena followed Frau Hoffman, almost as spectacularly with the hem of her skirt bunched up around her waist, Voroshilov sat up and drew in his breath. The women still seated in front of him were clearly his main responsibility – but his first priority had to be reconnaissance. In these kinds of situations, someone had told him long ago, a quick moment's thought and observation can save you from an eternity of death. And allow you to perform the same function for those you might be protecting.

He stuck his head out of the car door, therefore, with the most modern of hand-held weapons so close beneath his nose he could smell gun oil as well as Chanel No. 5 – and he knew which fragrance he preferred. But the instant he did so, a beaded ebony *sagila* war club that could have been taken from the tribal decorations on the walls of the Nelson Mandela Suite – and that had been in use on the continent since men began to walk upright – bounced off his shaven skull.

Like Paznak – in some respects at least – Richard hit the door handle the instant that the half-track hit the security limo, and leaped out into the shrieking bedlam of the night. His own

154

vehicle was still moving, but like the others it had slowed significantly as the whole cavalcade decelerated towards the burning car. The sound alone warned him that something bad was going on. But he didn't yet know exactly what – beyond the obvious fact that the lead limo had been involved in some kind of crash.

Whatever was up, Richard was certain of one shining, incontrovertible truth. He needed to be with Robin. The gap between them – a limo length and then some – was suddenly more than he could bear. He hit the ground at a run, stumbled and fell. He felt the seams on his tailcoat strain and spring apart at the shoulders. He felt his knees go through the perfectly pressed creases of his trousers and leave a good deal of white skin along with the black cloth on the tarmac. He didn't care. And he knew that Robin wouldn't care either, if he could somehow get them through this – whatever 'this' was.

He picked himself up, swung back towards the car. Saw Felix's face chalk-white against the shadow. 'Throw me a gun and for God's sake lock the doors!' he shouted.

A SIG Sauer, the twin of Voroshilov's, clattered out on to the roadway. And the instant that it did so, the car door slammed shut. Even out here, Richard could hear the terminal *snap* of the central security locks. He gave a wry halfsmile as he scrabbled the warm steel of the handgun off the still-hot tarmac. At least someone here knew the basic requirements of security, he thought. Someone willing to follow the *'Do what I say; don't do what I do'* rule. The basic rule of survival in these circumstances.

Richard came erect, straddling to give a secure shooting position. He held the SIG double-handed in front of him at eye level, and it was through the V of the gun's basic sight that he surveyed the suddenly silent scene.

The half-track held the security vehicle securely against the wall, imprisoning all the men within it. The rumble of its motor mingled with the sound of the fire as though they were part of some other situation altogether. In the guttering firelight, the military vehicle looked like a steel box on a tank track secured to the front end of a big Mac truck. The box's rear doors stood open and men were boiling out and in. Richard knew how many there might be for he had ridden in Kebila's half-track. The dying light of the burning car made it clear that these men were not in uniform, however. They seem-ed a ragtag group, armed with an assortment of weapons from clubs, spears and bows to disturbingly modern-looking military kit. And the military theme was echoed by the speed and precision with which they were working. And by the silence, too. They all knew what to do and were doing it quickly and efficiently with-out the whisper of an order or a command.

As Richard watched, seeking a specific target amongst the sinister, shadowy bustle, he saw a team fan out in pursuit of a group of people running away into the shadows of another little side street. He got a glimpse of a bald head he recognized as Paznak's, three unfamiliar ball gowns – and a pale flash of what he could simply not believe to be a pair of naked breasts.

But then, nearer at hand, he saw a second, silent group clustering like bees swarming around Robin's car. Voroshilov's familiar shining skull rolled out of the rear door and bounced on the roadway. Only a second glance revealed – mercifully – that it was still attached to his black-clad body. But even so, the pale sphere seemed like a football for an instant as it was surrounded by busy, booted feet. Richard dragged his gaze up. Just in time to see two feminine figures being pulled out of the car. He really only saw the frocks – one almost as hard to discern as Voroshilov's black-suited body. The other was all too easy to see, however. It was the shiny red silk of Robin's outfit. And he would have known that riot of guinea-gold hair anywhere. And, although he couldn't quite make out the words, the low tone of her icily outraged voice was utterly familiar.

Swiftly and silently, on tiptoe like a ballroom dancer, with tails flying, shirt front and cuffs gleaming, and the SIG still held steady at eye level, he began to move forward, his mind racing. Holding the gun in the ready position was probably unwise, for he was not likely to start shooting as things stood at the moment. Even Paznak seemed to have understood that, for he had vanished with his part-dressed charges as silently as Richard himself. This neighbourhood seemed so quiet, suddenly, that even distant gunshots would have come like thunder.

Then Robin stopped speaking. She was looking back towards Richard. Anastasia, by her side, was doing the same. As were the men surrounding them. He slowed, and carefully, quietly, calmly began to lower the SIG. There was only the sound of the burning car, like the blustering of a distant wind, covering the subliminal throbbing of the half-track's motor. And the faintest possible hissing behind him, as though some titanic black mamba was coiled there, ready to strike him down. He had an overwhelming sense of a huge and threatening presence. But he was too wise to turn and look.

The ice-cold point on the back of his neck came as hardly any surprise at all. 'Stop,' ordered the quiet voice of the man who held it. A voice as deep and resonant as the sound of a distant earthquake, but as close and intimate as a friend whispering a secret.

Richard stopped. Dead. The SIG was pointing at the pavement between his patent-leather shoes. Just as well, he thought.

'What I am holding to your neck is what you might call an assegai,' the quiet voice informed him. 'It is an old, traditional weapon with an ancient history; but it is both sharp and effective. It will separate the bones in your neck from the bones in your spine before you can tense your arms, your hands or your trigger finger.'

'I understand,' said Richard. His voice seemed rough and rusty all of a sudden. 'What do you want?'

'We have what we want. Are you Asov?' As the quiet voice interrogated him, he could see the team of men around the car guiding the two female figures away towards the fire-bright half-track.

'I am Mariner,' he croaked. 'Richard Mariner...' His throat ached almost agonizingly.

'Then you must bear a message to Asov, Richard Mariner. We have his daughter and her tutor.'

'No...'

The assegai's point moved forward infinitesimally. He felt hot blood go coursing down the back of his ice-cold neck beneath the high starched collar of his dress shirt. Was it just imagination that made him feel that the very tip of razor steel was nudging at the disc between his lower neck vertebrae?

'Don't talk, Richard Mariner,' demanded that deep, quiet, chillingly calm voice. 'Throw the gun into the middle of the road and then get down on your knees. I do not wish to harm you, but I feel you may leave me no alternative if I do not incapacitate you a little at least.'

The speech covered the time it took for Richard to comply, for he moved slowly and carefully. The point of the assegai remained embedded in the back of his neck, following his every careful move.

When Richard was on his knees, the voice

resumed, its tone more businesslike. 'Listen and tell Asov. We have his daughter and her tutor. He will hear our demands in due course. Tell Asov that how his women survive and how long they survive depend upon how he answers those demands.'

Thirteen

Red Dot

The half-track was reversing back down the side road before the point of the assegai was removed from Richard's neck. As soon as he felt the point slide out of his super-sensitive flesh, followed by yet another spurt of burning blood, he tensed himself to swing round. His first thought was to turn and face the man who had kidnapped Robin and Anastasia, but even though he tore himself round with wrenching speed, the roadway behind him was empty except for shadows and the Russians' limo. The headlight beams were so bright that anyone standing outside their glare was effectively invisible. The screaming of the half-track's engine had covered any departing footfall as effectively as the shadows in the derelict thoroughfare hid everything beyond the head-light beams from sight.

His next thought, driven by his mounting rage and outrage, was for the SIG and he rolled forward and up like an Olympic sprinter at the off. Scooping up the pistol, he raced forward to Robin's limo. But apart from the ungainly sprawl of Voroshilov's body dimly illumined by the courtesy light in the vacant passenger compartment, there was nothing to hold him here. He used the solidity of the heavy, gaping door as a further aid, catching hold of it left-handed and throwing himself forward, the V-shaped sight of the SIG in his right fist zeroed on the opening to the side street where the half-track had vanished. He could still hear it, however, reversing away just as fast as it had appeared, its motor screaming into the distance. By the time he got to the guttering hulk of the burning car, mere seconds later, the roadway was empty. And the howling note of the racing motor echoed off the dark and apparently empty house-fronts, coming down an octave as, somewhere in the far distance now, the gear was changed from reverse to drive.

Richard checked the burning vehicle first. There was no sign of the apparently injured driver who had staggered out into the road ahead of the little convoy. The man with the laden bicycle had likewise vanished. The bicycle, too, had gone – the solid vehicle and its load probably worth a good deal more than a human life. The car itself, bonnet up and engine compartment full of burning rags, was a rusted skeleton. From this close he could see that its tyres were long gone and it was sitting on red-flaking wheel rims.

Richard turned. He glanced across at the bodyguards' scraped and battered limo lying against the wall, the vehicular equivalent of a comatose wino. The courtesy lights inside were on, and although it was hard to see details through the opaque crushed glass of the side windows, there was life and movement in there. Movement which would no doubt soon find a way out on to the pavement, for it should be easy enough to punch through the windows even if the doors remained wedged shut. At which time Max and Felix would be back to full protection. Though a further glance back down the street showed that they were still sitting there, safely locked in their car with headlights blazing and engine idling.

He abruptly found himself wondering what exactly they had seen of the atrocity. A back view of the man with the assegai and of his companions in the brightness of the headlights at the very least. Perhaps their faces, though he doubted it. Clothing; uniforms. Perhaps enough for some kind of identification; some kind of a lead...But that was a faint hope best left in the future. In the meantime, he wondered how long it would take them to realize there was nothing stopping them racing back to the safety of the hotel compound, no matter who they had to leave out in no man's land. 'Well, I hope my guys can hold you still for a few more minutes yet,' he said to himself out loud. 'Until I finish this final piece of business here, at any rate.'

Richard had one last immediate priority. And having paused for little more than a minute while his shock-sharpened mind seethed with observations and deliberations, he was off at a flat run across the road, the burning car at his back, racing through the space between the first two cars to fulfil it. As he neared Robin's, so Voroshilov pulled himself unsteadily erect, shaking the battered dome of his shaven skull.

'Move yourself, Voroshilov. You're in deep trouble and unless you help me get Paznak and the other women back in short order, you'll be looking for another job.'

Richard didn't slow as he called this. Tails flapping, sleeves tearing further and further away from shoulder seams, studs flying off his shirt front like bullets, he pounded into the dark mouth of the alley opposite the road along which the half-track had come and gone.

'Paznak!' he bellowed at the top of his considerable voice as he entered the claustrophobic little side street. 'Frau Hoffman!' But only echoes answered him, seeming to come from all around. Mockingly from behind as well as in front of him. He had called too early and the power of his voice had hardly travelled forward at all.

He was surprised and a little disappointed when Voroshilov did not appear at his shoulder and come charging into the dangerous little alleyway with him as he took another deep breath and plunged into the stifling darkness. But a couple of minutes later he was grateful for the fact. And he continued to be grateful for a couple of minutes further after that, until the downside of the new situation began to register more forcefully.

First, everything around him was suddenly bathed in blue-white light and the snarling of a motor behind him made him realize that Voroshilov had been quick-thinking enough to commandeer the limo, and bring it round in Richard's footsteps, headlights on full beam.

Richard could now see that the roadway ahead of him was empty. The only movement that registered was the wavering of his own gigantic shadow. In derelict sections of cities that he knew, there was always a wealth of animal life. Had this been somewhere in London, Shanghai, Hanoi, there would have been rats, mice, cats, dogs, foxes perhaps. A sense of furtive movement vanishing swiftly. Diamond gleams of reflected brightness. There would have been pigeons, gulls, magpies, flapping, pecking and calling.

Here there was nothing. Certainly nothing of that size. Flies, perhaps – but few enough of these to gleam like sparks in the headlights. Ants. Beetles. Roaches, he supposed. Though he could see none. And, more importantly, perhaps, he could see nothing at all for even insect life to feed upon.

'Paznak,' shouted Richard again, wishing briefly that he could remember the Russian's first name. Too well aware also that even his most deafening foretop bellow would be lucky to rise above the gathering roar of the motor revving in the confined space.

And even as he called, immediately behind him, close enough and loud enough to make

165

him jump like a cat on hot bricks, the limo's horn blared out, drowning even the disorientating cacophony of the motor for a moment. He glanced over his shoulder, wondering whether the overwhelming blare of sound was some kind of a warning to him. The headlights dazzled him at once and he stepped blindly aside, stumbling up on to the pavement.

The long car with its sinister black windows eased level with him at once and slowed. He hesitated, with the door handle convenient to his immobile left hand. The SIG, still pointing out at arm's length, was almost resting on the high white roof. But he didn't want to get in. He had to be able to listen out for Paznak or the women and the interior of the car would deafen him. Even more effectively than the horn and the motor were doing. He decided that his best course of action would be to fall back in behind it, suddenly very grateful for the thought of having the armoured body as a kind of mobile foxhole.

And the need for protection came immediately. As the car waited for him to make a decision, so a fusillade of shots rang out in a familiar forces' three-tap. The bullets slammed off the windscreen, leaving a neat pattern of little spiders' webs grouped around the driver's face. Richard automatically stepped back. Behind him was the entrance into one of the deserted houses, with its door still miraculously there – though splintered and sagging. The jutting brickwork of the doorway gave him the welcome illusion of cover.

'Paznak!' bellowed Richard again. 'It's Voroshilov and Richard Mariner.' The engine revved over his hoarse calls, the note of it rising and falling as the shocked driver slipped it into reverse and then back into drive, no doubt at Voroshilov's bidding.

Richard frowned with concentration, his mind, used to situations like this, holding him still for a moment more of calculation before the swiftly gathering tidal wave of adrenaline he could feel gathering in his system swept over him. Would the men who had kidnapped Robin be using a military three-tap like that? Well trained though they seemed to be – and well armed with guns as well as clubs and assegais – Richard doubted it. The person most likely to be shooting like that would be the militsia-trained Paznak. Paznak, panicked, spooked and all too aware of the need to protect his no doubt unhappy charges. Paznak, blinded by the headlights so that he was shooting only at the formless glare pursuing him. Deafened by the motor so that he could not hear the voices promising help.

Paznak somewhere close by, at ground level, dead ahead, therefore.

And confirmation came an instant later, in the instant before the second military three-tap hit starred the screen immediately in front of the driver's nose. The faintest line of ruby light. A dot reflecting off the glass just where the bullets hit home. Richard stepped forward and swung square-on to the fusillade, as though the beams of the headlights could protect him from bullets as effectively as they hid him from sight. There, in the lower window of a jutting house-front maybe thirty metres dead ahead, the tiny red beam glittered and was gone so swiftly that it might never have existed. The only gun with a red-dot sight that Richard had seen so far was Paznak's Glock.

The limo's driver ran out of courage then – courage or fear of Voroshilov. The gears ground into reverse. The motor whined like an amateur tenor straining for a high note and the long white car skidded in place, the smoking tyres spinning helplessly as they tried to overcome the forward inertia of the massive, armoured body. Then they gripped the hot, pitted surface of the rotting roadway and the limo howled backwards. The great square bonnet swung dangerously sideways and Richard leaped back into the doorway, bashing his shoulders, skull and tender neck against the sagging wood while the headlight-housing and bumper beneath it scraped along the brickwork all too close at hand. The nearest door slammed open, screeching along the wall in a shower of sparks. Richard involuntarily heaved back again and the rotten doorway behind him gave way. He stepped back. Back and down. The door might have survived the depredations of the wood-hunters. The floorboards had not. Beneath the little sill of crumbling brick which was all that remained of the outer doorstep was what felt like hard mud. Richard leaned forward and glanced out of the gaping doorway. The car was weaving drunkenly away, its door flapping like a broken wing. Immediately in front of it, scant metres away from Richard, Voroshilov was picking himself up like the intrepid survivor of a road accident. As soon as he straightened, the limo's headlights died and the whole road was plunged back into Stygian blackness.

Footsteps spat across the pitted tarmac, coming Richard's way with a certainty that assured him Voroshilov had made good use of that instant of brightness after he had picked himself up. 'Here,' called Richard even so, his low voice guiding the Russian over the last few steps as surely as the Benin Light had brought *Prometheus* into Granville Harbour. Having called, Richard had the presence of mind to feel his way back from the doorway so that when Voroshilov came tumbling in through it he was well out of the way.

'Shit!' said the Russian feelingly if softly. 'You're a hard man to keep up with!'

'You're doing a good enough job,' said Richard easily. 'You bring your SIG Sauer with you?'

'And extra nine-mil loads. I noticed you were carrying the same gun so that'll help us both if things get any more complicated. But that's not all...' There was a tiny *click* and the room was full of light. 'I brought the torch from the limo's breakdown kit.' He fiddled with the settings, switching from full beam to neon work-light to orange and red warning flashers.

'Great,' said Richard feelingly. 'Now we can all have a breakdown.'

'Most amusing. This is the famous British stiff upper lip, yes? A jest in the face of danger?' The beam found a gaping inner doorway and the pair of them picked their way across the hard earth of the floor, stepping up over the raised brickwork that had once contained an inner door frame. The next room was like the first, crumbling bricks and sagging plaster. No ceiling to speak of. No floor above the red earth that had once been concealed by long-gone floorboards laid on beams whose ghosts patterned the red mud floor.

'Seems to work for James Bond,' said Richard quietly, stepping over the sill behind Voroshilov. He paused for an instant as something huge welled up within him and threatened to overwhelm him. Fear for Robin and what might even now be happening to her. When he could breathe again he was surprised to find that his eyes were full of water. 'But talking of breakdowns,' he persisted as soon as he felt his voice would be steady, 'what in God's name has spooked Paznak so badly?'

'He is Slav. He is not of warrior blood like a Cossack such as myself. And I must admit that when they were giving out brains, poor old Paznak was not the first in the queue.'

They were at the corner of a third room now, the dark promise of a room stepping out over the pavement into the defensive position from which Paznak had blindly fired the Glock. The silence told them the room was empty now. But the smell of gun smoke told them all they needed to know. Voroshilov flashed the torch beam towards the window and there six brass casings gleamed. Richard crossed to the nearest and stooped. 'Still warm,' he whispered. 'Nine mil. Has to be him. Let's go.'

The torch gave them confidence that they would be able to move faster than their quarry. 'But even so...' persisted Richard as Voroshilov flashed the torch around, hesitating to obey Richard's brusque command. 'Yes. There is something badly wrong. He has lost or broken his earpiece so that I cannot communicate with him. Though this may be a black spot for communications – I cannot get a reply from either of the other cars. All he is trying to do is to protect three women, two of whom seemed when last I saw them to be more than half naked. Such a thing might distract him but is not too likely to frighten him. Even the sight of Frau Hoffman in all her glory should not really *frighten* him; after all, he has seen what she wears to sunbathe round the pool.' And on the word *pool* the torch beam settled on the floor beside the next inner doorway – the only other way out of the room. On the red mud there was a wide stain of darker colour. Once again it was Richard who crossed to it and tested it with his fingertips. He rubbed the thick redness between fingers and thumb, raised it to his nostrils.

'It's wet and warm,' he whispered as Voroshilov crossed to stand close beside him. 'Hard to be certain of the colour but it certainly smells like blood.'

'Paznak's?' wondered Voroshilov.

'If it's not, we'd need to be careful,' said Richard grimly, wiping his fingers in his coat tail. 'AIDS may be endemic.'

'I think we should risk calling to him,' answered Voroshilov, nodding acknowledgement. 'Do you agree?'

'Certainly. *PAZNAK!*'

'Mother of God! Where did you learn to shout like that?'

'Shush!'

'I think I am deaf in my left ear...'

'Voroshilov! Shut up! I think I hear them...'

In the silence that seemed to echo through the derelict terraces after Voroshilov stopped speaking came the faintest distant whisper. 'Here! We're here. Help! Help!'

The pair set off as fast as they dared. Both men were unsettled by even these most recent events – let alone the kidnapping – and were all too well aware that they could still be in the tightening coils of a trap. Richard at least knew that the torch in the dark house, like the limo on the dark road outside, was a mixed blessing. Just as it let them move quickly and confidently, so it also gave clear warning of their approach and a very precise target indeed. But they had to rescue the women. They had to find Paznak. They had to discover what was going on.

Richard decided that if whoever was waiting for them would know that they were coming in any case, then he'd let them know for certain. As it was a woman's voice that had called, his next bellow was, 'FRAU HOFFMAN?'

The reply was louder, stronger and much nearer. But there was something not quite right about it. 'Do you think they have cellars in these houses?' he whispered to Voroshilov.

'God knows. I'm not even certain they have inside plumbing.' He shone the torch up at the flimsy wreckage of the ceiling as he spoke. 'They sure as hell don't have any staircases left to let us go up and look.' And somewhere in the tiered darkness up there Richard thought he saw a star. Venus, perhaps, decided his deeply pre-occupied mind: there was a distinctly ruby gleam to it.

But when Voroshilov's torch beam came down to shine straight ahead, it called Richard's mind back to much more earthly matters. For it showed only a blank wall. 'End of the line,' whispered Voroshilov.

And, as the Russian spoke, Richard saw the strangest thing – a tiny line of brightness that shone down his cheek between his cauliflower ear and his bristling moustache like the blood he imagined on his own neck and back: as though the Russian had somehow cut himself shaving.

'JUMP!' yelled Richard, and Voroshilov did exactly that – so that it was not quite the end of the line for him after all. The three-tap of

173

bullets slammed between them into the red mud of the floor. Or rather, two bullets did. The third of the pattern resulted only in the telling *click* of an empty weapon.

Richard moved on his own word, of course. He jumped left, followed by the beam of Voroshilov's wildly swinging torch. He landed on his left foot and turned lightly on his toe – at last in the style of Fred Astaire – to find himself confronted with a gaping door out into the long-dead overgrowth of the back yard. But there, revealed for an instant before Voroshilov had the wit to switch the torch off, was a sight that brought a tiny revelation. A stone step. The bottom step of an outer staircase too sturdy and solid for the vultures who had stripped the terrace to take.

Richard ran up it silently, hoping that Voroshilov would have the wit to follow him. Almost immediately, he arrived on a little stone balcony that jutted from the side of the house like a ledge on a square brick cliff. There was starlight out here and the promise of a rising moon. Even after the brightness of the torch beam, he could see the solidity of the wall and the straight-edged vacancy of the doorway. He pressed his shoulders against one, right at the square edge of the other, and he held his breath and waited. Above the thumping of his heart he could hear a range of sounds all too close at hand. Hoarse breathing. Quiet whimpering. A strangely unsettling creaking. In time his pupils would expand and in a very few minutes the

174

moon would rise, so if he was patient he would have enough light to take him into the room behind him even if Voroshilov didn't arrive. But he didn't have to wait for the moon after all.

An instant later Voroshilov loomed up beside him. 'On three,' he whispered.

The two of them whirled on the third beat. Richard's SIG was in his favoured two-handed grip, but Voroshilov's was one-handed with the torch in the other. As their shoulders met in the middle of the doorway, he pressed the torch button and flooded the room with blinding brightness. The effect was so sudden and yet so clear to Richard's night-adapted vision that it remained in his memory like a photograph, as vivid as the last vision of Robin standing helplessly beside the limo, surrounded by her kidnappers.

Frau Hoffman sat on a ledge of flooring little more than a metre wide. Her hair was a mess and her gown in tatters. Bambi and Irena were crouching beside of her, their arms wrapped around each other, hair and clothing in no better state. Faces white and eyes wide with terror. A little way away from them, towards the centre of the room crouched Paznak, the left side of his madly working face a mask of blood. The flesh between the point of his jaw and his hairline had been simply bashed away – the ear and the earpiece with it. On the floor in front of him, like a low defensive wall, lay the blood-spattered body of a native boy in ragged uniform who

175

was covered in dust and apparently dead. Above the boy, Paznak was pointing his Glock at them, the ruby beam of its red-dot sight like a rapier blade between them. But the gun was in empty mode. Skeletal and useless.

Then Voroshilov broke the stasis. 'Paznak, it's us,' he said, shining the torch beam up on his face. The gesture was wise and the tone of voice soft enough to quiet a startled Cossack pony, but the result was unexpected. Paznak started back as though confronted with a nightmare. The floor beneath him gave way and he vanished with a roar and a cloud of plaster dust.

Fourteen

Post-mortem

Granville Harbour's central hospital was as isolated as the central police station and as ill-supplied as the neighbourhood stores. But the Granville Lodge had a clinic for its guests rivalled only by the President's, with a live-in medical team on twenty-four-hour call. It was here they brought the battered Paznak, the hysterical women and – at Richard's insistence – the dying boy.

Richard needed to insist most forcefully just to get the boy down the stone steps and into the car which had come back for them when the shooting stopped and the driver's fear of Voroshilov replaced the blind panic of being under fire. The frightened women – who also worried about AIDS in the local population – felt that they had risked and suffered more than enough so far this evening. Eventually he had simply overruled their hysterical orders and laid the boy in the comfortably carpeted footwell, with the tailcoat as a pillow and a range of rags, mostly torn from his own evening shirt, to fashion makeshift bandages. But then the exhausted

Richard, all too well aware of the scarecrow figure he was cutting, had to insist even more forcefully still to get everyone tended properly when they got back to the convoy on the main road.

Max Asov had apparently decided to sack both Paznak and Voroshilov the instant he saw what was happening at the women's limo, and none of their actions later made him willing to change his mind. As the icily outraged Felix Makarov observed, good security men were ten a kopek – so why put up with foot soldiers whose only real ability seemed to be to recover from bad situations they had got themselves into in the first place? The fact that his own men had been rendered helpless and had remained utterly inactive until they broke out of the crushed limo just in time to welcome the ubiquitous Major Kebila to the scene of the outrage apparently made no difference.

'Leave them here,' Makarov snarled to Asov as Richard presented the blood-bedabbled pair to their erstwhile employer while they ushered the weeping women out of the back of their limo and into the back of the battered-looking military ambulance Kebila had brought with him. 'Let them die in the gutter like this terrorist scum!'

Even the limo drivers gaped at Makarov's brutal words. Richard was outraged.

'That is out of the question, Felix, and you know it. We may not be the SAS or the Spetsnaz but these are our men. We take them home.

178

And as for the boy, we know nothing about him. Until we can perform some kind of post-mortem on what has gone on during the last half-hour, and discuss matters with Major Kebila here and his superiors, we need to keep all our options open. And everyone possible alive.'

'Nonsense,' raged Makarov, ruthlessly ex-FSB, ex-KGB to his fingertips. 'We need to pistol everyone who cannot or will not help us and move on. It is a rule that has served us well. Once you shoot enough people in the head, something always seems to turn up!'

Richard stood silently, looking the Russian square in the eye and willing himself not to mention the seemingly endless debacle of Chechnya, where application of Makarov's rule did not seem to be serving anyone particularly well, until at last Makarov looked away.

'I have no doubt you hope to gain intelligence from this child,' he allowed, speaking more temperately. 'But all you will gain is another reason to watch your back.' His stare swept over Voroshilov and Paznak like a winter gale from Siberia. 'I expect you feel some kind of loyalty to these inefficient imbeciles into the bargain. But all you will gain is two more use-less hangers-on. And you will have to keep a close eye upon every move they make, for fear they will trip you at a crucial moment.'

Richard looked around the circle of security men who stood beside Kebila's soldiers, scan-ning the shadowed street and house-fronts now

179

that it was far too late. None of them flickered an eyelid at Makarov's brutal rendition of their terms of employment. Perhaps they thought that when the going got tough they would do better than Paznak and Voroshilov had.

But Richard frankly doubted it.

'We will need all the help and intelligence we can get if we're going to find Anastasia,' Richard persisted, switching his attention to Max Asov.

But Anastasia's father seemed to be as icily outraged as his business partner. 'What we need,' he spat back, 'is to clear away all of this debris, get organized with Major Kebila and his superiors – get President Banda motivated into the bargain if we have to – and then hit these people so hard that they come *begging* to give her back. Starting with this little scum...'

The raging Russian reached into his jacket and for a moment Richard thought he was going to pull out a gun and shoot the boy where he lay. But by the best of good luck, it had been Asov's SIG that had come clattering out on to the road and when he felt nothing more than an empty holster under his arm, he froze, his mad eyes fastened on his weapon where it rested securely in Richard's fist.

Major Kebila stepped between the two men. 'Even were it advisable, Mr Asov, I could not permit you to execute one of my people in full public view. Mr Mariner is right. We need to know exactly what went on here before we take any further action. Therefore we must move

180

quickly. And check things out very precisely. Then, at least, we will have a better chance of knowing who to hit, and where they are. And in any case, like all kidnappers, they will be in contact...'

'They will,' added Richard earnestly and forcefully, feeling the ghost of that assegai point like ice in the back of his neck. 'That was the message. Wait for their demands...'

'Precisely. And when that contact is made it will give us more clues still. I give you my word, Mr Asov, and you, Mr Makarov, that when we know who has these women, we will hit them without mercy until, as you say, they beg – *and beg on bended knee* – to give their hostages back.'

'As you wish,' Asov acquiesced gracelessly. 'But those two buffoons are no longer in my employ. Take them where you want, Major, and treat them however you will. But give me back my guns.'

Major Kebila hesitated, apparently shocked by the brutal dismissal. A little silence fell, broken only by the throbbing of the army trucks in the background, the sobbing of the women sitting apparently untended in the back of the ambulance and the choking gasps of the dying boy.

'No, I don't think we can allow that either,' grated Richard, every bit as angry as the Russians. 'If Mr Asov can sack these men so quickly, then I see no reason that I can't hire them equally quickly.' He turned to Voroshilov who stood, gaping, spraddle-legged and hunched, with the SIG dangling from his right hand and the semi-conscious Paznak draped over his left shoulder. 'Welcome to Heritage Mariner, gentlemen,' snapped Richard, without moderating his own Arctic tone. 'Now give Mr Asov back his guns and let's all get to hospital before it's too late to do anything for the boy.'

Quickest to recover and most eager to help once they got to the Granville Royal Lodge's clinic was Frau Hoffman. No doubt she was equally aware of the ridiculous figure she had cut in the incident and of the fact that she – even more than Paznak and Voroshilov – had failed to live up to her employer's stern requirements. It may well also have occurred to her that a man whose wife had just been kidnapped – no matter how exceptional a man he might be – would be much more hesitant to hire someone such as herself than he had been to throw a lifeline to the battered ex-security guards. Unless she played her cards right, she could find herself abandoned here with no papers, money or support.

Given all that, however, it would have taken someone of much less insight than Richard, Asov and Kebila to be fooled by the self-serving spin she put on her version of events. Nevertheless, at the earliest possible opportunity, she gathered her hotel hospital robe determinedly across her bosom, leaned forward earnestly across a little table in the clinic and

182

launched into her version of events.

'Of course I will be happy to repeat all this more formally later, but I felt it would help you to know at once what happened. And as Paznak is *hors de combat*, I am the most reliable witness, I believe.

'I saw what was happening at once, and felt it my duty to make sure that Miss Bogdana and Miss Irena, Mr Asov's and Mr Makarov's companions, were safe with Paznak. I was particularly careful to assure myself that Anastasia was in the safe keeping of Mrs Mariner and Voroshilov before I went. You should remember that the young women were terrified and hysterical, and on the run, with Paznak close behind. Anastasia was calm, as was Mrs Mariner – calm and controlled. And I had every expectation that if Voroshilov felt he could not guarantee their security personally, he would have the wit to close the door and lock the car.'

Voroshilov was seated like a half-deflated balloon beside the comatose Paznak, who was receiving pretty extensive surgery to his ear and the side of his face. The work was being done by a trainee nurse because the doctor was in the clinic's little surgery fighting to save the wounded boy, and the two fully trained assistants were up with Bambi and Irena in the Russians' suite. Their attendance was the price Richard had paid for his retention on the doctor. Kebila had stayed with them too, for neither of the gustily sobbing women looked like any kind of a witness.

The deflated ex-security man could not yet summon up the energy to challenge the gabbling woman. But he shot her a glance from between the shaggy slats of eyebrow and moustache that would have killed a bear at half a *verst*.

'I saw no detail of what actually happened to our car or its occupants because a crowd of terrorists started to pursue us at once,' persisted the self-serving Swiss hausfrau. 'As soon as he saw them coming, Paznak ran, and the two young women, not unreasonably, took to their heels as well. With this scrum of well-armed thugs between me and the cars I had no option but to follow. And as I could no longer help Anastasia, I naturally felt responsible for the two that I could help. Especially as Paznak seemed unable to do so.'

'And so you all ran up the alleyway?' Kebila was tiring of the relentless self-justification. He leaned forward and Richard could almost hear him admonishing *Just the facts, ma'am* like a detective from an old TV series.

'Yes. That's right. I was able to overtake Paznak quite quickly...'

'Was he falling back to get between you and your pursuers, perhaps?' probed Richard gently. 'To protect you while you escaped?'

'Possibly...' *But not very likely*, said her dismissive tone.

'But you ran on. Then what happened?' Kebila wanted to cut to the chase.

'Miss Bogdana stumbled and fell into the path

184

of the pursuing mob.'

'Her shoes were designed for dancing, not sprinting,' nodded Kebila. 'No doubt you stopped to help her...'

'Miss Irena was screaming with hysteria by now. I felt it would be better for me to help *her*...'

'So Paznak stopped for Miss Bogdana,' Kebila probed.

'It was his duty to do so! And then the leading terrorists were upon him at once. He was struck on the head. With some kind of a club, I think. But he opened fire. It was very strange. There were several men grouped closely around him and he seemed to push his gun hard against them as he shot. It was surprisingly quiet. They broke away. Several of them fell down. He got free and ran towards us with Miss Bogdana, who was crying and screaming also. Some of the men stopped with those lying on the ground behind him, but several more came on. I saw at once that we needed to get off the street and many of the doorways in the houses beside us were open. So I helped Miss Irena in and called to Paznak that he should follow us with Miss Bogdana. And so he did—'

Kebila interrupted the story at this point, turning to look at Richard – possibly because Richard gave a hiss of pain as a nurse began to swab his neck with disinfectant. 'You went up the street on foot and by car. Did you see any dead men lying there?'

'No. The street was empty.'

'So. Either Frau Hoffman is mistaken about the first encounter or the terrorists are well enough organized to remove their dead and wounded pretty quickly.'

'Which would make the boy even more crucial if they left him by accident.'

'Indeed,' said Kebila thoughtfully. 'Let us hope he survives and proves cooperative.'

'It also explains,' growled Voroshilov, 'why Paznak was so defensive. He was expecting them to come after the boy on top of everything else...'

'A good point. As with the boy, we will have questions for him in due course. In the meantime, Frau Hoffman...'

The tutor resumed her story. 'It was very dark, but his gun had a little beam of light and we were able to follow that. Even so, the terrorists caught up with us once again. They had no torches. Nor any guns as far as I could see. It was very dark and extremely confusing. And I was doing my best to look after the young women, of course. But our pursuers had clubs, I am certain. Paznak was hit in the head again. In the same place as before, I think, but he kept firing until they broke away. He must have fired at least ten shots in all, in both attacks. At last they broke away and fled. I think it was because they realized that *they* were being chased. We heard shouting. It sounded to me like someone calling Paznak's name but I cannot be certain. And the revving of a motor. Paznak did not seem to hear anything. He had let Miss Bogdana go during the second attack. Now he caught up the nearest person, probably believing it to be her. But it was a boy that the terrorists had left behind in the confusion.

'Paznak held on to the boy they left behind and tried to use him as a shield. After the shouting and the revving of the engine came the most terrible brightness. Paznak said something about the rest of them coming in a half-track vehicle and started shooting again. Out of a window and right down the street at the approaching headlights. The shots were very loud this time. They hurt our ears. In the brightness I could see for the first time how badly hurt Paznak was. But he told us to get away if we could.

'So we ran. He followed, bringing the boy. He was walking strangely, and he was shouting in a strange mixture of Russian and English by this time.

'We found the stairs and he told us to climb. Something about high places, fields of fire, advantage of surprise. I kept the girls with me, and I took the boy as well, for I had seen how hurt he was too. Someone called my name and I answered once before Paznak told me it was a trap and I should stay quiet. The blows to his head may have damaged his brain as well as his ear. In any case, Paznak crawled out into the middle of the room, pulling the poor boy behind him, and fired some more shots. Two, I think.

'Then Mr Mariner appeared, with Voroshilov and the torch...'

'The Glock's got a seventeen-cartridge load,' said Voroshilov suddenly. 'And Paznak didn't have a spare. That sounds about right. Nine at them, eight at us.'

'But the boy,' Kebila insisted quietly. 'He was with the men who attacked you? Right from the beginning? He could not have been an innocent bystander? Could not, for instance, have been hiding in the house you went into and ended up getting shot by accident?'

'Paznak couldn't have been trying to get him out to safety as well, could he – after having shot him by accident?' probed Richard further.

'No. I am certain!' She looked at them almost defiantly, like a child caught in a lie.

Richard looked away, still much less than satisfied. But it looked like this was the only version of events they would get unless either Irena or Bambi – Bogdana – had seen something important, which he frankly doubted. So that was that until Paznak woke up – if he remembered enough to make any sense. Or until the boy came out of surgery – if he ever did.

Or, of course, until the kidnappers made contact.

Fifteen

Conference

The Nelson Mandela Suite seemed huge and empty. Everywhere Richard looked seemed to be filled with Robin's absence. His own clothes lay scattered, awaiting his organization, or the tailor's or Robin's. Her clothes and possessions were neatly packed away; all but invisible. Only her fragrance filled the air, making her as vividly present as a ghost.

Pushing all feeling down for the time being, fearing that it would disorientate – incapacitate – him, Richard strode through the reception area tearing off the remains of his evening shirt and shrugging off the white evening braces. Then he reached back and tore off the bulky bandage on the back of his neck.

A moment later, he was standing in the shower with the water at the hottest setting he could bear. As the power of the jets thundered down upon his head he fought to clear his mind, to achieve some kind of distance from the terrible situation he was in, to decide on his immediate priorities for command and action. Unlike Max and Felix, and, apparently, Major

189

Kebila, Richard believed that hitting the kidnappers hard and soon would be of no help at all to Robin and Anastasia. Quite the reverse. The women were in all likelihood somewhere in the shanties, or even on their way up into the delta, and the only thing likely to keep them safe and well was the promise of negotiation.

But keeping them safe and well was only the most basic beginning. The main objective must be to get them out. Bring them back. And that of course meant that someone had to go in after them. Not a massive attack force but a surgical extraction team. Not a gun-happy army but a special-forces unit. Not a company – a commando.

Richard switched the water off and stepped, steaming, into the bathroom. The bell on his door was buzzing with a persistence that made him think it had started to sound some time ago when he was deafened by the shower. 'Coming!' he called, wrapping one towel round his waist and catching up a second to drape over his head like a cowl. On his way past his bedfoot he grabbed his dressing gown, swinging it on as he crossed the main reception room, and so when he actually got to the main door itself he looked like a boxer about to enter the ring.

He glanced through the spyhole and paused. Of all the people he had been half expecting, Morgan Hand was the last. And yet there she was, with Voroshilov looming uneasily at her shoulder. Richard hit the catch and the door swung open. 'This is an unexpected pleasure,'

190

he said, reaching up to towel his hair dry one-handed. 'What can I do for you, Morgan?'

'I came as soon as I heard,' she answered striding into the room, her tone sympathetic and her eyes busy. 'You'll want to keep on top of things if I know you and I thought I'd better put myself and my command at your disposal at once.' She was not in uniform but her costume of silk blouse and slacks looked both stylishly feminine and businesslike – like many of Robin's favourite combinations.

'Thank you,' he said, sincerely. 'Welcome to the team. Voroshilov, how's Paznak?'

'Asleep.' Voroshilov shrugged. He had not had the opportunity to shower or change, and was still redolent of gun smoke and adventure. No doubt his kit as well as Paznak's would turn up dumped somewhere like the corpse of a murder victim. Richard realized he had better either transfer the tab for their current accommodation or find them new rooms soon.

'And the boy?'

'Also asleep. You must expect a visit from the management soon about them. There is some question of payment. Accommodation. Medical fees...'

'I'm not surprised. Hang on a moment, will you? Voroshilov, there's a minibar. See what the captain wants then help yourself and pop in here for a moment when you've done that.'

Richard hesitated in his bedroom, getting a grip of his whirling emotions and trying to decide on some kind of a plan. He discovered with disorientating shock that he felt almost helpless. The simple responsibility of sorting out Voroshilov's accommodation and looking after the boy seemed almost overwhelming. He stood, indecisive, looking to left and right, as though punch-drunk already. Without a plan he had no idea what he should prepare for. Without any idea of that he had no notion of what he should wear. If he didn't make his mind up and get some clothes on then he would find himself just sitting in here as naked and helpless as a baby, while God alone knew what might be happening to Robin.

Richard pulled the towel off his head and looked at it. There was no blood on it, though the back of his neck still burned and itched. He shrugged off his dressing gown and as he did so the second towel lost purchase on his slim hips. Socks and underwear, said his subconscious automatically. It was pretty basic stuff, but it was an important first step. He was hopping on his left leg pulling on his right sock when the buzzer sounded again. 'You want me to get that?' called Morgan.

'Yes. Let in Heritage Mariner people but I don't want to talk to anyone else for the moment. Then get on to reception and check the status of Voroshilov and Paznak's rooms. Tell them Heritage Mariner will foot the bill for the time being. And for the boy, if he comes out of surgery...'

As he spoke, Richard reached for more clothing. Like the socks and underwear, what he chose was selected because it was substantial and hard-wearing, though he was as yet utterly unaware of the fact. He pulled on a double-woven cotton check shirt, therefore, patted the breast pockets automatically and fastened the double-buttoned cuffs – but he left the collar open in deference to the wound in his neck. 'Who's there, Morgan?' he called as he heard a confusion of voices crossing the reception room outside.

'Everybody, I think,' she called in answer. 'The rooms are sorted.'

'The team's all here, Richard,' confirmed Jim Bourne's familiar tones.

'Get yourselves settled,' ordered Richard. 'I'll be out in a moment.' He looked at the battered Rolex Robin had given him just before their wedding and which had hardly been off his wrist since. 'Conference in five minutes,' he said automatically.

He caught up the fawn cotton trousers he had been wearing this morning but threw them down again, unaccountably impatient with their flimsiness. He started sorting through the clothing from the grip that Robin had put aside for the laundry to press. There was a much more substantial suit there. Well-built big brother to the fawn fashion statement. It was at the bottom of the pile because it needed least attention. He pulled it out and slipped the trousers off the hanger, shaking the legs wide and hopping his feet into them one after the other, pulling them up and buttoning them shut. Even the belt was wider, stronger, decorated with loops and catches as though specifically designed for a big-game hunter – or a mercenary soldier. He cinched it tight and reached for his hairbrushes. The face that stared at him out of the mirror was lean and angular, blue-jawed, lined and ruthlessly determined. It masked the hurt outrage and confusion he felt. But it was a convincing mask. It would do.

The instant he finished brushing his hair, there was a tapping at the bedroom door. It sounded like the sort of knock that might be given by a gorilla trying to be subtle. 'Come in, Voroshilov.'

The Russian came in frowning with worry, clearly expecting that Richard had thought better of his offer of employment and was about to show him the door. 'Voroshilov, you said you swept this place?'

It took a moment for the Russian to realize Richard was talking security rather than room service. Then, frowning, he nodded.

'I assume you took out any devices that might let competitors or other interested parties into our secrets?'

The nodding continued.

'Might you have overlooked any that could communicate, for instance, with a concerned associate with our best interests at heart?'

Richard could almost see Voroshilov's lips moving as he worked his way through the jungle of English verbiage. It was like talking to Callum McKay. Subtlety not his strong point.

194

But Voroshilov got there. 'It is possible that Paznak may have missed two devices in the main room and one in here,' he admitted, as sly and subtle as a starving wolf on the winter steppe.

'I'd be very grateful if you could disable them for me, please.'

Voroshilov immediately knocked over the bedside lamp at his left elbow. It shattered on the floor and he stepped on the shards.

'Could we be a little less untidy next door?' Richard asked amenably. Voroshilov, still sheepish, nodded silently and turned away. Richard looked at his retreating back and down at the mess on the floor. He would call room service later, he decided – and take care what he asked his big new blunt instrument to do in future.

Then as Voroshilov exited and Felix Makarov's brutal warning about watching him and Paznak echoed in his mind, Richard turned back to the bed and the clothes he still needed to put on. The tailored jacket that went with the trousers was half-lined, festooned with pockets and constructed of material designed to withstand the bite of a crocodile by the feel of it. His desert boots stood neatly by the bed – but they were flimsy companions to this morning's outfit, not this one. He slipped them on, however. If he wanted boots to match what he was wearing, he would have to buy them – or borrow them from the largest of Major Kebila's combat-ready command. And that reminded him...

'Voroshilov,' he said, striding out of the bedroom at last, 'did you ever give those guns back to Mr Asov?'

'Not yet,' admitted the Russian, looking up from the innards of an eviscerated telephone. 'I brought them all up from the back of the limo. I went round the security arch. You want me to give them back now?'

'No. Don't.'

There was a little silence, then Jim asked, uneasily, his eyes travelling from Richard's stout clothing to Voroshilov's suspiciously covert actions, 'What have you got in mind, Richard?'

And when Richard replied, frowning with mild confusion, 'Nothing, Jim. I've nothing in mind at all...' He actually thought his words were true.

'Right,' said Richard brusquely a few moments later, 'first question. Where is she?' He looked around the circle of faces, meeting each pair of eyes as they all thought about his question. Like a gifted schoolmaster he knew better than to hurry the answer or pressure his questionees. 'Best guess and any other thoughts.'

'Well, I'm afraid that rather depends...' began Jim Bourne.

'On a number of things,' emphasized Charles Le Brun.

'I see that,' agreed Richard gently. 'It depends on who has her. On why they took her. On what they expect to gain – and from whom. Is this directly targeted, or is there a hope that pressure will be put on President Banda? Are they seeking money, power, publicity? If money, then power? If publicity, then credibility? Is this a terrorist act, a criminal act or a political act? I see that it *depends*. But the first and most important question is still – *where is she?*'

Simeon was a little more adventurous, though he was still unwilling to try for a direct answer. 'There aren't that many local factions – criminal or political – who would dare do anything like this. And almost none of them have access to military equipment like that half-track.'

'All political forces other than his own are criminal, according to Banda anyway,' observed Jim, relaxing a little. 'But that half-track does make it look political. I'm pretty certain that the security forces in general and the army in particular are too well paid to get involved in anything simply criminal. And I really cannot see them being careless enough to simply lose an armoured half-track.'

'I agree. They don't seem to be careless. And they are hardly likely to get involved in anything criminal as things stand at the moment. Anything that dangerously upfront anyway,' said Richard. Then he paused, thinking of Colonel Hercule Nkolo and his brother, Harbour-master Herold. 'But if it's political, and sufficiently powerfully political to have pulled in some security units, then does that mean it comes back to the Doctor? And if it does, then where is his HQ? Where is the Doctor likely to be holding the girls?'

'Wait a moment!' cautioned Jim. 'Let's not get ahead of ourselves here. Someone of the international standing of Dr Chaka is hardly going to get himself mixed up in something like a kidnapping!'

'Is there nothing he wants badly enough to risk it? There's no such thing as bad publicity, after all. But you're right. If it's Dr Chaka or his people, then it has to be something vital. Something that Max Asov can do or stop doing. Voroshilov – any ideas?'

Voroshilov shrugged. 'Even if there was something, he would never let anyone like me and Paznak know about it. I've never been at a conference like this with Mr Makarov or Mr Asov. If they thought I had any ideas at all about their plans they wouldn't have sacked me, they'd have killed me.'

Richard nodded. No surprise there. But a good thought. 'Morgan, we might be more exposed here than we want to be. Get on to *Prometheus* and get her ready. I want to be able to go aboard her at a moment's notice if I have to and take all of these people with me. She won't be as comfortable but she will be safer if we want a secure base for any reason. Use the facilities.' He gestured at the big TV. 'Get First Officer Oblomov up and get things under way there – but be as subtle as you can.' Oblomov technically worked for Heritage Mariner – but his heart might well lie with the Russian consortium; and the same might go for many of the crew.

'Then it's back to you guys,' he said, turning back as she rose to obey. 'Jim, Charles, Simeon, any gossip? Any thoughts? Any ideas? If you can't think of anything specific, then get on to Patrice Salako at the paper or Miss Uhuru at the TV studios.

'The rest of you – is there anything in the contracts to give us a clue? Any references to anything you can think of that might have special political significance? Enough so that the country's only real opposition party would come out from undercover and go to these lengths to stop it? Go through your copies with a fine-tooth comb and a fresh slant. What is Asov up to? Why might the Doctor want it stopped? We'll be wiser when someone contacts Asov, and I guess he'll want me at least there when they get through – it'd look pretty suspicious if he didn't, given the circumstances. But I'd be happier to be ahead of the game before the call comes through, if at all possible.'

'If...' insisted Jim. 'If...And besides, what makes you think that Asov is the only target? They took Robin as well as Anastasia, didn't they? Why shouldn't you be subject to their demands as much as Asov?'

Richard shook his head. 'It's not much of an edge, but we'll keep this need-to-know for the moment. No one outside this room must know. But no. They didn't kidnap Robin. At least not knowingly. They were expecting two women – Anastasia and her tutor. That's exactly what they supposed they were taking out of the car.

That's why the message they left with me was for Max Asov and Max alone. And as far as I know, that's exactly what they think they've got – his daughter and her tutor. They think they have Frau Hoffman, not Robin, and if I know my darling wife she won't be in any rush to tell them the truth unless she can see some pretty clear advantage in it. They might well have no idea they actually have Robin at all.'

No sooner had he finished speaking than the half-assembled phone gave a strangled squeak. Richard picked it up and held it to his ear with some difficulty. 'Mariner.'

'Asov. They've made contact. My suite. Come alone.'

Sixteen

Contact

Richard had no intention of doing what he was commanded by Max Asov – or by Felix Makarov, for that matter – even under these circumstances. But he didn't want to rub the Russians' nose in it either. So, although he seriously considered taking Voroshilov with him as the closest employee he had to a bodyguard, he contented himself with a taciturn, 'Jim, Simeon, they've made contact. Let's go.'

The man who admitted them to Max's suite was Fedor Gulin. Gulin had always reminded Robin of a toad, and Richard agreed that he shared many features with the amphibian. Everything, it seemed at first glance, except webbed fingers and green skin. Squat bald head joined directly to squat body without benefit of neck; huge eyes and mouth, though the mouth still not quite big enough to contain the tongue; spots and pustules; a vaguely slimy appearance...

Gulin glared at Richard's companions but did not have the immediate authority to forbid them. 'Evening, Fedor,' said Richard striding past the repulsive man with no intention of waiting for a response. 'Where's Max?'

Max was in the main reception room with Felix and their whole team. Richard noted this distantly as he strode across the massive, crowded space. He also noticed the similarity to the Nelson Mandela Suite in size, scale, layout and decor. But all of his concentration was on the half-dozen men by the DVD player.

Major Kebila stood at Colonel Nkolo's shoulder but he looked much more in command in spite of pips, braid and such. Behind them stood a little four-man squad of Kebila's command, their stony faces and smartly held weapons growing familiar to Richard. And it seemed that it was Kebila's men who had made the discovery of the kidnappers' message. Which looked to be a DVD, where he himself had been half expecting the more traditional disguised voice on the phone or perhaps even a note. Interestingly upmarket, Richard thought. Hidden message there for a start.

He also suspected acutely that Nkolo had only joined in because the President and his senior staff were so worried about the situation and its possibilities for bad publicity – and destructive outcomes. They clearly wanted to be seen to have been doing all they could under the stern judgement of history – especially if anything went wrong.

Everyone else's attention was on Kebila too; so much so that Asov hardly seemed to notice Jim and Simeon, let alone object to their presence.

'The disc was in a dead man's hand,' said Kebila, clearly continuing something he had been saying just before Richard and his team arrived. 'It was addressed to Mr Asov in what we call Matadi script, French and English. These men discovered the corpse during a sweep of the area of the kidnapping itself.' He nodded to the four smart soldiers at his back. 'They do not speak English or French so I shall explain their testimony for them.

'They have said that they were patrolling on foot, though they had a half-track as backup. The area was of course quiet, and, they thought, deserted. One moment the roadway was empty and still, exactly as we left it when we returned to the hotel here.

'They returned to the half-track to summon a removal team to come and get the burned-out car for a thorough forensic examination. Then, next moment, when they went back to the burned-out vehicle to search it for clues themselves, the dead man in question was discovered sitting in the driver's seat. He had arrived during the minutes my men were away from the crime scene, they are certain. And he clearly did not get there under his own steam. They found it very disturbing, almost supernatural. They returned to the half-track and called for backup. But they had the presence of mind to take a series of crime-scene photographs and to bring the disc with them. We have since recovered the vehicle, of course, and performed a closer examination of the deceased.

'He had died from a gunshot wound. Close range, to the heart. His clothing was marked with powder and was charred from the discharge. The bullet went straight through his chest, leaving a surprisingly small exit wound. My firearms experts tell me it may well have carried enough force to do serious damage to anyone standing close behind him. Two birds with one stone. Perhaps three or more.

'Recalling the testimony of Frau Hoffman, it seems most likely that this is one of the pursuers killed by the Russian Paznak, though neither she nor he recognized him from the photographs. We will show these to the boy when the doctors permit. He is still in a deep coma and so it would be useless for us to press the point. It seems certain that the man died in the street during the attack, however, and was immediately removed by his associates. Then replaced by his associates to ensure our immediate attention and drive home their message.'

'Waste not, want not,' said Max shortly, impatiently. 'Can we see what's on the disc, Major?'

Kebila glanced at Nkolo, whose attention seemed to have wandered a little. 'May I play the DVD, Colonel?'

'What? Oh, yes. Certainly. But, gentlemen, as you watch it please remember that we are dealing here with a little criminal gang trying to make some capital and some profit out of the relationship between our beloved President and international big business as represented by yourselves. There is no need to worry about meeting any of the demands contained in this. The whole of the President's government, from the security services to all the relevant ministries – and of course the armed services themselves – will be fully engaged in finding and destroying these scum.'

Having delivered himself of this carefully rehearsed speech, the colonel nodded to Major Kebila, who slid the disc into the machine. Part way through the speech Richard realized, disorientated, utterly irrelevantly, that Hercule Nkolo reminded him most forcefully of Fedor Gulin. Except that his low forehead and fat cheeks were bright, smooth and shiny, not patterned with mountain ranges of pustules and cratered like the face of the moon.

Richard's mouth went dry as the disc slid on to the little plastic tray and the tray retracted into the DVD player. He blinked several times to clear his eyes and focused on the massive TV screen with all his considerable intelligence. He had never, in fact, scrutinized anything so closely as he watched the screen during the next few moments. Ideas, insights and questions burst into his head as he watched, but they were ruthlessly filed away for examination, comparison, discussion and answering later on.

The screen cleared abruptly with an eerie echoing crackle as a soundtrack came alive. The picture steadied as the crackling faded to the faintest hiss. And the most unexpected vision of all filled the TV. A well-made-up young woman sat at a desk looking steadily straight into their eyes. There was some kind of a flag behind her but Richard did not really register the detail at first, for he was sidetracked by the face itself. For a moment Richard thought it was Charlotte Uhuru. But no. It was a stranger who shared what he supposed must be typical Matadi tribal features with the lovely broadcaster. The high cheekbones, the long chin and slightly angular jaw. The long nose and the back-sloping forehead emphasizing the slightly aristocratic tilt of the whole head. The wide eyes and the deep mahogany skin.

She was dressed in conservative tribal clothing. What looked like a cotton robe dyed rich russet with black marks giving it the appearance of leopard-skin. She wore a simple matching headdress. She wore no rings or jewellery. Richard focused on the wall behind her. He noticed now that the flag was coloured green and blue in a stylized representation of a river winding through jungle, with the letters PPLD in the centre coloured red. The woman's head and shoulders with the flag behind filled the whole of the screen, except for the thin line of desk at the bottom just wide enough to contain her folded hands.

'Mr Asov,' she said quietly in well-modulated French, clearly reading from a carefully prepared script, 'we have your daughter Anastasia and her companion. We mean them no harm and we propose to return them to you none the worse for their experience as long as certain conditions are met. We will contact you again in twenty-four hours by which time we expect the following things to have been put in hand. First, we expect that soi-disant President Liye Banda will have formally recognized the People's Party for the Liberation of the Delta. Secondly, Liye Banda will have expressed his willingness to recognize Dr Julius Chaka as the Leader of the Opposition in the current puppet parliament. Thirdly, he will have set a date for elections to a properly democratic government – such elections to be overseen by scrutineers from our own reformed Electoral College, the African Union and relevant international democratic communities.'

The wide brown eyes looked unflinchingly out into the room, but it was clear the gaze was focused on only one man there. 'You know that you are uniquely placed to bring pressure on the President, Mr Asov,' continued the quiet, cultured, disturbingly confident voice. 'These demands are neither unreasonable nor un-achievable given your current position and that of your associates. Fourthly and finally, Mr Asov, you and these associates at the Bashnev-Sevmash Consortium will withdraw all your men and equipment from the delta. You will publicly commit to rectifying the environmen-tal damage that your work there has done so far, and paying full compensation to the indigenous people whose lands and lives you have come so close to destroying for ever. That at least is a fair and even bargain. The life of your child for the lives and futures of our children. Long live the PPLD! Long live Julius Chaka!'

The soundtrack stopped. Kebila froze the picture before it faded. The woman sat like a lovely painting gazing out of the frame of the TV.

'No one at Granville Broadcasting will admit to knowing this woman,' said the soldier quietly. 'And yet she has access to facilities that only they possess as far as we know. The background to where she is sitting has been cleverly concealed by that rag of a flag and seems anonymous to us. We are assured that the recording could have been made anywhere – in a studio or in a private residence. It is unlikely to have been made outside or in the bush because there seems to be so little background noise. Our analysis of the soundtrack is ongoing but there seems at first hearing to be no extraneous sound. No sound at all, in fact, except the woman's voice. This seems to be a very carefully prepared piece of work indeed.'

Richard saw the relevance of that last observation at once, and his thoughtful frown deepened as his mind raced ahead, seeking the implications of something no one else seemed to have understood yet. In another forum he might have taken the lead and moved the discussions on. Not here. Not now. Not as things currently stood.

'Have you any comment on the demands, Mr Asov?' asked Major Kebila gently.

I'd start with the demands, thought Richard,

208

watching events narrow-eyed. *I'd start with the fact that they haven't even mentioned the authorities – let alone warned you against approaching them. They're either very clever, very confident – or very, very stupid.*

And they don't seem the least bit stupid to me...

'What comment could I possibly make?' snarled Asov, his face suffused with an anger more intense than any Richard had ever seen him betray. 'It is outrageous, preposterous. That a legitimate businessman whose only plan is to bring wealth and employment into the country should be made the target of such an outrage. I have some demands of my own and I will be putting them to President Banda in person at the earliest possible moment. And they will possibly involve you, Major Kebila. Probably you, Colonel Nkolo. And certainly General Bomba if the President listens to me. Because I want these people found and killed. Not negotiated with, not appeased. Exterminated. I want them, their associates, their women and their children if necessary bombed back into the Stone Age.'

'They mostly live in Stone Age conditions already, Mr Asov...' observed the major icily.

'Then I want them bombed back into pre-history,' snarled Asov. 'I want them bombed until it's like Jurassic Park out there.'

As Asov's outraged words rang around the room, Colonel Nkolo's personal phone began to sound. He pulled it out and put it to his ear. Came to attention as he listened. Snapped it shut when the message finished as though he were putting a weapon on safety. He turned to Kebila. 'The President wishes to see us immediately.'

He swung round to look across the room.

'And we are to bring Mr Asov. Mr Asov *alone*.'

But Max under presidential orders was no more obedient than Richard had been under Max's. 'No,' he said. 'Mr Makarov will come with me. And...' His gaze swept around the room. Met Richard's burning stare. Shifted away. 'Mr Gulin. Also we will bring along Mr Vrithov and a couple of his well-armed associates to wait in the chopper as our insurance. I assume,' he continued, icily, 'that we have stopped all this nonsense with limousines...'

Seventeen

Plan

Back in the Nelson Mandela Suite, Richard filled in the others on what had transpired in Max Asov's rooms then picked up where he had left off his thinking there. He used the mental activity of dominating the conversation as a much-needed cover for his mounting rage and frustration. It was bad enough that Robin had been caught up in this – but to have been kidnapped by mistake, as a kind of an accident, it came close to bursting his heart. And the widening gulf between him and his erstwhile associates only made matters worse. On the one hand he was outraged by Asov's failure to include him in the group visiting President Banda. On the other hand he suspected acutely that he would not actually want to be included in the conversation Asov and Makarov were about to have – much though he would have given to know what was said.

Robin had never liked or trusted the Russian businessmen. How right, it seemed now, she had been. But Richard's reaction to this inner conflict was typical of him. He had to keep

211

busy, he felt, or he would simply explode.

'I've never been involved in a situation like this before,' he grated at once, therefore. 'So all I really know about it comes from films and TV shows. But I thought it was standard practice for kidnappers to warn their victims' nearest and dearest not to alert anyone or to notify the authorities. These people, whoever they are—'

'The People's Party for the Liberation of the Delta,' said Jim, quietly.

'Maybe,' allowed Simeon at once. 'More than maybe, in fact, because if they don't want anonymity, then they must want publicity and that makes it obviously political, doesn't it? PPLD and Dr Chaka have to head up the list. In fact, as far as I can see, they more or less *are* the list.'

'OK,' agreed Richard impatiently. 'But there has to be some distance between Julius Chaka and the actual kidnappers, doesn't there? I mean it's all very well calling in the African Union and the wider democracies to oversee the elections they say they're hoping for, but what sort of a political campaign begins with a serious criminal offence like kidnapping? How can Dr Chaka risk that kind of publicity? What kind of a reaction from any kind of democratic observer is that going to bring?'

'Pretty negative,' allowed Jim. The two words seemed to kill the conversation, but Richard simply could not keep still. He continued pacing around the room, as though – big though it was – it could never contain his restless energy. And he carried on talking, voicing thoughts when they were still part-formed.

'Unless,' he said, thoughtfully. 'Unless...'

'Unless what?' Simeon demanded on behalf of the assembled team.

'Unless what's going on up the river is so evil that a kidnapping looks allowable in comparison,' began Richard slowly, his voice gathering pace and certainty as he spoke. 'Or, of course, unless President Banda lets Max Asov have his way and General Bomba goes upriver mob-handed and creates such carnage that the original cause of the situation just gets lost in the horror.' Richard shook himself, paused for a moment and looked around the frowning faces. 'Either way, we need more intelligence. We need to know what Asov, Makarov and their consortium are actually up to in the delta.'

As he finished speaking, Richard's gaze lit upon Voroshilov. 'Voroshilov,' he said at once. 'Have you any idea what's going on in the jungle?'

'No,' answered the Russian. 'Like I said earlier, that's the kind of thing Mr Asov and Mr Makarov kept really close to their chest. Paznak might know something but I have no idea.'

'Why might Paznak know something?'

'He's not quite as fit as me. He was Gulin's watcher. If there's a weak link it'll be Gulin and the vodka bottle. I got the idea that Paznak had heard things. But we never discussed anything. Most of the time working for Bashnev-Sevmash security, the *less* you know the safer you are.'

'But you don't work for the consortium now,' said Richard thoughtfully. 'You work for me. And so does Paznak.'

'You want me to go down and see how he is?'

'That might be a good idea, yes. Yes, please,' he added decisively.

Voroshilov went out, moving swiftly and silently for such a big man. Was there a new spring in his step, wondered Richard, or was it just his imagination?

He turned back to the others and started talking again at once, ideas falling into shape even as he uttered them. 'The supposition that this is a carefully thought-out and meticulously planned action is really inescapable,' he continued. 'I don't know whether anyone on Asov's team noticed – or thought it through if they did – but it seemed to me that the DVD had to have been made some time ago. Perhaps even before the kidnapping itself. I really can't think of any other way the kidnappers got it back to Major Kebila's men that fast. It was only a matter of an hour or so, if Kebila was telling the truth about having worked on it already before he showed it to us. I don't know how long it would take to set up something like that and burn a disc, but I'd be surprised if it could be done from scratch in so short a space of time. Therefore it had to have been at the very least in an advanced state of preparation long before the kidnapping took place.'

Richard paused. Looked around the room.

Shrugged. 'I'm just not sure what exactly that notion implies. What actual hardware would the PPLD need to produce something as impressively professional as that? And how would they need to go about it? Would they have needed a studio, as Asov and Kebila seem to think? Would it need to be nearby? Could they edit bits in and out – like the names of the kidnap victims – or would that be just too obvious in the finished product? Are any of you really up to speed with the latest media technology?'

They all shook their heads as he gazed around them. Then Morgan said slowly, 'I don't know, Richard. But I think I know a man who might.'

Five minutes later the jarringly cheerful countenance of Third Officer Callum McKay filled the screen of the videoconferencing facility. Richard had half expected to see *Prometheus*'s radio operator. But no. Apparently the Third Officer knew even more than Sparks about this kind of thing.

'Yes,' he admitted cheerfully. 'You got me, Captain. I'm a total computer nerd. What can I do for you?'

Richard explained the situation and what seemed to have happened so far.

'Well, if it was me,' allowed McKay thoughtfully if tactlessly, 'all I'd need is a fairly up-to-date laptop with Internet access and a DVD burner built in. Nothing fancy or particularly expensive. Pretty standard kit. If I were being tricky I'd maybe want a webcam for ease of communication. And ideally some kind of secure comms line to stop people eavesdropping on me. It's amazing what sort of information people send out unprotected into the ether. Makes even the British government look careful. On the other hand, if I'd got it all set up anyway I could use one of the pre-prepared carriers if I wanted. Jesus, I could even put it on MySpace or YouTube...'

'Right,' said Richard, glancing around the blank faces and the shrugging shoulders in the Nelson Mandela Suite. 'Then what would you do next?'

'Well, like I said, I'd have previously set up my studio facility, have cameras ready to roll so to speak – though a little webcam at the far end would do just as well. Or a cellphone with Internet capability. And have my newsreader – so to speak – all primed and ready...'

'OK, we understood that. Then?'

'Then I'd just signal to her – on a video link like the one we're using now, if I had a webcam my end as I said. Or on a cellphone if I didn't. I'd log on to the site she's broadcasting from with my laptop and get her picture up on the screen. She'd read out the speech as prepared, putting in the names of exactly who I'd taken, and I'd burn it straight on to the DVD with the computer's disc burner.'

'And where would this studio arrangement have to be?' demanded Richard.

'Anywhere.'

'Do you mean that literally?'

'Yup. Anywhere in the world with access to

the Web. Which is, of course, worldwide; so yes. Literally anywhere. It could even be on the International Space Station, I guess. Or the Moon, in theory—'

'And you could make the DVD – burn it – in real time?' Richard interrupted impatiently.

'I don't see any reason why not.'

'So how long for the whole process?'

'Well, I haven't seen the finished product so I can't estimate how long it might take to set up the studio end, so to speak. But once you'd established your web link and briefed the news-reader on what details you wanted revealed, then almost real-time, as you said. However long the disc runs for plus whatever time it took to make contact, agree the script, get a decent take – say two or three for safety's sake – and finally get the disc to wherever it was found. You could do all that in an hour, maybe ninety minutes easy. The only other element is how far from the original crime scene you'd have to go to get a secure location and a decent signal for your laptop.'

'Right,' said Richard decisively before Mc-Kay could get sidetracked into any more specu-lation. 'You've given us lots to think about. Thanks for that. We'll call back if we need clarification.' Richard broke the contact and looked around the room again. 'Where on earth does that get us?'

McKay's innocently cheerful intervention had gone some way to freeing tongues, if not to-wards lightening the mood. 'It emphasizes the political nature of the thing,' said Simeon slowly. 'I simply cannot conceive of any local – locally organized, locally funded and locally equipped – criminal gang getting their hands on this kind of hardware and the expertise to use it like this.'

Richard nodded, but it was Jim who said, 'I agree. No one outside government circles and security forces has had access to that kind of equipment since President Banda threw out the last of the international NGOs. Médecins Sans Frontières, I think it was.'

'Except the broadcasters,' emphasized Richard.

'I doubt it. Too tightly controlled. The whole of the press is. Patrice Salako at the newspaper is nowhere near the free agent he seems. And as for Charlotte Uhuru...'

'And yet,' said Richard thoughtfully, 'I noticed a strong similarity between Miss Uhuru and the woman on the DVD. That alone might make it seem local. Matadi features...'

'No,' said Simeon forcefully. 'You're wrong there. Matadi features are very distinctive – pale skin, almost ivory in some lights, short chins, broader noses and full lips. And very distinctively long, almost oriental eyes. Charlotte Uhuru isn't Matadi. She's Hutu. Her family were originally from Rwanda. Fled the troubles before she was born.'

Richard realized he had seen an almost perfect Matadi face, just like Simeon had described. In Fort Zinderneuf. It belonged to Dr

Celine. And thinking of the doctor tricked off something else in the restless snake pit of his seething brain. Something that someone had said at the time. Something that seemed as though it might be important now. He opened his mouth to ask the question...

The door buzzer sounded. Richard closed his mouth and decided to take the opportunity of answering it while he mulled over the implications of all this new information. But his thoughts went on to the back burner at once, for Voroshilov had not merely visited Paznak. He had brought him back with him.

Although the right side of Paznak's head was swathed in bandages, his eyes were clear and his first words showed that he was well past the disorientation that had made him shoot at them so wildly. The grim lines of his Slavic face showed that he was beginning to become all too well aware of the situation he and Voroshilov had found themselves in. 'Is it true?' he demanded in thickly accented English, facing Richard belligerently, nose to nose, as though it was all the Englishman's fault.

Richard guessed all too acutely what Paznak was talking about. 'Yes it is,' he said. 'Mr Asov fired you and I hired you. You work for me now – or you're freelancing on your own out in the city. Flat broke, unarmed, with neither papers nor local contacts. It's your choice. And now's the time to make it.'

Paznak swung round to Voroshilov, his face working, all-too-painful belief beginning to fill his slab-square cheeks with blood.

'I've made up my mind, like I told you,' Voroshilov told him less than helpfully, still speaking English. 'We've worked as a team since the old days of glasnost. But you can end it now if you'd like to. I stay. You go if you want.'

'One other thing,' persisted Richard, almost gently, all too well aware that he was dangerously close to wasting time and losing momentum, but well aware into the bargain that there might be considerable benefits in winning Paznak over to their side, 'if you stay, then you're a Heritage Mariner man all the way. One hundred per cent.'

'Body and soul, same as the rest of us,' said Morgan Hand, helpfully.

'Mind and memory,' added Simeon Bourgeois.

'And everything that you bring with you becomes ours,' concluded Jim Bourne, his voice suddenly sounding unsettlingly like that of Satan tempting a wavering soul. 'Every little memory and suspicion. Every little Bashnev-Sevmash secret.'

'Not,' added Voroshilov witheringly – and Richard never really worked out whether his words were calculated to cause the effect they did or not, 'that anyone would trust a stupid Slav like you with any really important secrets!'

'I know plenty of secrets!' countered Paznak angrily. 'More than you have any suspicion about!'

'Well, bring them to the table,' insinuated Jim,

unsettlingly demonic still, becoming some-thing out of a Le Carré novel. The interrogator George Smiley, perhaps. 'Let's see if we can do a deal.'

'What is the deal that's on the table between Makarov, Asov and President Banda?' asked Richard forthrightly. 'What will they be talking about when they've discussed the likelihood of getting Anastasia and my wife back alive?'

Paznak hesitated, his long dark eyes sliding from one face to another, calculating the odds like a gambler at a roulette wheel; like a mer-chant in an eastern market.

'No papers,' hissed Jim Bourne. 'No way out. No friends. No job. No money. No gun.'

'And you know they'd send Ivan Vrithov after you the minute they knew you were out on the street,' added Voroshilov. 'It would probably be a race between Vrithov and Kebila to see who could get to your sorry ass first.'

Paznak caved in. Started speaking language so far out of character that at first Richard won-dered if he had slipped back into Russian. 'They'll be talking placers; especially lateritic environments upstream which are apparently full of gold,' said Paznak baldly. 'Diamonds in the alluvial deposits on the river bed. And they'll be talking coltan and cassiterite.' He looked around their stunned faces. Then, hav-ing taken the first step, he proceeded in a con-fessional rush. 'Gulin used to spout all this stuff when he was nursing the vodka bottle and I was nursing him. I wasn't really interested at first, but he went on and on about it, so I started a bit of investigating of my own. I mean I used to be a detective, for God's sake. And wet-nursing Fedor Gulin is just so fucking boring!' He took another breath. Glanced at them all, but didn't meet any eyes. Especially not Voroshilov's.

Voroshilov looked to Richard as though he too had just been hit in the head with an ebony war club as his so-called stupid Slavic friend went on. 'The Benin Light crude in the offshore fields is only the tip of the iceberg; it's designed to provide the funding for the upriver work. They're planning to spend their oil fortune getting gold to precipitate out of the river itself while they dig up the river bed looking for diamonds under something called a false bottom. And they'll be tearing coltan and cassiterite out of the mines in the delta. President Banda must have been talking to someone down in Congo or over in Rwanda and suddenly realized he was sitting on another, even bigger fortune, if he can get someone ruthless enough to get upriver and grab it for him. Like they have in Kivu, Katanga, Ngungu, Kalima and the rest. Most of the coltan is supposed to go east across the continent and out of Somalia to China, where they use it in PlayStations, MP3 and MP4 players, new-generation cellphones and so forth. Cassiterite comes bound to iron deposits that are worth a fair bit in the States, but the cassiterite itself is the prime ore for tin and it's easy enough to separate from the iron. And you just know what the market for tin is like – for the Heinz company alone! And that's before you get into the industrial solder market with no more lead-based solder allowed worldwide, and rustproofing motor cars everywhere from Detroit to Shanghai, stopping off at Datsun on the way.'

'So the delta could be worth more than the oilfields!' whispered Simeon, awestruck. 'Who would ever have imagined such a thing?'

'Distilling gold, you say,' added Charles Le Brun. 'Gold out of the river water.'

'In huge amounts if they do it right, Gulin thinks. It washes down from the mountains inland and dissolves because of the tropical environment.'

'And diamonds!' whispered Morgan, her eyes gleaming at the very thought.

'How long has this been going on, Paznak?' demanded Richard, frowning, his mind whirling like a Catherine wheel on Bonfire Night as he tried to calculate the implications of what the Russian was saying.

'It's been a fairly long time in the planning. Getting field men up the river and into the delta. Setting up the basic outposts to test the theory on the ground. But it's all still small beer.'

'Big enough to have done some serious damage, if that DVD is anything to go by,' countered Richard.

'Obviously. Smashing up the river bed to look for diamond deposits would do that, I suppose,' Jim's precise accent interposed, his tone showing that he like Richard was fighting to see the

223

full implications of the Russian's revelation. 'And I guess that the mines are really *mines*, if you know what I mean. I don't think you can opencast for cassiterite. They must be sending people underground. In the middle of the delta that has to be incredibly dangerous work...'

'But they're only starting out,' emphasized Paznak. In for a penny in for a pound now that he had so emphatically turned his coat; as willing to be hung for a sheep as a lamb. 'As far as I understand it, the full financing is due to come from the first big oil shipments. President Banda will match them dollar for dollar, but it's a deal, not a charity. If they've got it right then the pack of them will make a killing big enough to make Wall Street look like a piggy bank.'

'But in the meantime,' whispered Jim Bourne, 'it's all up for grabs. Whoever gets the delta gets the deal.'

'The whole of the country has been looking west,' agreed Simeon. 'All the security, from General Bomba to Major Kebila and on down, has been working to funnel the Benin Light out and the oil revenues in.'

'Only now, if what you say is right and Gulin's drunken babblings are accurate, then the game's gone round one hundred and eighty degrees on them,' said Richard. 'Now it's not the oilfields that are the real prize. It's the delta. And while President Banda controls Granville Harbour, the refineries and the docks, someone else entirely controls the delta.'

He gazed round them all, his mind still whirling and sparking, seeking to get a handle on the implications of what he was beginning to understand. 'Dr Julius Chaka and the PPLD control the delta. Or they say they control it and have every intention of controlling it in the near future if they don't quite do so yet.'

'So why,' asked Jim Bourne, posing at the very least a $64,000 question, 'why in hell's name do they want to kidnap Anastasia Asov?'

Eighteen

Campaign

Had Richard really taken the time to stand back and get a global look at the situation after Paznak's revelations, he would have seen at once that he was always bound to go upriver into the heart of the delta. That's where Bashnev-Sevmash had their secret workings. That was where Dr Julius Chaka was. That's where the PPLD bases were. That's where Robin and Anastasia had to be. But to be fair, even had circumstances made this situation clearer to him earlier than they did, he would have wanted to test the theory; to be certain, before he committed himself, his friends, employees, his vessels and his company to his desperate campaign.

'We could sit here speculating all night,' he said in part answer to Jim's final question. 'But it would be little better than guesswork. What we need are cold hard facts. Or as close to cold hard facts as we can get.'

'Do you think Major Kebila knows what Gulin knows?' asked Morgan, apparently apropos of nothing.

'I'll bet General Bomba does,' answered Richard at once. 'Maybe even Colonel Nkolo. They were both invited to this meeting with the President and Bomba's family, of course. But I get the feeling that Kebila may not quite be in the same loop. Why?'

'Because of the boy. If what Paznak says is right, the boy could have some pretty vital knowledge. Any of the kidnappers could.'

'That may be why they were so careful to take their wounded,' suggested Simeon. 'I mean we can take it for granted that they'll be organized in classic cell structure so that no one will know anything more than a few names and a fraction of the big picture. But anyone who's been up-river might well know just a little bit more than that.'

'A vital detail...' agreed Richard. 'It could be anything.' As he spoke he was in action. 'And if Kebila knows just how big a deal he's dealing with the boy will be in Fort Zinderneuf before you can say *Beau Geste*.'

He opened the door and stepped out into the lobby. 'Better here than there, I'd say. Morgan. This may need a woman's touch. And Simeon, a friendly face. How's your Matadi?'

'I speak Matadi fluently,' said Simeon in fluent Matadi.

'I suppose that means you can speak it,' said Richard, hesitating at the lift door. 'Let's hope the boy's in a fit state to listen and respond. No, I think the lift's too obvious. And far too exposed if there's anyone ill-intentioned waiting.'

On that thought he wondered whether he would be wise to take Voroshilov's SIG Sauer or Paznak's Glock with him. But then his good sense reasserted itself – men with guns got shot at.

Men with guns got shot full stop.

Behind the Hepplewhite chair where he and Robin had first seen Voroshilov there was a modest door with the universal Fire Exit sign above it. Richard crossed to this and led the little team down.

They reached the back of the lobby swiftly and silently. Richard led them towards the corridor that led down to the clinic as casually as he could – all too well aware that nothing they did out in the public areas was likely to escape the notice of André Wanago or his team. And that meant Kebila would be alerted the instant the manager thought they were up to anything suspicious. Always assuming the guard the major had left on the clinic door didn't radio in a report at once, of course. In some places and situations Richard might have hoped for slackness or downright dereliction of duty from a guard on a boring detail. A carelessness that might have made it easy to get to the boy unnoticed through some cunning, sleight of hand or bribery. But not from one of Kebila's men, he suspected.

But there was no guard on the outer door. Richard held up his hand and his two companions hesitated at his back. With only the faintest squeak of crêpe sole on marble slab, Richard moved forward until he could see into the inner room. The guard was there and he was holding his SA80 in fire position, hugged tightly to his shoulder, pointing the automatic weapon at someone on the far side of his tense body. Richard could see no more, but he could hear a heated conversation. In a language as impenetrable to him as Greek was to Casca in *Julius Caesar*. Between an angry man – the soldier, he assumed – and an equally angry woman.

He gestured Simeon forward.

'It's Matadi,' Simeon confirmed after a moment in the merest thread of whisper. 'Whoever the woman is, the sergeant has her under arrest. She says she is only here to tend the boy. The sergeant says Major Kebila thought she might come and Colonel Nkolo and Kapitaine-commandant Moputo have left orders that she must be detained again. He says it was a mistake to release her after the atrocity at Fort Zinderneuf this morning. General Bomba has some questions for her. Kebila is on his way.'

'It must be Dr Celine,' breathed Richard, frowning, his mind full of unwelcome images from earlier – of the brave and apparently innocent doctor helplessly at the mercy of the ruthless general in an all too vividly imagined Fort Zinderneuf torture chamber. He briefly regretted his decision about the Russians' handguns. But then again. Perhaps this was a situation that called for brains before brawn.

He stepped back, crowding Simeon into the doorway, their shoulders walling Morgan in the passage. 'I say, excuse me,' he said loudly, striving to look and sound like a man who had just this second stepped into the room. 'Is the doctor here? My friend feels terribly ill. I think it must be something she ate...'

The sergeant swung round on the first word. He was a big, square man and filled the doorway. His SA80 was too big to come out past his massive torso so he had to lower it. Richard's wise eyes noted that, good soldier that he was, the sergeant had kept the safety on. For a nanosecond he was tempted to attack, but the flow of the words he kept on babbling somehow distracted him. Especially as his voice seemed to have been transformed into the cut-glass tones of a vapid Bertie Wooster addressing the faithful Jeeves.

A tall woman of familiar and unmistakably Matadi appearance appeared at the sergeant's shoulder. 'I'm a doctor,' she said in English as perfectly accented as his own. 'May I see your friend?'

'Wait!' snarled the sergeant. But he spoke in Matadi and although Richard recognized the tone, he did not obey the order. 'I say, would you?' he said and stepped forward once again.

The sergeant's gun came up then, but Richard was almost chest to chest with the soldier and the SA80 snugged into his armpit, still with the safety on. Once again Richard regretted the SIG and the Glock – either would have made a potent club. But no sooner had the thought occurred than it became outmoded. Dr Celine hit the sergeant on the back of the skull with a bedpan. The pan was heavy enamelled iron and the assailant was, after all, a medical woman so she knew just where to focus the greatest force. The sergeant slumped from vertical to horizontal while the weapon was still echoing like a modest gong.

Surprised though he was, Richard nevertheless had the presence of mind to close his arm down hard, hoping inconsequentially that the gun oil would not stain his jacket. The SA80 slipped out of the sergeant's grasp as the portage strap slid off his shoulder and the gun remained exactly where it was. Until Richard thoughtfully took it in his right hand and passed it back to Simeon, who hefted it familiarly. 'Do we need to tie him up? Gag him to stop him raising the alarm?' asked Richard.

'No. Pull him on here and put him on Baptiste's bed,' the doctor ordered shortly. Richard obeyed and was surprised to see the wounded boy standing fully dressed and rigid at the bedside, wide awake but clearly gripped by an overwhelming array of shock-sharpened emotions. He was tall, whip-thin. His head seemed far too big for his body, like a cannonball balanced on a rag-clad broomstick. It was difficult to judge his age, for his gaunt black features seemed only a little younger than Tutankhamen's, though they were in the classic Matadi mould. His eyes were wide, guarded, frightened and suspicious. Fair enough, thought Richard. The last white man he had seen had shot him. And a good number of his friends, come to that.

As Richard worked and Simeon handed the SA80 to Morgan then came through to help him, so Dr Celine swiftly put the bedpan aside and pulled a syringe out of a cupboard. 'This will keep him quiet,' she said and as soon as the comatose soldier was on the bed she injected the contents into his neck. 'This is where I should say that he'll wake up in a few hours' time with a terrible headache,' she said drily as she worked. 'But after the bedpan he won't notice the hangover at all. Who are you and why are you so willing to help me? This is the second time today...' She straightened on the question and looked Richard straight in the eye.

'Come up to my suite and I'll explain,' he said. His hands seemed to have taken on a life of their own. They were unlacing the sleeping sergeant's size-twelve boots as he spoke.

'I've heard that one before,' she said.

There was a directness about her that appealed to him. He remembered the first glance they had exchanged in Fort Zinderneuf. That feeling that they were old friends. That they had been more than that, perhaps, in some previous life. As she spoke he found himself wondering whether she felt the odd attraction too. 'And I don't have a lot of time,' she persisted. 'Kebila is on his way and he won't be coming alone. Baptiste here may be able to stand, but he won't stay upright for long. I have to find some place I can continue to tend him.' She looked around.

Her gaze seemed to reach out beyond the clinic, the hotel, the compound, into the darkness of the still benighted and dangerous city. 'Somewhere really well equipped. Somewhere safe.'

And without any thought at all, Richard said, 'I have somewhere safe if we can get to it. Somewhere with facilities as good as these.'

That same direct gaze looked deep into his eyes again. 'Then we do need to talk,' she said, decisively. 'But we have no time to waste. Baptiste and I will come up to your suite at once.'

This time they did take the lift, though Richard knew André Wanago would be on to his friend Kebila as swiftly as the sleeping sergeant must have been alerted by the sight of the woman and the unguarded boy. Baptiste would not have been able to make the stairs, however, though he was so skeletal that any of them could probably have carried him with ease. As they stepped out into the lobby, they were welcomed by the vision of Voroshilov back on guard. And the sight of him struck Richard. 'Dr Celine,' he said.

'I'm just Celine to my friends,' she answered.

'The man who shot Baptiste is in my suite with me. He's no longer any danger to the boy but...'

'It might be a shock to see him. Yes. Well thought.' Celine stooped and looked earnestly into the boy's wide eyes. She whispered rapidly as the lift doors slid shut behind them.

The boy answered in a couple of gruff monosyllables and the woman laughed. 'He would not have recognized him in any case,' she said, straightening. 'It was too dark to see what was going on at all. But now that he knows the truth, your friend had better watch out!'

'I think he'll be able to take care of himself,' said Richard easily, and opened the door to the suite.

Celine's arrival seemed to galvanize the team, thought Richard, putting the boots down on the table beside his laptop. Certainly those who knew anything much about Granville Harbour and its recent history. It was as though he had shown up with the man for whom the suite was named. Or had arrived in downtown Calcutta with Mother Theresa in tow. And a combination of Celine's priorities and Richard's unthinking offer also changed the track – and the immediacy – of their plans.

But it only brought nearer something that had always been almost inevitable, Richard suddenly understood. The Royal Granville Lodge might make a suitable base for Max Asov and Felix Makarov, but it no longer suited him. Quite the reverse, indeed, for his plans were clearly going to diverge even further from theirs. And only trouble could come from plotting two such widely divergent courses in such dangerously close proximity. Besides, Richard had still not recovered from the simple shock and outrage of Major Kebila's first arrival. Though to be fair they had been subsumed in a

great deal more overwhelming shock and outrage since.

But for the first time since he had pulled on
his socks and underwear after the shower he
had taken upon returning without Robin, Richard had a clear and immediate plan. 'We're on
the move,' he announced. 'We go as quickly
and secretly as possible, but we take every
Heritage Mariner employee with us and we take
Celine and Baptiste as well.'

'But where are we going?' demanded Charles
Le Brun.

'No. I assure you. The woman and the boy are
with Captain Mariner and the sergeant is sleeping like a baby. I tucked him in myself. There is
nothing anyone here can do until you arrive.'
André Wanago broke contact with Laurent
Kebila, put the handset back in its cradle and sat
back in his big leather office chair. No sooner
had he done so than the intercom from the front
desk buzzed urgently. He depressed the button
with a long, perfectly manicured index finger.
'Yes?' he demanded in impatient Matadi. He
had left orders not to be disturbed.

'The Heritage Mariner team are pulling out.
They want to leave at once.'

'What?'

'They are standing here with their suitcases
packed. Everything...'

'All of them?'

'Apparently so, sir. And with everything they
brought, as far as I can tell. We had no warning.

235

They didn't even use a porter...'

'I'm on my way.'

'But they want their papers, their accounts, transport to the airport. And they want it all now!'

'Stall them. I am on my way.'

But even as he pulled himself, frowning, to his feet, André thought better of his promise. Even were the front desk eager to help, processing everything at such short notice could take an hour and more. He eased his long, slender frame back into his seat and picked up the handset once again. He pressed the recall button with his thumb and put the instrument to his ear.

'Kebila.'

'It is André once again, Laurent. Things have taken an unexpected turn here since we last talked.'

The major gave a bark of grim laughter that rang through the ether over the grinding rumble of a half-track running at full speed. 'Captain Mariner and Dr Celine were bound to be a challenging combination. The fact that they seem to have got the better of Sergeant Major Tchaba warned me as much. But what on earth have they managed to achieve in less than ninety seconds?'

André explained.

'And you are certain they are all there? All the Heritage Mariner people?'

'My night manager seems to think so.'

'And only the Heritage Mariner people? No

unexpected locals. A striking woman, for instance? Or a wounded boy?'

'Ah. I see your point. I am on my way to the front desk at once. How long will you be?'

'I will be as quick as possible. Both General Bomba and Colonel Nkolo are trying to attract my attention and I don't know how long my comms equipment can continue to malfunction. I think your information may have rendered it completely useless for the time being, however. I really do not want to be distracted from this situation – even by regimental superiors or general officers. It is extremely fortunate that neither of them has this number.'

'My very thought, Laurent. I will call you back the instant I have more information. In the meantime I will hope to see you soon.'

'You may bet on it, André.'

With his mind racing, André hung up once again, shrugged on his jacket, shot his cuffs and ran lightly up the stairs that joined his office with the main reception area. The distant promise of dawn bled upwards in the eastern sky beyond the crystal windows and above the steaming delta. Reception was deserted except for the last of the night staff and the first of their morning replacements. So that the crowd of departing guests standing amid the modest mountain of their luggage seemed almost threatening. There should have been ten counting the missing Mrs Mariner. There were nine. André performed two head counts as he crossed the echoing space, making assurance doubly

237

sure. The newly arrived American from the tanker in the harbour was there. But the Russian thugs were not. They would be something else for Laurent's men to take care of when he arrived. Captain Mariner towered impatiently in the midst of all, however. And there was no sign of Dr Celine or the wounded boy. Though some of the cases were capacious enough to have held them, André noted. Possibly even the missing Russians too.

'Captain Mariner. How may I be of service?'

'Ah, André. We're checking my people out. This unfortunate business with my wife has ruined all hope of completing our business. I no longer need to part with the vast sums needed to keep half a dozen useless lawyers in the lap of luxury. I don't even know where Mr Asov and Mr Makarov have got to...'

'They have remained overnight in the presidential compound...'

'Indeed. Well, we do not propose to remain anywhere any longer. We want our papers and our accounts. And transport to the airport at once, if you please.'

'Of course. I will send for the limousines on the instant. General Bomba still has command of the helicopters, unfortunately.' He shrugged accommodatingly. 'But it will take a little while for us to complete all the formalities, I'm afraid. May I suggest that you all leave your cases here and return to the comfort of the Nelson Mandela Suite? We will call as soon as everything is prepared. In the meantime I will have an early breakfast sent up. With the compliments of the management, of course...'

Nonplussed by André's urbane quick thinking, the bellicose Englishman capitulated. 'Very well,' he acquiesced. 'Call us just as soon as you're ready.' And he turned, and led the whole troupe towards the lifts.

'What do we do?' asked the night porter, not a little awed.

'We prepare the accounts, cretin, and get ready to bid farewell to these troublesome people. Though they may not all be going precisely where they are planning to go. Now get on to the phone and order everything as I said. *Vite!*'

In fact André simply meant for the porter to rouse the night chef into preparing an early breakfast, but the porter roused the garage into the bargain.

So that simple good luck sealed the only little loophole in Richard and Celine's plan.

Nineteen

Commando

'What in hell's name is this?' snarled Laurent Kebila as the half-track finally ground to a halt outside the Granville Royal Lodge. The battered vehicle with its dusty camouflage paint-job and its mud-spattered bodywork sat like an ogre at a wedding behind a pair of pristine white limos. As the driver to whom the question had been addressed shrugged his ignorance, the exhausted major slammed his fist against the glass behind his shoulder. *'Out!'* he ordered the well-armed squad in the back. 'And *you* go and tell those monkeys to move. I won't have time to hang around here after I've picked these people up!'

Both men swung down from the cab at once. As Kebila sprinted up the red steps with his tight little command at his back, the driver strolled stiffly across to the nearest limousine, whose boot was open and half-filled with luggage. 'Hey, monkey,' he called in military Matadi, 'my boss the major wants you to know that if you don't get these pretty toys out of his way at once he's as likely as not to drive his

240

half-track right over the top of them! And believe you me, he could do it too!'

It was only when he had finished delivering himself of this speech that the driver got close enough for a good look at the chauffeur he was talking to. Who, as he straightened up, turned out to be a tall white man with thick black hair, Brylcreemed to a rule-straight parting, a pencil-thin moustache and big jug-handle ears. And the strange white chauffeur was holding, in an extremely businesslike manner, a very danger-ous-looking Glock handgun with a literally dazzling red-dot sight.

Laurent Kebila paused at reception. His men formed up automatically amid the last of the hand luggage. André was there with his men, frowning over the paperwork, which they were filling in as slowly as possible. André glanced up as the major approached. 'They're all in the Mandela Suite,' he confirmed. 'I sent breakfast up half an hour ago just after I called you for the second time. Nothing to report since then.'

'Except for a couple of bloody great limou-sines immediately in my way! I've left orders for them to be moved at once. Now give me the pass keys, please. I have no intention of knock-ing on the door!'

'Well...' André handed over the keys, then shrugged. 'The limousines add to the illusion that we are fulfilling their request. And I have reserved seats on the eleven thirty flight to Paris for them all...'

'You may be certain, André, that they will by no means all be flying out today. Some of them will never be flying out at all, in fact, unless they're very careful indeed!' And on that threatening note the exhausted and all too clearly stressed-out officer led his four-man commando to the lift. They stepped in. The doors wheezed shut.

And the instant that they did so, what looked to André like the whole of the Heritage Mariner contingent burst out of the stairwell door. Looking neither to right nor left, as well drilled, focused and efficient as the major's soldiers, they crossed the reception area and went out through the doors. In the instant before the security alarm went off, André was just able to see that the missing Russians were on point and rear guard, both seemingly very well armed indeed. And there in the midst of the tight little group, almost as tall as their grim-faced leader, was the familiar figure of Dr Celine.

André reached for the internal phone and pushed the button marked Mandela. As the instant connection began to ring and ring and the redundant alarm began to shrill, the great glass doors beyond the security gate opened and closed. A zephyr of hot, humid dawn breeze reached the awestruck André. Even through the almost soundproof glass and over the insistent alarm he could just hear the sound of doors slamming and of engines starting. No problem about having the limousines moved, then, he thought. He was concentrating so hard on what

242

was going on outside that Laurent's enraged reply almost made him drop the phone.

'What now?' snarled the angry officer.

'They've gone. All of them. Dr Celine, the boy I guess, the Russians, all of them. They must have been waiting on the stairs. Watching. They appeared the instant you got in the lift...'

'I can see they've gone! That they're not here, at any rate. Where have they gone?'

'I don't know. To the airport, I suppose. They've just got into the cars and—'

'Right! I'm on my way down. I'll stop them before they get to Customs and Immigration. I'll stop the fucking flight if I have to. Tell my driver to have the half-track running and ready to go...'

The raging Laurent may have said more. André didn't hear. He was on his way towards the front door. Pausing only to switch off the alarm, he strode out on to the steps outside. Strode out and stopped. He had expected the limos to be gone of course, but he had thought that their drivers would be driving them. Not sitting dejectedly on the red tile steps beside an extremely sheepish-looking soldier.

And it had simply never occurred to him that the half-track would be gone as well.

'Of course I know how to drive it!' Voroshilov shouted over the roaring of the over-revving motor. 'Paznak and I were trained in the militsia. It's not so different to one of ours!'

'Then I can probably drive it myself,' said

Richard. 'I drove a T-80 main battle tank once.'

'Ha! You and James Bond! Did you drive it through St Petersburg with an angel on the top of it?' Voroshilov emphasized his scorn for the Englishman's boast by grating the gears and making the half-track lurch so badly that there were howls of protest from the back.

Richard held his peace, tightened his seat belt and concentrated on the tourist map of Granville Harbour that he had taken from the welcome pack in the Nelson Mandela Suite. It wasn't long on detail, but they weren't trying to follow any back streets. He glanced up just in time to see the limos turn right and flit away up the ridge towards the airport like a pair of doves greeting the dawn. 'We go left here,' he ordered. 'And by and large, downhill is always good.'

There was nothing complex in the plan that he and Celine had dreamed up. Steal some transport. Send most of the team to the airport and hope for the best. Get the rest of them with Celine and Baptiste down to *Prometheus*. The tanker's medical facility was almost as well equipped as the Granville Royal Lodge's. And in Celine they had the doctor required to tend Baptiste. In the tanker also they had privacy to plan, and a measure of freedom to enact those plans without any interference. And absolute security. The massive vessel might be moored within the harbour and would prefer to be helped out by the small flotilla of tugs that had helped her in. But if push came to shove she could cut her lines and her losses and sail for home – albeit painfully slowly under side- and bow-thrusters at first. And only if the anchorage was clear.

She had enough supplies and bunkerage aboard to get to Melbourne or Montevideo, let alone to Milford Haven. And she had an extremely well-equipped gun locker whose contents were now supplemented by the Glock, the SIG and the sleeping sergeant's SA80. There was simply no way to board her or to stop her short of a full military action. And if it ever came to that, Richard reckoned, there was probably nothing that any of them could do.

The half-track lurched out of the diplomatic district and was waved through the police road-block without a second glance. Which was lucky, because Voroshilov showed no sign of slowing, let alone stopping, and he missed the police car's rear bumper by a hair's breadth. Then, true to Richard's simple direction, Voroshilov kept the square olive bonnet pointing downhill and surprisingly soon they could see the mercuric stillness of the bay. Dawn soared up across the sky in front of them all peacock blue with scarlet eyes where cloudlets hung, but somehow none of its splendour was reflected in the dead water dead ahead.

'You think they'll come through to *Prometheus* on the videoconferencing circuit when they get the next message from the kidnappers?' asked Voroshilov, sufficiently relaxed with the half-track now to be thinking about something other than his driving.

'Yes,' said Richard simply. 'They have no reason not to that I can see. And several reasons to do so. At the very least it'll be a good way of making sure they know for certain where I am and what I'm up to. And – who knows? – they may have a sense of decency somewhere. Robin's only in this mess because she stayed to help Anastasia. And they must know as well as President Banda that I will make just as much trouble for this godforsaken country as they could ever do if anything goes wrong. They'll want to cover their backs, won't they? All the way down the line.'

'All the way down the line,' agreed Voroshilov wisely. 'So you're just going to sit aboard this tanker and wait for the call, huh?'

'Oh, no,' said Richard dreamily, beginning to sound at last like a man who hadn't slept in more than twenty-four hours. 'I don't think I could possibly do that. Those are the dock security gates dead ahead. Let's see if you've worked out how to stop this thing yet, shall we?'

Richard ordered that they leave the half-track parked on the dockside at the foot of the gangplank. It had served its purpose in getting them safely through the city with its twin nightmare dangers of police roadblocks and armed kidnappers, but it hadn't quite reached the end of its usefulness. 'That should save a phone call at least,' he observed. 'I should

246

imagine that Herold Nkolo will be on to brother Hercule the moment he sees it.'

'And they'll be in contact with *Prometheus* pretty quickly after that,' agreed Jim Bourne. Simeon and Charles nodded their agreement as the group lugged their kit up the towering side of the vessel. The limos had contained the legal eagles – a brace in each. They would all have fitted easily in one, but that would have left too much transport too easily and immediately available to Major Kebila, Richard had reckoned. And the fact that they had made it to first base showed that his planning so far had been sound.

Richard escorted Dr Celine and the tottering Baptiste to the ship's infirmary and saw them safely ensconced before returning to the bridge, where the rest of them had gone, following Morgan like a herd of sleepy sheep as she resumed her command.

'We need to get some rest,' said Richard. Then he turned to the wide-eyed Third Officer McKay. 'Callum. You hold the watch. Wake us if anything important happens. Wake us in any case at the end of the forenoon.'

'If you're not sure then wake me first,' ordered Morgan, glancing at Richard's grey-chinned, haggard face.

'Aye, aye, Captain!' said Callum. And he meant it.

At noon, local time, with the sun immediately

247

above the communications mast and the haze-distorted foredeck seeming on the point of melting into the steaming bay, they met in the owner's office to plan. Away to forrard, the delta hulk deceptively quiet and cool, like an infinity of green shards scattered across the lower sky. Four hours' sleep, a quick shower and in some cases a shave had revitalized all of them to some extent, and Richard most of all. He was sparking with energy and, as ever, keen to be in action.

But he could only really get down to business when Morgan arrived, back in her captain's uniform. He had a better idea than Jim, Simeon and Charles what the tanker might offer in the way of supplies to help them in any enterprise they decided to undertake, but only Morgan could give them the details. Voroshilov and Paznak might be excellent armaments men should such things as guns be required, but they only had the SIG, the Glock and SA80 to play with for the time being. A thorough search through the gun locker had revealed nothing of even faintly comparable fire power, though several boxes of the ubiquitous 9mm ammunition had Richard looking askance at the Russian first officer, who had held the keys, while Voroshilov got their own guns loaded, zeroed and ready to go.

'There are some very angry people waiting to talk to you,' she announced cheerfully as she arrived.

'Anyone vital?'

'Alphabetically: airport, army, Bomba, customs, harbour master, hotel...'

'Anyone I need to talk to?'

'Wouldn't have thought so. Shall I pull up the gangplank? Major Kebila's on the way, apparently. Alex Magnus and Hal Cornelius have been in touch. The good major apparently decided to let the four of them go on the Paris flight. Left more than an hour ago. They should be somewhere over the Sahara now.'

'Overflying the real Fort Zinderneuf perhaps,' said Richard, his voice light with relief at having got the lawyers out at least. 'Now, the first thing I think we need to look at is the gun cupboard manifest. We have ammo for guns that don't seem to be there any more.'

But no sooner had he spoken than the ship's tannoy sounded. 'Captain. Third Officer McKay here. We have visitors...'

They didn't take up the gangplank. They invited Kebila aboard. Kebila unarmed and alone. It was an invitation that the still outraged officer was happy to accept, for he had matters he most certainly wished to discuss. Property he wanted to recover. Which upset Voroshilov, who had grown quite attached to the SA80 that, after the half-track, seemed to be first thing on the major's list. Perhaps it was just as well that once Kebila had recovered the sergeant's gun he did not think to ask for his boots back as well. But, like Richard, no sooner had the major got the bit between his teeth and begun to list his grievances and what he proposed to do about them than he was interrupted by the tannoy. The words 'Dr Celine' froze on his lips as Callum McKay's voice boomed out:

'Captain and owner to the bridge, please. We have a conference call from Mr Asov and Mr Makarov.'

Richard and Kebila locked gazes like duellists interrupted at a vital point. 'That'll be the second contact,' said Richard, his voice hoarse, his tone dead. Kebila nodded. And all of them were off at once.

Prometheus did not possess a 45-inch flat-screen TV. The sounds and pictures from the hotel were therefore beamed to the largest computer monitor, and the earnest face of the same newsreader, sitting in front of the same PPLD flag, obscured the irrelevancies of the spot price for Benin Light crude. But not before the frowning face of Max Asov had made use of the webcam and the microphone. 'Richard! What is this? Felix and I get back here after a hard night negotiating with President Banda and half his government only to find you've vanished and pissed off not only the hotel staff but a considerable section of the armed forces into the bargain! Is this any way to go about getting our women back? What are you playing at?'

'Put on the DVD, Alex. We'll talk when we've watched it. As I assume you have already seen it yourselves.'

Richard glanced across at Kebila. Had the major and his contacts seen it too? Was that the reason he had been so slow to come after Richard, the half-track and the gun? As he looked at the apparently preoccupied soldier, so his gaze was drawn to a movement in the doorway at his back. Celine moved silently into the frame and stood watching the screen with the rest of them.

'It is now six hours since we made first contact,' said the woman on the screen. Her voice was quiet and calm, simply a newsreader reading the news. 'In that time there has been no cessation of work in the Bashnev-Sevmash mines.' Her calm dark face vanished. In its place appeared a picture of grainy over-brightness. Lines of men toiled in and out of a gaping portal under yellow sodium security lighting. Jungle loomed in apparent monochrome behind them. The churned mud glittered as though diamonds had been strewn there. In the lower corner of the picture was today's date and a time just after midnight. The picture vanished to be replaced by another. This one showed a series of dredgers strung out across a river like the footings of a huge invisible bridge. Every vessel was belching white smoke into a black and starless sky. Upstream the water seemed as black and untroubled as the heavens, flowing under giant fingers of lazily trailing foliage. Downstream it roiled in sickeningly pallid shades and the trees overhanging the water were burned, decaying, dead. The date in the corner remained the same. The time ticked by without a pause. The picture returned to the newsreader. 'Perhaps you hesitate to follow our orders because you doubt we have your women,' she said. Once again her face vanished. Two women sitting side by side replaced her. Their shoulders, crushed together, lined the bottom of the frame. Their hair just brushed the top. Their faces almost filled the screen, with just a hint of background almost lost in the blackness behind them. Robin's face was closed and unreadable. Disturbingly so to Richard, who was finding it very hard to breathe. Anastasia's wide-eyed and petulant. Not least because every stud, bar and ring had been removed from it. The date and time in the corner ticked on, unvarying from the earlier shots of the mine and the barges. Then it was gone again as the newsreader returned. 'We are serious people engaged on a serious project. The future of our nation hangs in the balance and we will stop at nothing to have our demands fulfilled. Mr Asov. We know you have approached the President as we have asked but he will be slow to act unless you continue to do what we have said. And in the other matters you have been utterly inactive. You have until sunset to cease the workings you have just seen. Then we will take away your daughter's sight.' The picture of the woman vanished, to be replaced at once by the picture of a child that looked to Richard at least a lot like a younger Baptiste. The cannonball head sparkling with diamond drops of water that gleamed in its curls and ran down its cheeks. In the midst of it a pair of huge eyes stared unflinchingly into the light above the unvarying date and the clicking time. The eyeballs themselves were utterly white, starkly and shockingly so against the utter blackness of the skin. 'All we will have to do,' continued the voice over the unwavering picture of the blind child, 'is to let her swim in the river downstream of your barges.' The picture vanished, the newsreader was back. 'Finally,' she said, 'it may be that Mr Asov is dragging his heels, trapped between the requirements of his business and the call of family. It may be that Mr Makarov does not feel deeply enough involved to add his weight as we would wish. But that is not true for all of Mr Asov's associates, is it? Mr Mariner, we urge you most strongly to add your voice to ours before your wife shares Anastasia Asov's fate.'

Richard forced down every emotion ruthlessly, though he could feel his blood pressure soar towards stroke-point as he did so. 'Major Kebila. What if anything can you experts tell us about that disc?'

'I can tell you where it was found and how. Who discovered it and when—'

'Irrelevant for the moment. What does it reveal about where these terrorists are – and where they are holding the women?'

'Obviously that they have infiltrated the mines and the placer system—'

'And the President's security if not his closest circles. Yes, I can see that. And if they are at Asov's workings then they are in the delta. Is

253

there anything to give a more precise location?'

'Not that we have been able to—'

But Max Asov was back on the screen and his voice drowned out the major's. 'They are right about one thing! We spent the night talking to the President. He will send a task force into the delta before the day is out – before my daughter's eyes are put at any risk. And we have the means at our disposal to support him in his mission to wipe these people off the face of the planet once and for all!' The raging Russian's face vanished and the screen went dead but his voice still echoed.

'Does he?' asked Richard.

Voroshilov nodded. 'He has an army all of his own,' Paznak added. 'Bashnev-Sevmash security. Ex-Spetsnaz to a man. Armed and equipped like a special-forces unit. If he ordered them to move last night they should be here some time later today.'

Sparks shoved his head out of the radio room. 'I know it's embarrassingly low-tech,' he said, 'but I have a phone call for a Major Kebila. A General Bomba's been trying to reach him for hours and he wants to speak to him at once.'

With Kebila safely out of sight and all too obviously preoccupied, Celine came fully on to the bridge. 'What are you going to do now?' she asked Richard quietly.

'I'm planning to take a small commando up the river and try to talk the women out before Max Asov and President Banda light a firestorm and slaughter every living thing up there.' He gestured to the delta with his chin. 'We've some intelligence and some local contacts. Third Officer McKay may be able to see something Major Kebila's experts don't want to share with us. He did last time. We'll go in armed, just in case, but we'll want to talk first. If we can find the right people to talk to, of course.'

There was a tiny silence, filled by the sound of Kebila having a sizeable strip torn off by his general over the phone.

Then Celine said, 'Keep Baptiste safe here and let me join your commando. I'll show you exactly where to go. I'll tell you who to speak to.'

'How would you have knowledge like that – and why would you want to share it with us?'

Richard's question was subsumed in a sudden cacophony from the computer. Callum was playing back a recording of the videoconference Richard didn't even realize he had made. Max Asov's raging features filled the screen as he shrieked, 'We have the means at our disposal to support him in his mission to wipe these people off the face of the planet once and for all!'

'They're my people,' said Dr Celine quietly. 'And Julius Chaka is my father.'

Twenty

River

The river patrol came at them so swiftly and
unexpectedly that they had no chance of avoid-
ing it or hiding. They were still well out in the
bay, in the full light of the early afternoon, the
better part of half a kilometre clear of the overhanging foliage that clothed the nearest river-
mouth. At Celine's insistence, they had in fact
been much more interested in keeping well
away from the shanty sprawling along the far
bank, and keeping a careful distance from the
pirogues, canoes, dugouts, inner tubes and
motor boats that spread out from it like oil
across the water. It had not really occurred to
any of them to keep a watch for the Granvillian
navy at all, any more than they chose to think
about the Granvillian air force, which did in
fact stretch to more than a few dual-purpose
helicopters.

'An inflatable this size with half a dozen
strangers in it is bound to attract attention,' she
warned, frowning, but speaking about the shanties during the last few moments before disaster
swept towards them at the better part of forty

256

knots. 'We're like a new face in the neighbourhood. And you mustn't underestimate them just
because they live like that.' Her long eyes
glanced across to the bright-coloured jumble of
plastic and clapboard dwellings. 'They may not
have brick walls or metalled roadways organized yet. They may still use jungle drums, clubs
and assegais. But they've cellphones, computers and Internet access too.'

'Tell me about it,' said Callum McKay, who
was seated securely midships with the laptop in
position as he went through his recording of the
videoconference and the DVD once again,
looking for more detail to add to Celine's quiet
certainty.

'They also,' Celine continued severely, looking across at Voroshilov, 'have the most modern
weaponry. And if the rumours are true and my
father has returned with a well-trained army,
then those weapons will be up to battlefield
spec.'

'What sort of battlefield spec?' asked Charles
Le Brun.

'Well, I'd have to guess—'

Before Celine could give her best guess,
Simeon Bourgeois interrupted her. 'There's talk
of an armoured division.'

'A division's the better part of twenty thous-
and troops,' said Jim. 'I'd say a brigade at most.
Of armour. Maybe a division of troops in all,
battlefield and backup. Still and all, that's an
army out here. If it's properly organized, trained and equipped.'

'Back to your T-80 main battle tanks?' Voroshilov asked Richard. 'Not much use in terrain like that, I'd say. With or without wings.'

Richard paid no attention to him. He had seen what main battle tanks like T-80s could do in African jungles. And on wide savannahs too. Not to mention the havoc they could wreak in cities. 'We can be fairly sure they have access to at least one armoured half-track,' he said grimly. Then he sat up straight like a pointer scenting game. 'What's that?' he said, staring forward into the mouth of the river itself. He shaded his eyes with one hand and reached back with the other. Jim Bourne passed the field glasses to Celine, midships beside Callum, and she passed them forward in turn. Richard slammed their eyepieces home, automatically setting the digital mode to full magnification and minimum light enhancement. The vessel speeding towards them was a hydrofoil. It was painted battleship grey and had clearly seen better days. But the two twin .50 calibre machine guns on the up-tilted foredeck looked to be all too well maintained.

Spray flew from the twin blades that lifted the whole of its racing foresection out of the water and the little vessels from the shanty scattered wildly port and starboard. Those that did not move swiftly enough were tossed aside by the bow wave and swamped – or sucked under the keel to oblivion. Nothing between the patrol and the *Prometheus*'s twelve-man Zodiac was big enough to give it pause or make it turn aside.

'It's the river-patrol hydrofoil,' called Richard. 'We need full ahead as soon as you like, please.'

Charles and Simeon sat side by side in the stern, each one holding the tiller control of a massive Honda 6-cylinder outboard. Each one was hugely powerful. Working together, they generated a simply awesome force. And they ran screaming up to full throttle now.

'Callum! Hang on to your laptop,' called Richard. 'Jim, mind the chart. Voroshilov, the guns! There'll be water coming aboard!'

The twin screws bit the thick river outwash. The stern of the big black inflatable sat down at the vee of a green-brown valley of foam-webbed wake. It seemed that only Richard, crouching right to the fore like a massive figurehead, kept the bow in the water at all. But to be fair, the four big grips full of armaments and equipment, much of which had been recovered from the reluctant Oblomov, stowed between his feet and the third officer's probably helped as well. Especially with Voroshilov sitting on top of them like an overprotective mother hen.

True to Richard's warning, spray flew in from every angle as the solid composite of the hull beneath the all but indestructible inflatable gunwales seemed to find every wave, lump and ripple, making each one explode like a depth charge with the power of its passage. But the patrol hydrofoil came on with relentless arrogance, the curving track of its course seemingly destined to intercept theirs, no matter how fast the big twin Hondas raced.

Richard dragged his eyes away from the relentlessly approaching vessel and looked ahead, his mind racing as fast as the outboards. The water of the bay heaved sluggishly, swirled by the relentless outwash of the river. The dizzying array of vessels from the shanty formed no apparent pattern, hanging on the top of the current between here and the makeshift little jetties beside the plastic and clapboard dwellings of their owners like colourful flotsam carried out of the jungle.

But then Richard began to see how those on his right were running across his course away from the blades of the approaching hydrofoil, while those on his left were drifting as contentedly as lotus flowers on the current.

And immediately ahead, the water parted for an instant to reveal the dividing line. And, as if to emphasize what his eyes could see – and his whirling mind was racing to comprehend – a man stepped out of the dazzle just ahead of him, walking across the water like Jesus out for a Sunday stroll. 'Come left!' bellowed Richard, putting out his left hand like an old-fashioned driver semaphoring his intention to turn. 'Come left and get ready to raise the motors on my command!'

The Zodiac raced towards the man walking across the water, its bow high and its slick keel jumping from wave to wave. Richard all but forgot about the hydrofoil now as he concentrated on his countdown. The mud-brown water heaved again, thick as molten chocolate. The waves slid back. The walking man's feet gleamed for an instant, their soles and sides almost shockingly pink. 'Now!' yelled Richard, tearing his throat. And, 'Brace!'

The Zodiac slid up out of the water and on to the mudbank as though it had been just another wave. Such was the vessel's momentum and the smoothness of the slippery mud beneath it that the inflatable didn't even hesitate. It sped across the wave-washed wall of soft earth, past the startled stroller and down into the next deep channel in a flash. 'Down!' shouted Richard and the screaming propellers plunged back into their accustomed element. The Zodiac powered onwards past the shanty fleet, no longer so anonymous – no longer giving much of a damn.

The hydrofoil condescended to vary its course a little at the last possible moment, and skimmed away westwards along the length of the mudbank, with all the deadly arrogance of a thwarted shark. Jim and Simeon eased back on the throttles until the inflatable slowed and settled. 'You think he was after us?' asked Callum, more than a little shaken by the episode, clutching his laptop to his chest like a frightened child with a teddy bear.

'I don't know,' said Richard. 'They didn't start shooting at us. I suppose that tells us something. If we don't get buzzed by a chopper or overflown by something worse in the next few minutes we'll maybe know for certain.'

'Even if he wasn't keeping a careful eye on us,' said Celine quietly, 'someone will be now...' She looked pointedly towards the bank and Richard followed her gaze. In maybe fifty little vessels and a hundred shanties beyond, more eyes than he could readily count seemed to be fastened on them.

They entered the mouth of the river a few moments later and at Richard's direction they started heading for the shade and anonymity of the overhanging jungle. 'I want to get out of sight as soon as possible,' he explained. 'That hydrofoil may well be sending something airborne after us. Callum, can you get on the Net please and check up on any entries under Granville air force.' Then, with his orders still hanging on the silent, stagnant air, they swung over, and in.

And under.

Between the river's mud-cliff bank and the training fall of lianas, creepers and pendant branches that dangled in the water, there was a dim little tunnel. The dappled shade could hardly be said to be cooler, but at least the leaves broke up the bludgeoning power of the afternoon sun. But the free-moving air through which the Zodiac had raced to get here was replaced by a static, fetid, steamy atmosphere. Richard was forcefully reminded of childhood chest infections treated by trapping his head over a bowl of boiling water laced with balsam beneath a suffocating towel. The Hondas settled to almost idling as they pushed the inflatable forwards, with Richard on the alert for dangerously sharp obstructions.

And so the silence settled on them, almost as heavy and oppressive as the atmosphere. The silence was absolute, brooding, unsettling. Richard had never been anywhere this quiet. Even in the wastes of Antarctica – even adrift aboard an iceberg – there had been the eternal moaning of the wind; the restless whisper of sugary crystals as sharp as sand; the stirring and groaning of the ice.

The last jungle-clad river he had sailed had been in the Tanjung Puting National Park in Indonesia. There the forest had been alive with bird calls, with the howls and shrieks of monkeys, apes, orang-utans. It had been astir and alive with a bustling over-fullness of insect and amphibian life. In a tunnel such as this he would have been careful to watch out for scorpions, spiders, snakes and somnolent river crocodiles, all of them chittering, scuttling, hissing, slithering, belching, snoring.

'Here it is,' whispered Callum at last. 'The local air division of the Granvillian armed forces boasts...Let me see...Well, it has its own website and it's recruiting if anyone's interested. Quite a list of planes, Russian MiGs and Tupolevs; French Alouette choppers, which we know about; Chinese Chengdu F7s. Wait a bit though, Wikipedia says most of them are grounded. Well, by the look of it I'd say they had a couple of squadrons of single-seater

Chengdu 7s and maybe one squadron of Tupolev bombers. We'd only need to worry about
the Alouettes, I'd say, and only if they've turned them into makeshift gunships.'

His whisper faded away and they all strained
their ears above the grumble of the Hondas,
listening for the telltale judder of Alouette
rotors. But there was nothing. And being forced
to search the massive silence for an absent
sound simply emphasized the enormity of it.

Nothing.

Only a silence of seemingly unearthly propor-
tions. An absolutely threatening lack of sound
that had characterized the place in the darkness
before the long-ago dawn. A silence that
shortened their breath as effectively as the dead
stench. That cowed even Callum's next hesitant
whispers into silence. A silence in which they
were all uneasily complicit, like conspirators in
a massacre. A silence that stirred the short hairs
on the backs of their necks like ghosts.

It seemed that there could be nothing worse
than that brooding, implacable silence.

And then the drums began.

The drums began to sound so softly at first
that it was only the silence that betrayed them.
Yet when he realized consciously that the
whispering rhythm was stirring the stagnant air,
it seemed to Richard that the beating had
already been in his head for some time. And
deep within his breast dictating the rhythm of
his heart. Although the drums seemed far away
at first, the sound was more threatening than

anything he had ever imagined. Perhaps it was their insidious persistence. Perhaps it was their prehistoric wildness. Perhaps it was that indefinable shiver of atavistic recognition that distinguished the timeless threat from the brash modernity of the helicopter sounds they had all been listening out for. Or perhaps it was the way they seemed to move, their deep bass undertone running up and down the stream ahead, echoing from side to side. But gradually, it was borne upon them that what was truly terrifying was that the drums were getting louder. And that they were almost certainly talking to each other about them.

'I thought you said these people had cell-phones, Celine,' growled Richard, trying as ever to break the almost unbearable tension.

'Drums are cheaper. And you don't have to recharge them,' she replied. Beneath the easy tone of her words, Richard thought he detected nervousness, perhaps fear. And that of course added to the tension he was feeling himself.

'Any idea what they are saying?'

'Not really.' She gave that attractively Gallic shrug.

'The slightest hint would help. Like are they asking, *Where are they?* Or are they saying, *We know where they are.*'

'I really don't think it matters, Richard. If they don't know where we are at the moment, they soon will. They may be looking for us, remember; but we're certainly looking for them.'

'So the drums are our friends,' said Callum.

'You could have fooled me.'

As Callum spoke, the tunnel they were following ended abruptly. The riverside fell back into the ruin of a landing stage and a considerable bay opened up in front of them with all the suddenness of a magic trick. So much so that Simeon whispered, *'Hey presto!'*

On the red mudbank beside the rotting rust red of the landing stage lay the ruin of a paddle steamer. A sternwheeler that might have graced the Mississippi, long ago. Accommodation and bridge house rising through five blistered and flaking storeys to twin smokestacks leaning crazily across the sky. Stern wheel smashed and vandalized, picked over like a corpse beneath a vulture perch. Glass all gone, curtains and furniture hanging half out of windows like the innards of a slaughtered leviathan.

The path from its red-rusted bow led up the bank to the burned-out skeleton of a considerable building. Hanging crazily half off the blackened frontage of the ruin was a dead neon sign announcing CASINO.

It was as still and silent as everything else round here under the weight of the westering sun and constant stirring of the drums. But Richard had the strangest feeling that he was being watched. Observed. Scrutinized. He looked around narrow-eyed, but he could see nothing. 'Where do we go?' he asked Celine and she shrugged and pointed – upstream.

The next section of the delta was by no means as overhung, for they had passed into one of those streams that Richard had described as wider than the Thames at Tower Bridge. The banks rose up on either hand and the trees seemed to be taller, set further apart, almost cultivated-looking. There was a tacit agreement between them that the drums were probably telling of their whereabouts now, so they sat in the middle of the stream and opened the throttles. To be fair, this gave an illusion of safety – there was the better part of a hundred metres of clear water on either hand, too far for any of the weapons they had seen to reach them, except for the guns. And even there, they would need to be pretty accurate or delivering an overwhelming rate of fire.

Under the invigorating effect of the sense of security – no matter how illusory – and the headwind created by their speed, Richard soon started talking, trying once again to overcome the deadening threat of the drums. 'The last time I was on a river like this – the Mau, further south, between here and the Congo – we had to be extremely careful about hippopotamus and crocodiles. But I haven't seen any...'

'And you won't,' said Celine. 'There may be some away upriver, but there are none down here in the delta. Just as there are no lowland gorillas, apes or monkeys, no birds or snakes, no big insects or arachnids any more. Just about the only living things you'll find down here are the mosquitoes. And the people, of course.'

'That's astonishing! How on earth has that happened?'

'Millions of starving people with hundreds of thousands of guns. Everything made of any kind of flesh has been hunted, killed and eaten. The river's been fished out with harpoons, then lines, then nets, then grenades and dynamite. There's nothing left here, any more than there is in the bush. There's talk of cannibalism returning in some places up-country because they've eaten just about everything else. Even the cassava crop is dying out because of the pollution in the irrigation water. And cassava is the least nutritious staple crop there is.'

'That's horrific!'

'As far as the country's concerned, it's simply seismic. Millions of people moved out of the city into the shanties when things got bad. Then when things got worse they moved out of the shanties into the delta. Now the delta is a wasteland hidden under an inedible jungle, they're beginning to move back again. Desperate. Dying. Literally nothing to lose.'

'And your father's moving up behind them with an army. That's precisely the sort of situation that led to the fall of Rome.'

'Ha!' she laughed. 'Who says we never learn anything from history?'

And on the sound of that bark of laughter, the drums abruptly stopped.

With its motors throbbing unnaturally loudly in the sudden, overwhelming silence, the Zodiac swept round a bend in the river and the most unexpected sight of all confronted Richard's awestruck gaze, while at the same time a low rumbling swept over him, as though a volcano was stirring in the distance. The slopes of the banks that had seemed to him so similar to embankments suddenly became embankments indeed, flagged with great grey squares of stone. At the very point of the bend, again with that magically abrupt transition, the cultivated trees gave way to riverside buildings. Public edifices, the size of County Hall and the Houses of Parliament in London or the New York Central Library. And, dead ahead, a great bridge stepped from one bank to the other. Or more accurately, stepped out and stumbled. For its span collapsed into the water dead ahead of them, tearing up the surface like the first great cataract on the Nile.

Apart from the bags beneath Voroshilov the only heavy items aboard were the Honda outboards, and the simple plan was that if the river got blocked, as it was now, they would portage for a short distance. On Richard's signal, therefore, they steered into the right bank, where there were slipways leading up on to the embankment. They pulled the Zodiac up, emptied it and stripped it, then carried the contents and pulled the hull over to the slipway on the far side of the bridge. It was the work of less than half an hour. But as Jim and Simeon were refloating the vessel and remounting the motors while Voroshilov was re-stowing the bags and Callum was checking his laptop on good dry land, Celine climbed up to the top of the embankment itself, and called for Richard to join her.

'Welcome to Citematadi,' she said as he arrived up at her shoulder. As in London, only more so, the meandering river had built itself an elevated valley. So Richard and Celine were effectively standing on a low hilltop looking across a wide valley to the next rise several kilometres away. The city had never entertained pretensions towards a New York skyline. There were almost no skyscrapers. Instead an equatorial Paris lay at their feet, regimented roadways as precise as those in Granville Harbour chopping the place into city blocks. To right and left, a broad multilane highway ran along the elevated embankment, lined on the riverside by the cultivated trees Richard had noticed from the river below. Ahead of them stood the municipal buildings that had warned Richard so abruptly that they were sailing into a city. And beyond them, down the slope, across the valley and up the far slope, more buildings stood, etched to almost supernatural brightness by the sun beginning to sink westward behind their shoulders. Silent. Empty. Home to not so much as a rat.

But where the ravishment of Granville Harbour had still been under way, here the rape of Citematadi was complete. The buildings across which they were looking in the sultry afternoon silence were shells, as though the place was a set for a science-fiction film, in which Richard and Celine were the last couple left on earth.

There was nothing inside the empty brick shells. Here and there they had begun to spread and sag, outer walls collapsing without the inner bracing.

The roadways, from the narrowest alley to the most expansive boulevards, were grassed over. Lamp posts and street signs festooned with liana creeper and ivy. In Granville Harbour there were rubbish piles in gardens and at cross-roads. Here they had nurtured huge bougain-villeas standing taller than the sagging dwell-ings. And in the distance, where the outskirts pushed up hard against the jungle, the buildings gleamed pathetically against the overwhelming rainforest like dwarfs confronted by giants.

'Citematadi,' he breathed. 'A lost city. Like something out of Rider Haggard, Wilbur Smith or *Tarzan*.'

'It's less than fifty years old,' she said, her voice a wilderness. 'It was known as the Jewel of the River as recently as 1985. But it's lost and gone. We'll never get it back. Like your poet Shelley said: "Behold my works, you mighty – and despair." '

But Richard missed her last sad observation, his eye and his mind distracted by a diamond-brilliant glitter in the midst of that tall stand of trees dwarfing the pathetic buildings in the distance. A glitter such as field glasses might make, looking across into a westering sun.

And no sooner had the gleam blazed and vanished, than the drums began again.

271

Twenty-One

Delta

After Citematadi the tributary they were following widened rapidly until it seemed to
Richard they must have reached the river itself.
And that was entirely feasible, for the main
flow came along the north towards the hill-crest
of Granville Harbour while the major part of
the delta wandered away southwards along the
coast towards the Benin Light oilfields.

Under the renewed threat of the drums and
the certainty that they had been spotted and
were definitely being watched, Richard dictated
a course along the southern bank, skirting the
northern edge of the delta where the trees
shaded them to a certain extent. It seemed safer
to him; circumspect indeed, even in the face of
Celine's continued assurances that they were
safe.

They skimmed along the broadening surface,
watching the stream widen relentlessly ahead
even though the south bank opened and closed
to release a succession of further streams that
ran down into the massive wilderness of the
southern delta area.

But it was not only the river that grew so relentlessly. For all too soon they found themselves entering the kingdom of the trees that had dwarfed the outskirts of the ruined city. Hard against the southern bank, the Zodiac seemed more and more reduced to utter insignificance. The river rolled towards them, wider and wider still, making a great brown passage between the tallest trees Richard had ever seen. From his position in the bow of the tiny inflatable at the foot of the cliff-like red-mud bank, they seemed as tall as the skyscrapers Citematadi was so clearly lacking.

Now it was more than the insistent thunder of the drums that cowed them into silence. The Zodiac crept forward between these enormous growths like a beetle crawling up the aisle of a cathedral surrounded by soaring columns.

When Celine said, 'Here,' she had to repeat herself twice before he heard or fully understood.

They turned into a narrow side-stream – almost a U-turn – and at once found themselves rushing forward. Until now they had been pushing against the sluggish current of the great river meandering past them through the northern delta towards the shanties, the city and the sea. Now they had the much more lively flow of the twisting tributary pushing them forward with all its restless power down into the vastness of the southern heartland. And the trees seemed, if anything, taller still. The pounding of the drums was loud enough to drown the throbbing of the engines and the rushing of the water as they whirled forward ever more swiftly. But after five minutes, as mysteriously and unaccountably as ever, the fearsome pounding simply stopped.

Oddly, Richard began to feel a stirring of excitement now. The speed was much more to his taste – especially as the sun was lost away across the western bay and it seemed like evening here already. Only repeated glances at his watch assured him that there were still some hours to the threatened deadline. Each time he looked at the battered Rolex he glanced at Celine and every time she met his eye she gave him a pale but reassuring smile. The first time that their eyes met after they had turned into the little tributary, she leaned forward. 'Nearly there,' she whispered, able to do so now that the drums had stopped. 'It will be soon now.'

And yet time continued to pass, until, of all things, Callum McKay shouted, 'STOP!'

Richard signalled to Jim and Simeon. The Zodiac swung over to the bank and beached at the nearest available landing point and the first moment possible.

'What is it?' demanded Richard.

'We're there, near as dammit. We must be! I just thought you'd like to know.' He glanced at Celine. 'Forewarned is forearmed, after all.'

'Yes,' she agreed, her voice tranquil even under his suspicious stare. 'We are nearly there. But how do you know?'

He held up the laptop triumphantly, its screen

274

bright amid the gathering shadows. He had frozen the picture of Anastasia and Robin sitting glumly side by side. With busy fingers flying, he isolated the area between their heads. 'Look,' he enthused. 'I just isolated and enhanced that area between their heads and...'

There, just visible amid almost impenetrable shadows, was something that looked for all the world like an elephant's leg. Speaking non-stop, Callum pushed his buttons and ran his fingers over the mouse-pad until he had isolated the elephant's leg from the picture. He showed then how he had copied it over into another file and enhanced it to the top of the possible range, elucidating every detail as he went.

And then he explained how he had asked the computer to enlist the help of the Internet in finding out what it might be a picture of. 'It took longer because it looked so much like an elephant's leg that I started with fauna,' he explained.

'But then, there seemed to be so little fauna around – and Dr Celine explained how it had all been eaten anyway – that I thought I'd try flora.' He pushed one final button. 'Hey presto,' he exclaimed triumphantly.

And the screen seemed, disorientatingly, to vanish. For the picture that filled it now was a perfect colour photograph of the gigantic trees with which they were surrounded. Under the picture came the caption, 'Unique to very limited areas of rainforest in the delta region of...'

'Well done, Callum,' said Richard, genuinely impressed. *'Well done!'*

'Well done indeed,' agreed the soldier who stepped out from behind the nearest tree. 'That was a very ingenious thing to have done, young man, though some of the detail of your explication was lost on me, I must admit. I am not really a computer expert myself, though I have many men who are.'

The instant the stranger started speaking, a squad of well-armed men fell in behind him.

The effect was so disorientating, the appearance so sudden and the action so swift, that not even Voroshilov had a chance to grab a gun. Jim, Simeon and Charles had little chance to do more than gasp and gape.

'I wonder if there is anyone quite so quick-thinking and computer literate on President Banda's staff – or in the employ of Mr Asov,' the stranger concluded wryly.

The unsettlingly amiable newcomer was tall – between Celine and Richard in size. Deep-chested and slim-hipped. Whip-lean, looking vigorously fit. His black skin glowed as though it had been recently oiled. He wore standard camouflage battle gear as punctiliously neat and perfectly pressed as Major Kebila's. He spoke English with a slight French accent but with easy authority. He wore the Sam Browne and side arm of an officer but neither his shoulders nor his beret bore any badges of rank. His face was long, his eyes slightly sloping. His nostrils and his lips were almost aristocratically thin. He favoured a short-cropped beard that was just beginning to grey at the angles of his square and solid chin.

Even though the man was in every respect the opposite of what Richard had been expecting, it came as no surprise at all when he added, glancing down at his watch, 'But my daughter would have brought you to me in plenty of time in any case.'

And Celine said, 'Hello, Father.'

They left the Zodiac and everything that it contained under guard, then they all followed Julius Chaka through the enormous trees for another few hundred metres. 'Welcome to Delta Force One,' he said as they stepped out into a clearing, but his voice was all but lost in a distant rumbling. The sound had none of the threat of the drums but it had instead the relentlessly unvarying power of a military barrage. The clearing was full of canvas-sided tents. Far too many, by the look of things, to house the squads of soldiers busy about the place. There were trucks, what looked like tanks. Accommodation, transport and equipment for a regiment, perhaps. But no regiment in evidence.

'Where is my wife?' demanded Richard. 'Where's Anastasia?'

'Not here, I'm afraid,' answered Dr Chaka. 'But they are both safe and well. And would be so even had you not taken a hostage of your own. Where is my grandson?' He turned as he uttered the question, his voice icy, his face folded in a frown, framed by a pair of helicopters that Richard for once could not identify.

Richard gaped, genuinely nonplussed. 'I thought all your relatives were dead, except for Celine.'

'Except for my daughter and her nephew, my grandson, who has been kept safely away from danger until the fiasco of the kidnapping...'

Richard recognized Julius Chaka's voice then. And experienced another half-expected revelation. This was the man who had held the assegai to the back of his neck while Robin and Anastasia were taken away.

'Baptiste is safe, Father,' Celine assured the angry man. 'Largely thanks to Captain Mariner. He is on board the *Prometheus*. In the ship's medical facility.'

'What do you mean *not here*?' Richard's patience was beginning to wear thin. The wound on his neck had suddenly started throbbing once again. And Chaka's anger at the loss of his grandson seemed to ignite an answering outrage in Richard. And all this civilized social chit-chat was not helping at all.

'It is far too dangerous here,' Chaka explained more quietly, almost mollified by his daughter's assurances. 'Or it soon will become so, I should think.' He hesitated, then turned decisively. 'Come with me. I believe you deserve something of an explanation.'

He stepped into the passenger seat of an elderly open-topped jeep. 'Climb in, Captain,' he invited, though his words were all but lost beneath the asthmatic coughing of the motor as the driver started up.

Richard shrugged and climbed aboard. 'Jim,' he invited in turn. Though he might well have gone for Voroshilov if the Russian had had his SIG in its usual place. In spite of the irritating civilized small talk, he did not feel at ease. Quite the reverse. But the alternatives to courteous compliance were severely limited. For the moment at least.

They bounced through quite a sizeable camp, with more tents, vehicles and equipment on display, but few men. And Richard noted with gathering concern that the ancient, asthmatic jeep was amongst the youngest and fittest of the hardware on display. But of course nothing he could see here was anywhere near the top of his list of priorities.

'If our women aren't here, where are they?' he demanded, raising his voice to a near shout.

Chaka consulted his watch once again. 'In the shanties,' he answered shortly. Richard strained to hear and could hardly believe what he heard.

'In the *shanties*?'

'The safest place I can manage. Until I get them into Fort Zinderneuf.'

'I'm not even going to ask,' bellowed Richard. 'I'm sure you're going to explain.'

'Why don't we let her explain a little herself?' said Julius Chaka then. 'Would you like to talk to her?'

Richard was simply stunned by the almost

279

casual offer. 'Talk to her?'

'Of course. I'm afraid we have not got the time to set up a video link, but she has access to a cellphone.' He pulled a cellphone from his belt. 'As do you.' He pressed a button and held the little instrument to his ear. Then suddenly he was speaking in Matadi. A few crisp orders were enough. He took the little phone from his ear and handed it over.

'Robin?'

'Oh, Richard...Thank God!' Her voice was strong and vibrant. In spite of how she had looked on the DVD, this was no kidnap victim, cowed and terrified. Richard's heart came close to bursting with relief.

'How are you, darling?'

'I'm fine. And so is Anastasia. We'll see you later if everything goes to plan. Don't worry about us. I must go now. Take care.'

The line went dead. Richard stood, a great weight lifted from his shoulders, reassessing his options. Realigning his allegiances.

Returning to the same question, albeit from a different point of view: 'I'm sure you're going to explain?' he asked, handing back the little cellphone.

'Oh, I plan to do much better than that,' said Julius Chaka.

The jeep swung into the riverbank as soon as it exited the camp. It drew up a few moments later at what Richard recognized as the top lip of a cliff. The sound was simply overwhelming

280

now. Julius Chaka gestured Richard and Jim to follow, and he leaped down out of the jeep. The smaller cousins of the bougainvillaea bushes in Citematadi replaced the massive trees on this side of the encampment. The three men eased their way through to a well-camouflaged vantage point on the very crest of the cliff-top.

And perhaps the most magnificent sight that Richard had ever seen. The cliff-top they were standing on was the end of a great almost semi-circular curve of cliff. It was not as high as Angel Falls or even Victoria Falls, but it was wider than Niagara. And although only one river plunged over the precipice it did so in perhaps a dozen tributary streams.

But then, in a sight that was unsettlingly familiar, the streams all gathered together at the cliff-foot. A trick of geology that had created this wonderful place dictated that the sloping valley down below should contain them, funnel them, braid them, almost, into one great flow again. A river almost as broad as the waterway they had come up after Citematadi, under the tall trees. And in place of the ruined span, it was straddled by the invisible bridge from the second DVD. The bridge whose footings were the Bashnev-Sevmash barges.

Upstream of the massive vessels the water ran clear and brown. Downstream it was still a sickly chocolate milk. A little breeze stirred and brought to Richard's nostrils the most stomach-wrenching stench he had ever smelt. A mixture of caustic and effluent like the contents of a

281

thousand chemical latrines concentrated into one.

He looked at his watch. If Asov was going to call a halt and save his daughter at the price of his profits he had better do so at once.

But the barges worked on relentlessly until Julius Chaka knelt, placed a little silver ball upon the ground, checked its placing and alignment carefully, then led them away again.

As the outskirts of Delta Force One's camp loomed out of the gathering shadows again, the thunder of a dozen waterfalls receded so that Richard was able to ask, apparently irrelevantly, 'If this is Delta Force One, how many others are there?'

'One.' Chaka seemed amused by the question – or rather, by the acuity behind it, now that Richard's mind was no longer quite so occupied with his worries about his wife.

'And the other one is beside the mines you want closed?'

'A little further away, but yes.'

'Far enough so that when the bombardment begins, they'll have time to clear the workers out, before...'

Chaka wrenched himself right round in his seat and faced Richard, almost nose to nose, his dark eyes gleaming triumphantly. 'It is thinking like that which has got you here!' he shouted. 'But it is time to go home now.'

The jeep wheezed to a stop beside the only helicopter Richard did recognize. A twin-rotored Chinook. The chopper looked in almost every regard the opposite of the jeep. Much more, in fact, like the man who owned and commanded it. Approaching middle age it might be, but it was shiny, powerful, extremely well maintained and ready for hard service.

The Zodiac was in a cargo net that would dangle beneath the long body when the aircraft was aloft. The rest of Richard's little commando was safe inside, strapped into their seats. Not quite under guard, but coincidentally surrounded by soldiers who just happened to be holding SA80s.

Richard accompanied Chaka to the foremost seats immediately behind the cockpit and as they buckled in, the soldier commanded, 'Go!'

Richard never saw precisely what switch the pilot pressed first, but even before the engines coughed or the rotors fore and aft began to turn, the massively amplified sound of drumbeats began to echo from speakers beneath the fuselage. Like a late-medieval monarch using organ music to mask the most secret conversations from prying ears, Julius Chaka was using the rhythm of the timeless drumbeats to camouflage the throbbing of his helicopters.

Richard had assumed that the Chinook would take them directly downriver to Granville Harbour. But as the aircraft lifted out of the clearing and low over the tops of the skyscraper trees, so it skilled away eastwards, upstream, towards the distant mountains where the stream was born. The vertiginous, cloud-capped peaks were little more than a purple smudge on the far horizon now as evening began to creep up from their foothills across their east-facing slopes, away in the far, dark heart of the continent.

Richard would have asked what was going on, because, although he was beginning to understand Chaka's plans, he had yet to think them through properly. But the thundering of the Chinook's rotors would have made talking difficult. The added sound of the over-amplified drums made it impossible. But Chaka made it unnecessary.

As soon as the Chinook was in level flight, he took a laptop out of a pouch on the side of his seat and opened it. In spite of his words to Callum earlier, he seemed to Richard to be pretty familiar with the slim machine. Within a very few moments, the laptop screen was split into eight separate pictures, each bearing an identification number. Straining over to get a clear look at the flat LCD, Richard immediately recognized one of the pictures – no, two. There in the top-left corner closest to him was the view across the magnificent falls. And top right opposite it, the familiar picture of the mine entrance from the second DVD. And there, below the view from the falls – clearly it had been a little webcam Chaka had positioned in the bougainvillaea bush – was the much closer image of the barges, again from the DVD, that had reminded him of the footings of a bridge. The rest of the pictures were roughly similar – anonymous pictures of camps. Delta Force One and Delta Force Two, if he was guessing correctly.

But no sooner had he worked out what the pictures of the encampments represented than they began to be blown apart. With a suddenness that was utterly unsettling and a ferocity somehow made worse by the fact that it was impossible to hear anything other than the beating of the drums, the picture of camp Delta Force One was full of flame and flying debris. Then, one by one, the webcams filming the destruction went to black, their transmissions failing as they were themselves destroyed.

It was possible to work out that Delta Force One was being hit because the camera on the cliff-top was shaking with the earthquake impact of the destruction being rained down on it. And the second webcam, the one whose picture had been on the DVD, showed a huge column of smoke on the cliff-top behind Max Asov's barges. And, suddenly, planes. Slim silver fighters streaking low above the treetops, pouring down fire. And larger, heavier slower bombers framed like vultures against the empty evening sky. The destruction was overwhelming. Awesome in its fearsomeness and its totality. The camera on the cliff-top abruptly stopped working. All the pictures of Delta Force One were black now, except for the one last camera on the far bank of the river that looked steadfastly up past the barges to the volcanically blazing column of smoke on the cliff-top.

Then, with a kind of slow majesty, all the

worse for its seemingly operatic inevitability, a Tupolev bomber came out of the smoke, low over the cliff edge. A rogue aircraft, apparently lost and out of control. It swooped across the picture on the laptop screen like the last of the long dead vultures of the place. Heading straight into the unflinching eye of the camera it crossed the river, as though searching in the lower sky for the roadway on that invisible bridge above the barges.

No sooner had it passed the blazing cliff edge than figures started jumping wildly into the river and swimming for the nearest shore, as though they had been forewarned of what was going to happen next. As they probably had, thought Richard, glancing up at Chaka's still, closed face, and down again.

The Tupolev's bomb doors opened. A series of fat black bombs tumbled lazily into the air. As though in slow motion they swung their blunt points downwards. As though hanging from the black bound circles of their fins, they fell. And in series, from distance to foreground, the barges vanished into towering columns of water, smoke and flame. Until the last picture of Delta Force One, like all the others, went abruptly and permanently dark.

And the instant that it did so, the camera pictures of Delta Force Two and the Bashnev-Sevmash mine workings beside it began to shudder in their turn. And men came boiling out of the mine like an army of panicked ants.

Chaka leaned over to Richard, so close that he

could smell the perspiration and the cinnamon on his breath. 'Now that,' said Chaka, his lips stirring against Richard's ear even though his voice seemed to be coming from far away among the implacable, warlike drumbeats, 'that's what I call friendly fire...'

Twenty-Two

Heart

'They called her *La Cœur Matadi*,' said Julius Chaka, looking down.

Richard could hear him at last because the pilot had turned the drums off and eased the throttle back as the Chinook began to descend. The cargo net with the Zodiac touched the ground beside the wreck of the paddle steamer and someone hit the release.

'*The Heart of Matadi*,' said Richard. 'A very romantic name. But she must have been a romantic boat.' He took a deep breath and asked the question he had been bursting to ask for nearly half an hour. 'When you said *friendly fire* you meant exactly that, didn't you? At least some of those pilots are in with you.'

'Have you seen the way everything works under President Banda?' demanded Chaka, suddenly aflame with outrage. 'From the civil service to the police, the intelligence services, broadcasting and the armed forces. It's not how good you are, it's who you know. People getting promoted through influence, bribery or nepotism, not through hard work, dedication, talent. That's a very dangerous situation. It's why people like Banda never last long term, any more than the French monarchy in the 1780s or the Tsars in the early 1900s. It only takes someone like me to come along and promise to reward merit, and suddenly everyone that really keeps things going is over on the other side.'

'Or, put another way, someone like Danton or Napoleon; Marx or Lenin. But it can't be as easy as all that, surely!'

'No, you're right. It's like a kind of magic trick. You need to prepare. But no one must suspect *what* you are preparing. Then, *abracadabra!* And hope for the best.'

As they exchanged this brief conversation, the Zodiac settled, shrouded in the cargo netting, then slid a little way down towards the river as though drawn inexorably to the water. Then it stopped, a tangle of rope and webbing, in the shadow beside the long-dead heart of the river.

The chopper heaved back upwards, hopped over the burned-out wreck of the casino and settled down towards the emptiness of what would have been its car park.

Here, as everywhere else along the riverbank, Richard thought, the jungle was overwhelming the works of mankind like the sands of the desert in Shelley's 'Ozymandias', the poem he had half-heard Celine quoting as they looked down across Citematadi.

But then, as the aircraft's wheels came close enough to kiss the rotting concrete flags, Richard gave a sudden exclamation of surprise so deep that he doubted his sight for a moment. His sight and his sanity. For what he had taken to be jungle was no such thing. True, there were trees thronging the distance, elephant grasses and wall after wall of bushes in between. But nearer at hand the trees were joined by netting. The jungle was extended by a low-slung sky of netting. Netting on the size and scale of a three-ringed circus tent and then some. And the netting was covered with camouflage.

He looked across at Chaka and grinned with scarcely believing wonder. *'Abracadabra,'* they both said at once.

From the air, there was nothing but a wilderness of jungle behind the old burned-out casino. From ground level there was a regiment of tanks. Richard saw ten of the big T-80s at a glance, with backup vehicles in plenty – from petrol bowsers to Land Rovers. And all the men who had been missing from Delta Force camps One and Two. And there was something else there too. Something so vital and so obvious that Richard could hardly believe he hadn't thought of it.

There was a road.

Richard climbed down out of the chopper at Chaka's shoulder and went and stood in the middle of it, looking first one way and then the other. It looked like a six-lane highway as wide as a motorway at home. Grassed over, yes, in places. Broken up and all but impassable in sections, certainly. All but impassable. But not quite impassable. Stretching away along the river towards the distant mountains on one side. Running straight into the heart of the shanties on the other.

And the instant Richard realized that, his mind took another simple leap forward, even as his memory leaped back. To the back of Major Kebila's half-track swinging so suddenly north towards Fort Zinderneuf. Revealing for that instant the extension of that same straight roadway through the middle of the shanties, past the very gates of Fort Zinderneuf and right into the heart of the city itself.

But even so. Smuggling a whole regiment of tanks along a roadway to within striking distance of the city, unsuspected...

'The authorities never come further than the shanties. Why should they? The shanties are where the trouble has been centred, after all,' said Chaka, reading Richard's mind with unsettling ease. 'And remember, the senior security officers are all most interested in staying on the right side of the President. In staying right *beside* the President, in fact. Like General Bomba, like Colonel Nkolo. Like Kaptaine-commandant Moputo. Like the courtiers at the courts of Louis XVI and Tsar Nicolas. Or at the court of King Charles I of England, come to that, before Oliver Cromwell and Co. arrived.

'Keeping the tanks hidden here for a day or two has been easier than I supposed. Like raising the New Model Army.'

'But *getting* them here...' Richard still could

not get his head round that particular feat of strategic magic.

'The tanks were surprisingly easy to move. You are familiar with this model of the T-80?' It was back to *Dr* Julius Chaka suddenly. A pedant with a slow-witted student. Chaka led him across into the shadow of the netting to stand beside the nearest camouflaged monster. It smelt of oil and metal – both of them hot. 'This one is my command tank,' said Chaka.

Richard was glad Voroshilov wasn't there challenging him to drive it. Simeon strolled round from the far side. 'May I take a closer look?' he asked.

Chaka waved expansively as Richard continued enthusiastically, answering his question. 'Well...I've come across them before, let's say...' Richard reached out to touch it as though it was an enormous steel horse while Simeon clambered up its side like a child on a climbing frame.

'Then you know that among their many other features, the biological and chemical-warfare protection systems render them completely airtight. And watertight, therefore. And these particular tanks come equipped with a snorkel system...'

'You brought them down the river!' Richard was amazed that he hadn't thought of it sooner. He had seen it done before.

'Down the road as far as we dared then down the river under water for the last few kilometres and up at the landing stage here. If you look very closely beneath *The Heart of Matadi*, I believe you will see some very strange marks on the bank indeed. Everything else just crept along under cover of darkness. Just as we all plan to do tonight, as I'm sure you guessed.'

'But if you're all set up to break into the city – with a regiment of tanks, for heaven's sake! – what on earth was the point of kidnapping Asov's daughter? Especially if you had no intention of hurting her – or holding him to your demands?' Richard swung round and confronted the confident general, his own anger returning with the memory of the confusion, hurt and worry that the phone call to Robin hadn't quite cured.

Dr Chaka came out once again, leading Richard back out of the camouflaged encampment as he spoke.

'Where has the President sent his air force? The one weapon in his arsenal that a tank commander might legitimately fear?'

'Down into the delta.'

'Precisely. And would he have done this without the Russians on his tail? No! And in the unlikely event that he recalls them soon, they will be low on fuel and out of munitions. Useless to him, should someone choose to attack his city tonight. And the army? Where is the army? With their own light tanks and various ranges of tank-busting equipment? Where are they?'

'I assume the army is combing the delta looking for the terrorists who kidnapped Asov's daughter so that he can wipe them out like the Russians demanded.'

'Precisely. Russians, I might add, whose bad temper has been irritated almost to the point of madness by the apparently accidental destruction of all their upriver possessions by the very forces they were relying on to protect them. Far more irritated, I grieve to say, than Mr Asov would have been to find his daughter dead and his barges and mines still working. Russians who, in consequence, have sent their own security forces into the delta to ginger up General Bomba's dangerously useless soldiery.'

'So there are no troops left in Granville Harbour?'

'Apart from the ubiquitous police roadblocks, you mean? No. No troops and no security staff. There's just one squad of soldiers left, I understand. A possible thorn in our side, I admit. Because they seem to be armed with two Scorpion light tanks and several armoured half-tracks. A range of anti-personnel equipment up to and including several pieces of anti-tank weaponry. Thirty men or so all well trained if not precisely battle-hardened. They form the main contingent guarding the central police station in the place we call Fort Zinderneuf. Under the command of Colonel Laurent Kebila.'

'You mean major. It's Major Kebila.'

'Oh, I think you'll find that, one way or another, it'll be Colonel Kebila soon.'

* * *

Having delivered himself of this cryptic observation, Julius Chaka bustled off. It went without saying that he had far too much to do to spend any more time explaining his plans to innocent bystanders. Even though, Richard calculated astutely, the President in waiting felt a little guilty about the manner in which Richard had become caught up in his plans through Robin's accidental kidnapping.

But as things turned out, they only stayed apart for a brief amount of time. And all too soon it was Richard's turn to feel guilty.

After his talk with Chaka, Richard returned to the riverside and the Zodiac. In the real world, far removed from the heady magic of Chaka's regiment of tanks, the inflatable was an expensive piece of Heritage Mariner equipment. It needed to be checked. It might even need to be repaired. It needed to be taken back to *Prometheus*.

At first glance it seemed to Richard that all the others were gathered around it, unwrapping the webbing and netting. Voroshilov started checking in the bags for damage to the guns and equipment. Jim Bourne went back to check on the Honda he had been in charge of and automatically turned to Simeon to do the same. And it was only then they realized that Simeon was missing. 'Did you see where Simeon went?' Richard asked Charles Le Brun almost casually, suspecting nothing as yet.

Charles shrugged. 'I haven't seen him since we climbed out of the chopper,' he said. 'I think he went up for a closer look at the tanks.'

'Voroshilov?'

'No. Why should I? I have much more immediate concerns believe you me. Has anyone seen the Glock? The one with the red-dot sight?'

'Callum?'

'I saw him up by the tanks while you were talking to Dr Chaka. He muttered something about asking Dr Celine a question and went off after her. I haven't seen him since.'

Richard would never know what it was that made him suspect something was wrong then. Perhaps it was the way Simeon had been crawling all over the command tank – inside as well as out, now he thought of it. Perhaps it was the fact that Simeon had hardly spoken to Celine at all during the whole time together so far and yet now he just had to see her. Perhaps the fact that just a word from him could have informed Richard of who Dr Celine really was so much earlier – a word he had chosen not to say for reasons of his own. Perhaps it was the memory of the way he had looked at Charlotte Uhuru, the President's resident publicist – and would-be serious newsperson. The look of a man who might do anything to get into the sunshine of her notice; anything at all. Perhaps it was Voroshilov's missing Glock.

Whatever it was, something made Richard straighten. 'Jim, get this thing in the water as quickly as you can, would you?' he said, then he turned and began to walk increasingly rapidly up towards the car park behind the burned-out casino. When he heard the motor cough and the shouting start, he broke into a run. But still he arrived just an instant too late.

Richard raced over the crest and past the ruin to be confronted by a confused group of soldiers, watching the rear of a rapidly retreating Land Rover that was racing as fast as it could along the pitted road towards the distant shanties.

'Who's in that?' he bellowed, but they looked at him with uncomprehending suspicion. 'Does anyone speak English? French?'

'What is it?' demanded Julius Chaka, crossing the car park rapidly, also frowning at the unexpected – unwelcome – turn of events.

'Who's taken that Land Rover?'

Chaka questioned his men in a rapid spate of Matadi. They answered in the same.

'They say it was one of your men.'

'It has to be Simeon Bourgeois. He's the only one of my team not with us. I'm afraid he may be going to raise the alarm. How can we stop him?'

'It's a straight road. He's an easy target. It's a bit of risk but I can drop a 125mm high-explosive shell on him at any range between one hundred and four thousand metres.'

Richard felt his blood run cold at the thought. And at the growing certainty he voiced immediately. 'I think he's taken Celine with him.'

'Why did you let him take the vehicle?' snarled the general at his men. He was so shocked by

Richard's news that he asked first in English. Then in staccato Matadi.

He was overwhelmed by a flood of explanatory self-justification. 'Because Dr Celine was in it with him,' he translated, slowly, nodding his head.

'Did she look all right?'

Chaka asked his guards and was once again overwhelmed by Matadi explanations.

'She seemed strangely quiet but they thought nothing of it,' he explained shortly.

'So, he's turned the tables on you. On all of us,' said Richard grimly. 'Can you send someone after him? Another Land Rover? A motorbike?'

'Of course. The road is too bad to allow anything other than my tanks to go at full speed – except a motorbike, of course. A motorbike might catch him. But then what?'

'Can you alert your people in the shanties? Block the road somehow?'

He looked at his watch. 'No. The plan is in motion. It has a timetable it must stick to. But of course I can alert them...'

He pulled out his cellphone automatically. Only to replace it with a hiss of disgust. 'No signal! Which of you has a field radio?'

He translated into Matadi again and one of the men ran off to fetch one. Only to return, frowning with bemusement.

'He says there is only one clear channel,' said Chaka. 'Everything else is blocked. We are out of communication! How can this be?'

'You don't have time for this, Dr Chaka. You need to send someone after the Land Rover at once.'

'That is easy for you to say! I need to send someone who has no set function or responsibility within the plan. Someone who can move swiftly without using the road or causing an alert.'

'Then you need me and my commando in the Zodiac with some kind of authority from you that any of your people will recognize in case we have to go into the shanties,' said Richard. 'I can get down the river in the inflatable as fast as he can get down the road, by the sound of things. And if we can't stop him then nobody can.'

'Why would you do such a thing?' Chaka's eyes were narrow with suspicion.

Richard could see him mentally assessing just how much vital information he had already handed over. How he might well need to re-assess some truly vital matters – like whether any of Richard's little commando could be trusted. Could be relied on. Could be released. Could be allowed to live. He took a deep breath, his mind racing.

'Think about it!' Richard persisted. 'If he's gone, then he's gone over to the other side. He's taken Celine, no doubt at gunpoint. He's stolen a Glock from our kit. But he could offer Banda and the Russians so much more than Celine herself if he's fast enough on his feet. He's headed for the shanties with your daughter in one of your Land Rovers. You can't warn them he's coming or that he's a traitor. All they'll see is your daughter in your Land Rover and a man who knows the plan in detail telling them what to do. They won't know he's a traitor to the cause holding a gun on a woman he's just kidnapped. He could grab Robin and Anastasia too, pretty easily. If he can rely on you waiting until dark before you move he might even have time to get to *Prometheus*.

'Morgan Hand would trust him the same as all the rest would. She would hand over Baptiste without a second thought!'

Chaka blenched, and Richard could all too vividly sympathize with his shock. Kebila with his command and Fort Zinderneuf could only hope to slow him momentarily. Even President Liye Banda, if he called his air force back from the delta in time, would have a hard job turning him back.

But Simeon Bourgeois with his daughter and his grandson could stop him dead in his tracks after all. For if Max Asov in this situation had been all brain and ruthless ambition, Dr Julius Chaka was all heart.

Twenty-Three

Darkness

'Ach! I am idiot!' Voroshilov suddenly snarled. He slapped his forehead with the sound of a pistol shot.

Richard looked back from his accustomed position in the bow. 'What?' he demanded.

The Zodiac was speeding downriver even faster than it had come up – almost as swiftly, in fact, as it had sped down the smaller stream through the tall trees towards Delta Force One and General Julius Chaka. What current there was in the bigger flow sat under her counter now. The Hondas raced like a matched pair of thoroughbreds at a sulky race in the Kentucky Derby. An evening breeze had sprung up strongly enough to be causing a set of waves that ran down towards the sea as though the river's dark surface was more impatient than its slow, still depths. It was strong enough also to whisper in the trees nearby, though the sound came and went intermittently beneath the rumble of the Hondas, the relentless slapping of hull smashing through water and the hissing of the widening wake they were leaving upstream.

And even that steady little breeze was pushing the Zodiac seawards as she seemed to fly from wave-crest to wave-crest under the last of the light.

'What?' demanded Richard again.

'It was the command tank! How could I not have seen it?' demanded Voroshilov. 'The command tank has a battlefield capability to jam all frequencies except the unit command frequency. Simeon Bourgeois must have switched it on before he kidnapped the girl and stole the Land Rover. That is why the cellphones did not work. That is why even the radios did not work. How did you not see it? You said you knew the T-80 tank!'

'Calm down, Voroshilov. Calm down and think. If we had told Chaka that he could be back in contact with the world at the flick of a switch do you think we'd be here? Do you think he'd have let us come away like this?'

'You knew? You did not tell him *on purpose*?'

'You know me of old, Voroshilov. You know I won't be happy to sit around at someone else's beck and call when my people are in trouble. A little white lie to allow us some freedom of action. He'll work it out for himself, in any case. It may even be that he can still use those wretched drums of his for their original purpose and pass messages that can't be electronically blocked! Then he can call the people in the shanties either way. But instead of hanging everything on that one chance, now he has a backup whether he likes it or not: *us*!'

As Richard spoke, so they came past the downriver end of the overhanging tunnel that they had followed so carefully on their way upstream. This was where the drums had first begun to sound so sinisterly this afternoon, thought Richard and he strained his ears now, relieved to be moving through a world of sound and rush, instead of that soul-deep unsettling silence.

But instead of the timeless drum-rhythm he was seeking, the insistent buzzing of his cell-phone began. With hardly a thought he pulled out the little instrument and put it to his ear.

'Mariner?' he barked.

'Chaka.' The general's voice was distant but clear. 'It was the jamming facility in the command tank...'

'Voroshilov just worked that out.' Richard was still employing less than his usual total honesty. He still had tactical reasons for doing so. He might be a free agent once again, but he still needed Chaka's trust – perhaps his help – if he was going to get the women back again. And there was a fair chance he and the general would find themselves face to face again soon – and Chaka would still have a dozen battle tanks behind him. 'What now?'

The line hissed as Chaka calculated. Better that he was doing that well clear of the little group in the Zodiac, thought Richard. He still did not trust the look that had come into the general's face as they watched the Land Rover vanish down the road with the treacherous kidnapper Simeon Bourgeois at the wheel. 'Where are you?' Chaka asked at last.

'Just coming out of the main stream into the bay. Shanties to the right of us.'

'Good. Go to the nearest jetty you can get to, show the first person you see the pass I gave you and get them to take you to Patrice Salako.'

'The newspaper guy? That Salako?'

'He's with us. He can get you to your women – if they're still there. I'll call him now and update him. I'll tell him to expect Simeon Bourgeois and look out for you close behind.'

'Has he got the women?'

'He knows where the women are. He's your best bet for getting to them quickly.'

'Right. Contact Patrice Salako. Get the women. Get Celine away from Simeon. Sounds like a plan. What next after that?'

'One step at a time, Captain.'

'OK. What about you? You can't afford to hang about, General. Especially if Simeon Bourgeois manages to slip through our fingers and raise the alarm.'

'I'm coming into the city under cover of darkness.'

'Is that necessary?'

'It is the plan, Captain.'

'OK. But what does that mean, precisely? 19:00 hours? 20:00?'

'That will be my decision, Captain. And you may be sure I'll make it when the time comes. In the meantime you have much to do yourself. Good luck, Captain Mariner.'

Chaka broke contact – leaving Richard feeling, for the first time in many years, the full weight of his rank and responsibility. 'Head for the shanties,' he ordered. 'Nearest jetty we can manage.'

He looked down at his phone again. Now that it was working he had more use for it. The screen and buttons glittered in the gathering gloom. The clock on the screen ticked up past 18:00:00 and he glanced up at the darkening bowl of the sky immediately above his head. The sun was settling on to the horizon dead ahead – and he was careful not to look at that as he dialled. Maybe fifteen minutes more of daylight left, he thought as the connection began to sound.

'*Prometheus*. Radio operator speaking.'

'Owner speaking. Get me the captain, please. It's urgent.'

Jim brought them as ordered to the nearest jetty and Callum tied the Zodiac securely in place while Richard stepped up on to a narrow plank supported by a series of roughly secured oil drums. And, oddly, for the first time since he had laced them up before climbing aboard the Zodiac, Richard was glad of Sergeant Major Tchaba's boots. The whole crazy contraption sank beneath his weight as he strode forward into the narrow passageway leading back from the jetty between the buildings. Water washed up past the turn-ups of his almost indestructible trousers, but the boots kept his feet dry.

305

Fortunately he had made it on to dry ground before Voroshilov climbed out with the bag that he had filled with the kit and armaments he considered to be indispensable. The planks actually vanished deep under water beneath his weight and he slopped unhappily up to where Richard was standing. With both of them on it together the water would have come up to their knees. 'You want a gun?' he asked.

'Not at the moment. I have this.' Richard held up the pass that Chaka had given him. 'I could do with a torch, though. The light will be gone in a minute or two and I see no evidence of street lights. Or any other kind of lights, come to that. Tell the others to stay close. We don't have much time.'

Voroshilov hefted the grip on to his back with the handles over his shoulders like straps, then carried it vertically like a Bergen. Then with Richard in the lead and the Russian at his shoulder, they proceeded single-file along the narrow passageway.

Richard had no doubt that they were being watched, but no one approached them. Quite the opposite. Wherever they went there were whispers and scurryings as the residents of shanty town gave them a very wide berth indeed. 'How's your Matadi, Charles?' asked Richard.

'Not as good as Simeon's,' answered Charles, the tone of his voice in the shadows seeming to contain a worried frown.

'Even so, could you manage something like

We come from General Chaka. We come in peace. We are looking for Patrice Salako. Anything along those lines?'

'Well...' Charles began to shout in impenetrable Matadi. But there was no reply. In the distance, however, there was a sudden noise – shouting, shooting and revving motors. Richard frowned, not liking what he could hear one little bit.

The light was almost completely gone now. The pallid glimmer high on their left hand seemed little more illuminating than the rise of a new moon. Richard switched on the torch Voroshilov had given him and directed the beam at the ground immediately in front of the massive black steel-lined toecaps and moved forward through the stinking mud and mess as fast as he dared.

But soon, in fact, Richard found that he was literally following his nose. And it didn't let him down. For, in among the stenches of effluent, river, hot corrugated iron and unwashed flesh with which they were surrounded, he thought he could detect a strengthening odour of burning flesh and hair, reminding him of the conversation they had had earlier about Welsh smokies.

After a few more steps along the foetid little passage, Richard stepped out into the Market Square at the shanty's heart and found himself confronted by the butchery.

The Market Square was in fact the roadway that joined the casino to Fort Zinderneuf and the heart of the city – the only open space in the whole unplanned mess of dwellings. The butcher's stall stood in the middle of it – on what would have been the bush-filled central reservation between the six lanes of tarmac road surface. A corral containing a couple of scrawny goats lay beyond it. A simple wooden gallows stood for a slaughterhouse.

Richard saw all this at a glance. And saw also something else that made him pause and frown. The market was part filled with people. All of them standing still, as though he had wandered into a photograph. He looked around more narrowly, his hair stirring and his heart thumping uneasily. In the light of the butcher's fire he could see one or two stalls scantily dressed with pathetic piles of trash and junk. But one or two more – that had stood across the road itself like the flimsiest of barriers – lay scattered and splintered on the ground. There were bodies lying beside them.

Richard stepped forward, gathering breath to remind Charles that he should continue to call that they were here in peace at General Chaka's orders. But then he realized with a start of simple revulsion that what was occupying the butcher's fire was not a goat or a lamb. It was the body of a man. 'Voroshilov,' he bellowed and the pair of them ran forward. Around them the whole strange tableau sprang to life. The bodies beside the ruined stalls began to stir and scream. The crown near the fire swirled and shouted. The butcher himself came hurrying forward with the tools of his trade – two long poles with hooks at their ends. With practised dexterity he began to pull the burning body clear, scattering hot chips of wood and burning splinters all around.

Everyone else skipped back, barefoot or lightly shod at best. Protected by the thick corrugated soles, Richard ran unheeding into the circle of fire, squinting for a closer look at the body. It was just possible to see that, uniquely amongst the nearby men, the body was wearing a Western-style suit. The half-roasted flesh had been black – even before it had fallen forward into the flames. The hair had been arranged in crisp black curls, even before the flames crisped them even further. Whoever he had been, he was toast.

'I hope to hell it's Simeon Bourgeois,' Richard called to Voroshilov.

'Who else could it be? Though I can't see the Land Rover or the woman.'

'I can see where the Land Rover went,' said Richard, glancing up half dazzled from the smouldering man. Then he stepped up to the corpse as the local people stepped further back. Richard sank to his knees beside the smoking horror. His breath hissed in bitter disappointment as well as in simple revulsion. 'It's Patrice Salako,' Richard said. 'He's been shot several times. Looks as if he were dead when he went into the fire, thank God. But where are the women? How can we get to them now?'

Charles Le Brun joined them then with

Callum at his heels and Jim Bourne close behind. 'I'll see what I can find out,' he said.

Richard straightened, dusting smouldering ash off his knees. Still at the centre of the circle of fire, he pulled out his phone and flicked it on. With his hand trembling – a combination of shock and stress – he searched down the memory for Chaka's number, recorded automatically as an incoming call immediately before 18:00 local time. The clock in the corner of the screen warned him that it was coming up to 18:30 now. The number came up. He pressed dial and the contact-failed signal came up. Followed immediately by the no-signal warning.

'Damn!' said Richard. 'Missed him! But if he's switched the command tank's jammers back on, then that must mean he's on his way.'

But as it happened, Julius Chaka was by no means the only officer who was on his way. No sooner had Richard pocketed his useless phone than three armoured half-tracks burst into the heart of the shanty, grinding over the pathetic wreckage of the ruined stalls in arrowhead formation. Laurent Kebila remained in the passenger seat of the lead vehicle, safely behind the bulletproof glass, until the vehicles had disgorged three full squads of men.

In the face of the intimidating arrival, the people from the shanties simply vanished into the shadows. By the time his men had set up a protective cordon, and Kebila swung the

310

door of his vehicle wide, there was no one to be seen in the market square but Richard and his little commando. And the smouldering Patrice Salako.

Kebila swung down slowly, clearly considering his opening line with care. 'Sergeant Major Tchaba sends his compliments,' he said quietly at last. 'He is in Fort Zinderneuf at present. But he is looking forward to discussing with you the matter of a headache and some missing footwear.'

'He needs to discuss the headache with Dr Celine,' answered Richard with an apparent ease and calm he was nowhere near to feeling. On the one hand he had no idea whose side Kebila was going to follow. On the other, he was very well aware that Voroshilov might start shooting before anyone got a chance to find out.

'Oh,' said Kebila, walking slowly forwards, eyes everywhere, every bit, on every level, the human equivalent of a cat on hot bricks, 'I believe the good sergeant major may well be discussing matters with her as we speak.'

Richard's mind leaped ahead, extrapolating a whole scenario from one tiny nugget of information. 'So Simeon got through to you, did he? I thought he would try to warn President Banda himself.'

'Or the delectable Miss Uhuru. I see you know the man. At last. But no. I was the logical choice, was I not? I was close by. I command a safe haven. Like yourself to a certain extent, I am a free agent – or I am until General Chaka arrives with enough tanks to curtail the options for freedom of movement.'

'Simeon has the women with him...'

'Another reason for swiftness of action. I'm afraid that like many men, Mr Bourgeois found it very difficult indeed to handle more than one woman at a time.'

'So my wife is in Fort Zinderneuf too.'

'As is the lovely Miss Asov. Yes. Safe in my keeping until a range of family members and a few associates arrive.'

'Family members? Associates?'

'Ah, Captain Mariner, you cannot fool me! You know whom I mean. On Mr Bourgeois's warning, I have sent squads all over the city from the heights of the Granville Royal Lodge Hotel to the depths of the docks. They have orders to bring me Miss Asov's father. His partner, Mr Makarov, who has long been – as I am sure you know – Mr Bourgeois's *real* employer. And Miss Uhuru's, of course. Dr Celine's nephew Baptiste whom you stole from me at the same time as you stole my sergeant major's boots. Your own associates, Captain Hand and the Russian Paznak who will not let the child out of their sight even under threat of death, apparently. And of course I am expecting one more person that I need not send my men to collect. Little Baptiste's grandfather, self-styled General Chaka. With *his* associates. And their tanks.'

And Richard felt that, had he been just a little

more like Voroshilov, he might have slapped himself on the head – if he dared make a sound like a pistol shot – and shouted, 'Ach! I am idiot!'

Twenty-Four

Horror

Robin looked at Richard with something akin to horror. 'Richard!' Her voice rang round the holding cell where Kebila had interrogated Richard at the beginning of all this. 'What are you doing here?'

'Looking for you, my love,' he answered, easing himself stiffly into that familiar creaky chair. Of all the places or situations he had hoped to find her this was among the last. Neither the location, the situation nor the simple shock of her expression invited the long, lingering, loving embrace he had been looking forward to sharing with her when he found her at last. He had no more expected to find her in this strange belligerent mood than he had really expected to find her in this all too familiar cell, still wearing the dress she had put on to go to President Banda's reception.

If he had thought more about what was happening to her and less about finding her and saving her, he suspected, he would probably have foreseen both eventualities. Certainly, she was dressed still exactly as she had been dress-

314

ed in the DVDs. And he suspected Anastasia would be as well.

'I don't want to be looked for!' she snarled, striding away from him towards the vacant bunks against the wall, swinging the stained ruin of her presidential party frock's tattered hem across the cold stone of the floor. 'God, I don't even want to be found! I just want to be *rescued*! Taken out of here. Out of this whole bloody country!' Her chilly gaze flashed across to the armed soldier who was swinging out of the door and pulling it shut behind himself, having delivered his latest prisoner at Kebila's orders.

He thought of retorting, with a great deal of righteous anger of his own, *Just what the bloody hell do you think I've been doing for the better part of twenty-four hours* but *trying to rescue you!* But all he managed was, 'Sorry, darling. I've done my best, but...' He shrugged, then his shoulders sagged a little.

The door shut. The key turned. The guard slammed to attention in the corridor outside. The noises echoed away into a silence almost as absolute as the silence of the jungle before the drums began.

'Well...' she temporized, a little nonplussed by his hangdog look of near-defeat. She had never seen him look so exhausted or depressed in all their years together. The first glimmer arrived in her understanding of just what the ordeal had cost him so far. Was costing him still, in fact.

She returned to the seat at the little table opposite him. She sat down, rested the toes of her incredibly inappropriate strappy evening shoes on the toecaps of the huge army boots he was wearing for some unfathomable reason, leaned forward and took his massive hands in hers. Overlooked the fact that he was filthy, mud-spattered and oil-smeared. Did not wrinkle her nose at the fact that he smelt like an out-of-control barbecue.

'You'd better tell me all about it,' she said more gently.

'Well,' she said, sitting back ten minutes later when he was finished. 'It looks as though this is the right place for the situation to be resolved, doesn't it, my darling? It's where the real power in the city seems to lie. In all sorts of ways. For all the glitz of the hotels and the President's compound, this is where the real work seems to get done isn't it? And for all the fancy titles – General This and Kaptaine-commandant That – it's the middle-ranking men like Kebila here that do it. And I guess that by the same token Julius Chaka knows that if he's ever going to win through, it's here he has to make the difference. And it's men like Kebila he needs to win over first.'

'I'm sure he understands that, darling.' Richard leaned forward too, frowning with gathering intensity. 'I'm pretty certain he's built it into his plans already. But I don't think he has the faintest idea where Kebila stands yet. And he, like Fort Zinderneuf, as you say, is something of a lynch pin. I'm sure there are some men in the air force who have come over to Chaka's side some time ago. Like I said, Anastasia's kidnapping just seems to have been a ruse to get the air force down into the delta so they could leave the city unprotected while blowing up the Bashnev-Sevmash works. And then getting as much of the army as possible down there in turn to try and sort things out. Two birds with one stone and then some.

'But it would only work as well as it seems to have if some of the pilots were already on Chaka's team, as I said. I wonder if President Banda could ever be made to see that, though?' Richard mused, his eyes and mind beginning to come alive as he attained an emotional and intellectual second wind.

'See what?'

'That if he's going to stop Chaka then he needs to do it here. At Zinderneuf. With Major Kebila at his side.'

'He might do. But then again he might have delegated that work to Major Kebila in any case. That could well be what this is all about, after all.' Her glance took in the cell, the prison, the fort and all it contained in the matter of materiel and personnel – weapons and hostages.

Richard nodded. Perhaps that was what Julius Chaka had meant by the cryptic observation that had been rattling around in the back of his mind since the general had first said it. Perhaps if Major Kebila did manage to slow the tanks here long enough for President Banda to call the air force back from the delta then he would indeed be Colonel Kebila before the morning. If he was still alive, of course.

If any of them were.

Kebila himself disturbed them ten minutes later as they were really beginning to get to grips with their speculation. His news made further questions unnecessary for the moment. 'The people from your ship *Prometheus* are here,' he said shortly. 'I expect Anastasia's father soon, but my communications are down so I can only speculate. And, as I am sure you were about to inform me, Captain Mariner, I have no doubt that the failure of my communications means that the battlefield jamming system in General Chaka's command tank is within range of my equipment now. That would place him in the shanties where I picked you up so recently.

'So I will bring in all your friends and associates at once and hurry about my business. I have to finalize my preparations to welcome General Chaka in a very short time indeed.'

If Robin had seemed upset to Richard, Morgan Hand seemed absolutely outraged. Thin-lipped and pale with anger she explained to Richard how the Russian crew members had failed to back her in the face of Kebila's invasion of *Prometheus*'s sovereign territory. Still brooding about the recovery of the guns they had taken from the locker, perhaps; at the

318

orders of Asov or Makarov, no doubt, they had connived – by their lumpen inactivity and refusal to obey her orders if not by outright mutiny – with the arrest and detention of herself and her charge. Only Paznak had stood up to them and he was swiftly overcome.

Then the whole crew had been shepherded off under the guns of the soldiers before Paznak, Baptiste and she had been piled into the back of a half-track. Precisely where the rest of her crew were she had no idea. But her main priority at the moment was to discover where they had taken poor Baptiste.

'Hold your horses,' said Richard, glancing across at Robin to see if she shared his sudden worry. 'When Kebila's men took everyone off the ship, did they allow time to make all secure? I know she's set for harbour watch, but there are still safety procedures...'

Morgan blenched. Her face literally went white. 'My God! I didn't think of that! I was so focused on protecting poor Baptiste – it was so sudden...'

'Well, I expect Oblomov and Poliakov got everything stowed away safely,' said Richard bracingly.

'It's not that! We'd just been called down to the oilfields! I was waiting for your contact to confirm our movement. Mr Asov and Mr Makarov had been calling in, as you know. Big rush as usual. And they were talking to their men as well as to me. So no. We weren't rigged for harbour when the soldiers came aboard. We were part-way through preparation to move over to the pumping station and take on a full cargo of Benin Light.'

She took a deep breath and looked at her employers in much the same way as Mata Hari and Benedict Arnold must have faced their firing squads. 'I have no idea what Oblomov and Poliakov shut down. Or what they left open, either.'

Richard glanced across at Robin once again. 'Well, there's nothing we can do about it now,' he said decisively. 'We'll just have to get everyone back aboard and run a full set of safety checks at the earliest opportunity.'

Having delivered himself of this decision, Richard stretched until the chair groaned and considered standing up again, decisiveness and energy beginning to flow back into his long, lean frame in the wake of that intellectual second wind. He looked around the room, counting heads and checking familiar faces. Jim, Charles and Callum were there along with Robin and Morgan. All of them looked shattered. Jim and Charles were deep in conversation. As were Robin and Morgan suddenly. Callum sat on one of the bunks and opened his laptop. Then he frowned with befuddled bemusement until he remembered that Bluetooth and Wi-Fi signals would be jammed along with all the others – so the Internet was closed to him for the moment as surely as Major Kebila's communications equipment.

Paznak and Voroshilov were in the corner

closest to the locked and guarded door, hatching something by the look of them. They glanced across at him and caught him watching them. They glanced away again immediately like naughty schoolboys. Richard decided he had better talk to them first. At once, in fact.

Richard was halfway to his feet when the door opened and he found he was too late after all. Fedor Gulin, of all people, was pushed unceremoniously forward by the door guard who turned at once to exit – just as he had several times before so far tonight. But he hadn't taken more than one step when Paznak hit him. The guard, halfway through the door, hit the jamb and bounced back in. Voroshilov hit him on the head with a SIG he had somehow managed to smuggle in, and Paznak caught him before he hit the ground too noisily. Gulin, simply bulldozed out of the way, span over towards a startled Jim, fortunately too winded and surprised to shout.

Paznak pulled the soldier in and Voroshilov swung the door to with his shoulder, gun held vertical but ready, peeking out into the corridor. He darted his spare hand round to the outer side like a snake and whipped it back laden with a bunch of keys.

By the time Richard was fully erect, the sentry was out cold on the floor and Paznak had his sidearm and his SA80. Voroshilov had checked the corridor outside and was gone on silent tiptoe. Something in Richard's head said *This is madness.* But he crossed to Paznak's side. 'Where's he gone?' he whispered. Paznak looked at him as though he were very slow-witted indeed. 'After Anastasia,' he said.

Richard caught Jim's eye and signalled him over to the door with a jerk of his head. Jim glanced at the SA80 but Richard frowned. It was far too soon to start arming themselves, he thought. *Think first, shoot later* seemed like a good motto for the time, the place and the situation.

Richard crossed to the gasping Fedor Gulin, and looked him straight in the face. It was like interrogating Toad of Toad Hall. 'Do you know where she is, Fedor?'

'Anastasia? No! Why should I?'

'You didn't hear anything about her on your way here?'

'No! Nothing!'

'Fair enough. Now what about Mr Asov?'

'Gone!' Gulin shook his head to emphasize the word. 'He and Mr Makarov were on the last flight out. The rest are at the hotel or at the airport hoping it opens again.'

'They've closed the airport?' Richard frowned. This was news indeed. His mind raced, trying to assess the implications.

'President's orders,' Gulin explained. 'Closed it to commercial flights at least. He wants it available for when the air force gets back from the delta. Is there going to be a civil war?'

'Looks like it. Do you know what President Banda seems to be up to? Anything on the local news or TV?'

'Only that vapid woman Uhuru. She says the President is taking overall command himself. But no one I've talked to really believes it. Rumour has it that he's got the last of the helicopters from the hotel all tooled up with whatever weapons it will carry and he's ready to make a run for the border if anything goes wrong. That's what the hotel manager told me, at least.'

Richard nodded once, thinking that if anyone knew what was really going on then that man was likely to be André Wanago. 'But you're certain about your employers? Max Asov just turned tail and left his daughter here to rot?'

'He said he'd be back for her.' Right to the bitter end, poor old Gulin was protective of his masters' reputations. His voice quivered with outrage at the sickened tone of Richard's voice.

'I see.' Richard glanced across at Jim. 'Maybe Paznak and I had better grab a gun and go to lend Voroshilov a hand after all,' he said. 'Looks like we're the only hope Anastasia has in the short term. Robin, you must have been the last one here to have seen her. How was she and what do you think will be happening to her?'

'Hard to say. You know she was so moved by what she saw in the shanties that she gave them all her rings and studs and stuff? Every bit of jewellery she was wearing. I kid you not; navel ring and all. Gold, diamonds and rubies. Worth a fortune anywhere –but especially here. If she keeps that up she'll get into the Premier League with Dr Celine.'

'Dr Celine,' grated Richard. 'Now there's another lady I want to see safe and well.'

'God Almighty,' said Robin. 'It's like being married to Sir Lancelot.'

'If memory serves, that would make you Guinevere,' observed Richard as he reached for the SA80. 'OK, Paznak, you get the soldier's side arm. Let's see where Voroshilov's got to.'

As Richard eased past Jim Bourne he whispered, 'Everybody else stays here. And I do mean everybody. We three are being stupid enough for the whole of Heritage Mariner and a couple of lunatic asylums put together as it is.'

Richard was not really familiar with the SA80. It seemed strange to him at the very least to find the long curving clip behind the grip and the trigger. He assumed that the switch convenient to his thumb was the safety and flicked it a couple of times hoping he was setting it to safe – and was not actually setting the fire control to rapid. Especially as there was no trigger guard.

Then, settling the stock in the crook of his arm and holding the weapon upright so that he would only put the ceiling at risk should anything go wrong, he followed Paznak in Voroshilov's footsteps out into the corridor.

It was the silence that struck him at once. All of the other cells stood open and empty. There seemed to be no guards other than the one lying senseless on the floor of the holding cell surrounded by Heritage Mariner people. Paznak was moving along the corridor towards the big reception area with its bullet-riddled fans. But when he got close enough to see that it was as empty as all the rest he turned back, and Richard, nodding agreement, turned as well. Then, side by side, they went back to the inner end of the corridor and began to climb the stairs. Even if they found no one, Richard thought, at least they would command the high ground. But then, knowing Kebila – as he was just beginning to do – he thought there was probably a fair chance that the high ground was taken already.

Above the empty offices and assorted storerooms, the second flight of stairs led not to a third storey but to a flat roof. Richard and Paznak climbed to a door that stood ajar and eased out silently to find Voroshilov there. 'I've scouted the roof,' he whispered as though he had been expecting them. 'It seems quite clear.'

Richard glanced around. There was a wall behind them with a skeletal set of iron steps reaching up to the wall-top walkway as though this was an old-fashioned crusader castle with battlements. Beyond that there was a gravelly vacancy the size of a football field that sat on top of the police station itself. And one glance told him it was utterly deserted.

'So we need to go on up, do we?' he breathed.

'Yes. This is the back of the fort. As far as I can see Kebila has everyone else – including his most important hostages – right at the front. Overlooking the big main road. It's where the

325

tanks will have to come.'

Richard looked around uneasily. Voroshilov's assessment seemed accurate enough. But the situation seemed far too simple somehow. Richard was no great theoretical strategist, but if he were Chaka he would be sending a sizeable commando round the back while his tanks distracted the defenders at the front. And if he could work this out, then Kebila could work it out as well.

As the three of them hesitated there while Richard double-checked the position, Callum McKay came puffing up the stairs and blundered out through the door behind them. His arrival was so unexpected that he nearly got himself shot. But he was big with news that seemed crucial in all sorts of ways. 'I've something really important to show you,' he said, far too loudly under the circumstances.

'In a moment,' decided Richard. 'Voroshilov, we're too exposed to start having a conference here. We need to move.'

'Up or back?'

'Up,' said Richard decisively. 'We need to push on if we're going to be of any help to anybody. Callum, come with us. We'll talk as soon as we find a secure position.'

The first secure position they found was in a little lobby that stood for all the world like the entrance to a little lighthouse at the foot of a watchtower. They crowded in. 'What?' demanded Richard.

'The first thing is that they've taken everyone

out of the cell just now,' gasped Callum. 'I came out to show you this...' He gestured at the laptop tucked half-open under his arm. 'I saw them all being taken out when I was hiding in the stairwell.'

'God!' snarled Richard. 'And you didn't think to say...'

'You told me not to, sir! And the other news seemed so important too...'

'Well!' said Richard. *WHAT?*'

Callum simply opened his laptop and showed them a picture. The unmistakable Charlotte Uhuru filled the screen. The expression on her face for once was more arresting than her cleavage. She was talking urgently, but too quietly to be heard.

'So what?' snarled Richard, almost mad with frustration.

'She's saying that the air force has defected. It hasn't come back from the delta like the President ordered. The planes have gone south across the border and landed in somewhere called Kamina...'

'She's saying this *now*?' demanded Richard.

'Yes! As soon as the Internet came up I went into Granville TV's website and—'

'My God!' said Richard. 'They must be right outside! That's why they've taken everyone else into the bargain. Kebila's learned a thing or two from the late Saddam Hussein. He's built a wall of flesh! *Move!*'

Richard span out of the watchtower and pounded silently down the walkway leading to the front of the Fort. His mind was racing to the rapid beat of his heart – and the pair of them seemed to be driving his pounding legs.

If Chaka and Kebila were at stand-off now, if the major was playing his last desperate hostage card, then they were all in deep, deep trouble. For Chaka, man of heart though he was, could not turn down a country in the face of a handful of lives. Not even the lives of his daughter and grandson could weigh long in the balance against his mission to save the country. Perhaps that had been the horrific double bluff after all. Perhaps Julius Chaka did not need to be sending men in through the back door because he was simply going to blow the front door open no matter who was standing in the way.

And yet, Kebila's last defiance and Chaka's horrific decision would both be wasted if what Charlotte Uhuru said were true.

For Kebila had lost if his brother officers in the air force had defected. Simeon Bourgeois had performed his treachery and his murder but nevertheless had lost. Everyone standing beside President Liye Banda had lost.

And Julius Chaka had won.

But the two commanders, standing face to face with the frail wall of the hostages between them, would only realize that fact if someone somewhere was watching the *Charlotte Uhuru News Show* on Granville TV at this very moment. And of all the things that might be happening on a potential battlefield, that seemed to Richard the least likely. The least likely of all.

328

The whole front of Fort Zinderneuf was bathed in light. It had not occurred to Richard that the tanks would have headlights – perhaps even searchlights. But they did. And they were all trained on the front of the Fort. All along the top of the wall, utterly black against the brightness, stood a line of figures. Only such things as hair length, hairstyle and berets made it possible to distinguish some of them from some of the others. And, of course, the stark black outlines of the guns.

Right in the middle of that still, black line, Richard was certain he could see Kebila's beret. Celine's distinctive hairstyle. The slight figure of Baptiste. Anastasia's straight black dye-job. Robin's unique gold ringlets – the only flash of colour there...

Richard glanced sideways as he hurled forward and caught a glimpse of the roadway below stretching away towards the shanties by the river. He could see one tank – the last of a long line, obviously. It was surrounded by people. Thousands, perhaps hundreds of thousands of people surrounded the tank – and presumably the others as well. The delta and the shanties alike must be deserted, he thought. Every man, woman and child down there had joined Julius Chaka's army. And they were all standing silently outside Fort Zinderneuf now, waiting.

This was popular revolution indeed.

And Laurent Kebila must see that. He must.

Richard found himself bellowing, 'Major Kebila! Laurent Kebila!' at the top of his stentorian voice. 'It's over! The air force has deserted! Flown on south! They're not coming back from the delta. It's over!'

But, as he later told the story, if there was a fat lady involved anywhere in the situation, she hadn't started singing yet.

The Alouette came in low over the unguarded rear of the Fort. It started firing the instant it cleared the rear wall and parallel lines of 20mm high-explosive cannon shells tore through the flat roof of the police station. Nose down, travelling at full throttle, it sped over the front wall. Hostages and soldiers scattered right and left as the shells seemed to tear the walkway apart. Richard, spinning to look inwards, caught a glimpse into the chopper's cabin as it sped by almost level with him.

He recognized the face of the man screaming orders inside. He recognized General Bomba and Colonel Nkolo at his side.

The SA80 seemed to slam against his shoulder of its own accord. He found out the hard way that what he had fondly supposed to be the safety was the rapid-fire mode. He pulled the guardless trigger and all but broke his collarbone with the recoil. The chopper leaped over the front wall and whirled away.

'That was Banda!' Richard screamed. 'That was Liye Banda himself! I saw him!' He pounded forward.

Hostages were streaming back away from the

carnage. He ran on, looking desperately for Robin. He rounded the corner, calling her name and plunged into the confusion. The shells had struck on the far side of the central party but Laurent Kebila was down. Richard found Robin and Celine crouching over him. He arrived just in time to hear Celine say, 'He'll live. Robin, you look after Sergeant Major Tchaba. Try and stop his legs and feet bleeding. There's nothing we can do for Mr Gulin. He took the full force. The Russian gentleman had a face like a toad, I recall. It's gone now, I'm afraid. Anastasia, can you come and help me with these men here, please. We can still do something for them.'

Richard went down on one knee beside Robin. She glanced up from the mess that used to be Sergeant Major Tchaba's feet. 'We seem to have survived,' she said, her voice shaking. 'Things are pretty horrific back there. But you need to keep an eye out,' she emphasized, more firmly. 'And try to get the survivors organized. The chopper may be back.'

Richard stood up. Now that he knew she was safe, he was way ahead of her. He leaned against the battlements and cupped one hand round his mouth, 'President Chaka!' he bellowed. He reckoned Chaka would have turned off the jammers so that he could negotiate with Kebila over the radio. Richard needed no such luxuries. His foretop voice would reach the command tank with ease. And so it would have, but it was lost under the gathering drumming of approaching rotors and the thunder of 20mm cannon almost at once.

This time the chopper came up from the shanties. It came straight along the road at almost zero feet. Its target was no longer the fort, but the men and women thronging the highway. And the column of tanks at their heart. Once again, the attack was so swift and un-expected that there was almost no time to react. The shells exploded in parallel geysers of mud and fire, flesh and bone. Where they struck the tanks they exploded uselessly, raining more horror and destruction on those nearby. But they did not have the power to pierce the armour.

But the shanty people did not stand idly by. Those with guns shot back. And, as the chopper roared past the fort, so Richard and some of the soldiers emptied their clips into its flashing fuselage. Voroshilov and Paznak too added every 9mm shell that they could pump through the SIG Sauer and the Glock.

Then it was gone.

Choking on the powder stench, Richard lean-ed forward once again. 'President Chaka?'

'Chaka here,' came the deep and steady voice he had first heard as the point of an assegai pricked the back of his super-sensitive neck.

Abruptly, Richard found that Robin was standing beside him, her arm embracing his waist with almost enough force to snap him in two. And as he spoke, a slightly hesitant child's hand was pushed into his empty fist.

'President Chaka,' he bellowed almost jubilantly, 'I believe that Colonel Kebila was on the point of surrendering the fort to you when he was shot. Dr Celine says he will survive to confirm that fact in due course, sir. But in the meantime the Fort, the city and I believe the country arc yours. Oh. And your grandson would like a word when it's convenient.'

And it was at that moment that the fat lady cleared her throat, in preparation to giving song.

For Richard and for those at the Fort, it ended – all but the clearing up – with the brilliant flash of fire from the harbour. It was so bright that for an instant Richard wondered whether the vengeful Liye Banda had got hold of a nuclear bomb. But no. It was something much nearer to home. Something, nevertheless, that exploded with much of the force of a nuclear bomb.

Precisely which of the bullets fired at the Alouette actually pierced its fuselage no one would ever know. Enough to kill General Bomba and wound Colonel Nkolo certainly, though Liye Banda survived both brutal attacks. More importantly, at least one of the bullets destroyed several vital fuel and control lines immediately beneath the pilot's seat.

As the Alouette sped along the roadway through the heart of the city, leaving the horror of Fort Zinderneuf far behind, the pilot suddenly realized he had lost control of the machine. Seemingly with a will of its own, the chopper raced at roof height over the empty southern suburbs until the bay of the anchorage filled the pilot's view.

An ancient, dilapidated billboard slapped its top against the chopper's wheels. The fuselage shook and juddered. The shock of the collision jarred the already damaged wiring. The cannons opened up – also with a will of their own – at the same time as boiling avgas sprayed on to the overheated engine. It burst into flames at the same instant as the cannons began to fire.

At the same instant as the Alouette raced down towards the tethered hulk of *Prometheus*. Ex-President Liye Banda saw it filling the windshield and screamed. They were his last sight and his last sound.

The supertanker's decks were not armour-plated. The HE shells could easily pierce them, and they did. The tanks were all but empty below. The ullage between the surface of the ballast and the top of the tank should have been filled with inert gas pumped there from the ship's own motors. But it wasn't. It was full of the volatile elements from the sludge left over from countless cargoes she had carried since her last overhaul and interior clean. The original design had not been precisely followed in the shipyard beside Archangel where she had been built. The crew, crowded off at gunpoint, had not completed their safety checks or their cargo-security procedures. The volatile elements were incredibly explosive. And the cannon shells triggered them off.

But even so, the ship would probably not have exploded as it did had the Alouette itself not crashed at full speed, already burning and with all guns blazing, on to the deck immediately in front of the bridge house. The explosion of the crash was enough to complete the work that the 20mm high-explosive shells had begun among the explosive gases below.

Prometheus exploded. The hull simply vaporized. Many of the harbour buildings simply vanished along with it, but nobody was near enough to be harmed except for Harbourmaster Herold Nkolo, who was trying to empty his safe before the new president arrived.

A circle of sound and force spread though the air – even as far away as the Granville Royal Lodge Hotel, the walls shook and the windows cracked before manager André Wanago's staring shaken eyes.

The power of the explosion tore a huge hole in the soil of the bayside. But what it did to the bay itself nearly beggared description. It gave birth to a wall of water nearly ten metres high that spread out in a circle from the epicentre as though a meteor had crashed to earth where the vaporized tanker had been. The wall of water hurled forward into the gape of the river-mouth. It washed away what little was left of the billboard's smouldering footings. It washed over the molten mess which was all that remained of the fencing designed to keep the beachcombers out. It inundated the bank where the bay became the river and it washed away the shanties as though they had never existed, every clapboard wall and corrugated roof, every plastic sheet and crazy, rope-bound gable. It flooded over the roadway and extinguished the butcher's fire with one titanic roar. It lifted the corpse of Patrice Salako and carried it silently away into the soundless depths of the delta.

It flooded the trees along the river course as far as the old casino, filling the treetops with waterlogged canoes, pirogues and motor boats. And for the briefest of moments, unobserved except by the new moon and the timeless stars, it brought the *Heart of Matadi* back to life as the ancient paddle steamer sailed away on its crest, beginning to sink into the heaving depths as she did so.

And it washed away southwards across the anchorage, though it had lost its power almost completely by the time that it heaved into the oilfields themselves. Only one thing stood briefly before it during its first wild southward rush. It swept over the slug-shaped hump of the timeless island where the Portuguese had first piled stones seven hundred years since. It rose up higher as it approached the tower where English slavers had lit the first bright beacon. It attained the highest point of its great wild life where the island itself stood tallest.

And, with the explosion of its foaming crest against the hot glass nearly thirty metres, a hundred feet, high in the thick and shuddering air, it put out the Benin Light.